Readers' Comments

· ·

"'*Romance Chocolates*' is the author's sweetest endeavor; so erotic and delectable that one should come across it in the Romance or Recipe section of a bookstore, packaged in a fine chocolatier, or even propped on taupe chiffon in Victoria's Secret. What a delight for Valentine's Day, Christmas, birthday or any day for both men and women who would like to lose themselves in a velvety story of rekindled love. The stories here are soft and sultry: the type you long to read by an open window, enchanting fire or even candlelight since they put the reader in a warm and whimsical mood. These vivid vignettes take place all over the world and are often about regaining what was once lost only to be reclaimed and recaptured in a more wondrous glow than ever before. Each story swirls its own tale in such a way that it becomes a dance in the moonlight for even the oldest soul; soon to be transformed once again to youthful desire and dreamy determination. Since the anthology is often one of sensory exploration, the author wisely continues the theme by punctuating each story with a decadent chocolate recipe; this brings the experience full circle to the palate where one can truly feast on all that has been divulged!"

Pamela Palmer Mutino, Westchester, NY
Playwright, and Author of *"Swish: Maria in the Mourning"*

"Chocolate *is* the chemistry of love. How much more delectable can titillating be? The author's sweet stories bring excitement to a new height. Her tales enrapture us and bring us back to a place of good old fashioned timeless romance and love, resurrecting for readers the enduring message of attraction between a man and a woman. So many different couples, each with their own flavor, whet our imaginations here. Every story is love and confections topped off with a scrumptious piece of chocolate to consummate our appetites. Mmm ...what more could a woman want? *"Romance Chocolates"* is like a big heart shaped box of candy!"

Gloria Schramm, Long Island, NY

Freelance writer, and Author of
"Soul on Fire: Encounter with a Saint" (Mother Teresa)

Romance Chocolates

An Anthology Of Sweet And Hot Chocolate Love Stories For Every Palate

Sheryl Letzgus McGinnis

Romance Chocolates

Dear Reader,

Romance! Chocolates! What two things complement each other better than love and chocolates? Chocolate has been around for about 4,000 years and romance; well romance has been around since Adam and Eve.

Where would we be without them? Some have said rather than falling in love they'd rather fall in chocolate. I think I'd like to fall into both; and indeed have.

The name for this collection of short love stories is actually a variation of a saying that has been in my family since I was a little girl. The original saying is *"She's eating romance chocolates."*

Whenever my beloved aunt Lorna from Australia would hear a young woman relate a story to her that she found a bit fanciful or unbelievable or in fact just made up, she'd declare "She's eating romance chocolates."

That wonderful saying! It delighted me as a young child and it delights me to this day. No explanation needed.

Some of the following stories have kernels of truth in them from real life but are fanciful enough that they would have caused my aunt to exclaim "She's eating romance chocolates."

A book of romance stories could not be complete without a romantic poem or two or three. I've included a few of my favorites sprinkled throughout the book for you.

I hope you'll enjoy these little stories and even better I hope you'll enjoy them with some fine chocolate. There's nothing wrong with "Eating Romance Chocolates;" the poets and great authors have been feeding them to us for centuries.

Bon appétit!

Other books by Sheryl Letzgus McGinnis

"I Am Your Disease (The Many Faces of Addiction)"

"Slaying the Addiction Monster –
An All-Inclusive Look at Drug Addiction in America Today"

"The Addiction Monster and the Square Cat"
(a children's book about drugs and addiction
for ages 10 and up)

Her books are available at www.amazon.com, www.B&N.com,
and other websites in addition to the author's website
www.theaddictionmonster.com

The author can also be contacted at –
Sheryl@romancechocolatesbooks.com.

Please visit her website at
www.romancechocolatesbooks.com

Table of Contents

"At the touch of love everyone becomes a poet"

- Plato

A Brief History of Chocolate

"One of the most sought after treasures brought back from the New World to Spain by the explorer, Hernando Cortez, was the cacao bean. Although Christopher Columbus was the first European to see the cacao bean, it was Cortez, twenty years after Columbus's discovery, who brought the seeds of the bean to Spain.

The value of the bean had been overlooked by the Spanish king and his court until Cortez brought back chests full of them and their worth was recognized. Soon many different recipes were created for the cacao bean.

Chocolate is created from cacao beans thought to have originated in the Amazon roughly 4,000 years ago. Some people claim chocolate or the utilization of the cacao bean dates back 2,000 years.

Rarest and most prized of the three varieties of the cacao bean is the Criollo variety; sought after by the world's best chocolate makers because of its aroma and delicacy.

However long it's been around, when one is consuming chocolate one doesn't bother to worry about how ancient it is – just how delicious it is.

The ancient cultures of Mexico and South America were believed to be the first to make chocolate from the cacao bean. The Aztecs used the cacao beans to prepare a thick, cold, unsweetened drink called chocolatl – a liquid so prestigious that it was served in golden goblets that were thrown away after one use.

Cortez had a suspicion that if this bitter beverage were blended with cane sugar, not only would it be more agreeable to European tastes, but it could become quite the delicacy. He was right. The Spaniards mixed the beans with sugar, vanilla, nutmeg, clove, allspice, and cinnamon.

The resulting concoction became the drink of the nobility - a secret Spain managed to keep from the rest of the world for almost 100 years."

Forget gold, silver, diamonds and other precious jewels; just give me chocolate – and a good romance story to go with it.

(Some excerpts from www.fieldmuseum.org and www.chocolatelovers. com and the author)

Annabel Lee

It was many and many a year ago,
In a kingdom by the sea,
That a maiden there lived whom you may know
By the name of Annabel Lee;
And this maiden she lived with no other thought
Than to love and be loved by me.

I was a child and she was a child,
In this kingdom by the sea;
But we loved with a love that was more than love-
I and my Annabel Lee;
With a love that the winged seraphs of heaven
Coveted her and me.

And this was the reason that, long ago,
In this kingdom by the sea,
A wind blew out of a cloud, chilling

My beautiful Annabel Lee;
So that her highborn kinsman came
And bore her away from me,
To shut her up in a sepulchre
In this kingdom by the sea.

The angels, not half so happy in heaven,
Went envying her and me-
Yes!- that was the reason (as all men know,
In this kingdom by the sea)
That the wind came out of the cloud by night,
Chilling and killing my Annabel Lee.

But our love it was stronger by far than the love
Of those who were older than we-
Of many far wiser than we-
And neither the angels in heaven above,
Nor the demons down under the sea,

Can ever dissever my soul from the soul
Of the beautiful Annabel Lee.

For the moon never beams without bringing me dreams
Of the beautiful Annabel Lee;
And the stars never rise but I feel the bright eyes
Of the beautiful Annabel Lee;
And so, all the night-tide, I lie down by the side
Of my darling- my darling- my life and my bride,
In the sepulchre there by the sea,
In her tomb by the sounding sea.

~Edgar Allan Poe (1809-1849)

The hardest thing to do is watch the one you love, love someone else.

-Anonymous

Chocolate Kisses

(Semi-Sweet Love Stories)

Milk chocolate with a touch of spice

"You know you're in Love when you can't fall asleep because reality is better than your dreams."

~ Dr. Seuss

"Can it be that it was all so simple then,
or has time rewritten every line?

If we had the chance to do it all again tell me,
would we, could we?"

"A Second Chance at Love"

Looking back I knew I had to go. From the moment I first read the obituary notice in our local paper, I knew my heart would lead me to the funeral home. Knowing he would be there needing a meaningful hug from someone who truly cared impelled me to place my long held hurt feelings aside and go to him.

His brother-in-law had died; I'd read the words with a curious mixture of empathy and anticipation. The last name had pricked the hairs on the back of my neck when I'd read it.

Arguably, after twenty years of being apart, I was under no obligation to attend the funeral, but I knew I could never forgive myself if I didn't.

I didn't want to spend another minute wondering if the flames would ignite once again. All these years, I'd been living with the glowing embers of our ill-fated relationship. They smoldered steadily and unrelentingly within my heart. Had it been the same for him? I wondered. Or had there been others after I was out of the picture?

I'd tried to go on with my life, dating a few men here and there, even marrying and eventually divorcing one of them. But my heart always belonged to James; the memories of our love keeping me going through the rough times.

It seemed throughout these last twenty years my mind was consumed with memories of our lovemaking. I couldn't think of those times without the word 'torrid' always popping up because ours was definitely a torrid romance.

I missed waking up in the morning to my very own special alarm clock; James's naked torso standing over me as he would poke me in my face with his hardness, urging me to get up, to get ready for work.

Of course my alarm clock had one big drawback, or advantage, depending on my mood; it woke me up a half hour too early each day. Most of the time my mood matched his and James would climb back in bed and we'd be all over each other, acting like two horny teenagers, grabbing and fondling each other and making torrid love until we'd both collapse in a heap.

Ahh, those were the days. How I missed them, how I missed James, his lips, his hands, his strong arms, his ... well I missed every wonderful part of him, big and small although there were really no small parts on James; just all wonderful parts.

On that fateful Friday night under a drizzly Seattle sky, with an anxious heart I drove to the funeral home. Intermittent raindrops were skittering across my windshield. I found a parking space. I parked and sat there feeling the thumping and skipping of my heart, desperately searching for the courage to face the past and possibly, hopefully, the future.

I don't know why my hopes were so high; they certainly hadn't been these past twenty years. But then I hadn't been faced with the prospect of seeing him again, in the flesh, all these years gone by. I'd had a husband during ten of those years and had been busy raising my two children. I was busy living in the moment, not looking backward, not anticipating the future and trying very hard not to regret my breakup with James.

I'd stuffed my feelings for him down deep, in the basement of my heart ... or so I'd thought, until tonight. Tonight the feelings had suddenly and inexplicably left the basement and had ascended to the top floor of my heart; rising rapidly to the penthouse. There was no denying them. There they were and there was no stuffing them back down again.

Mourners passed by hurrying into the building. I knew it was now or never. It was time to pay my respects but also to see if a spark was still there for him; one that could reignite a long dormant fire.

Dozens of thoughts swept through my head as I exited the car; the Wondering What Ifs I always called these things. What if he isn't pleased to see me? What if he's with a new significant other? I knew he hadn't married. I wondered if he'd been waiting for me all these years, hoping I'd return to him.

He was the man who had rocked my world all those years ago and then had so callously unrocked it. Just like that! Poof! He wanted out of the relationship. We'd argued as most couples do but it seemed that he had begun looking for any excuse for a fight. When he'd finally said he thought it best that we go our separate ways, I agreed. Why did I do that? Why didn't I fight for our love? Why didn't he?

How could two people have such an out of this stratosphere love life and then just throw it all away? Probably because we were so young and all that mattered to us was sex. Apparently that was the only foundation we had, but it was one hell of a foundation. I found myself smiling at the memories and also finding myself becoming strangely aroused. Damn! He still had a stranglehold on me after all these years.

I walked into the funeral home, entered the foyer, and waited behind the other mourners, listening to the mournful sounds of the funeral dirge. With trembling hands I signed the guest book. Drawing my breath in deeply, with trepidation and tears spilling over my lower lashes, I walked from the foyer on unsteady feet and an air of uncertainty.

Anxiously scanning the mourners' faces my breath suddenly caught; my throat constricted so tightly I feared I'd choke and end up as another corpse in the room.

There he was. And he wasn't just there. He was making his way through the mourners. His eyes locked on mine; a look of gratitude and kindness playing across his still handsome face. His hair was gray now and worn shorter than I remembered it.

"Cathy," he whispered in my ear as he hugged me tightly; holding on to me for what seemed like forever.

I hugged him back with an enthusiasm that had been missing in my life for far too long. It felt so right. I held his hazel eyes with mine, looking up at his 6'3" frame packed with about 15 or 20 pounds or more since last I'd seen him. Standing at 5'10" myself we were a good match.

"Hello James," I whispered. How are you? It's been so long."

"Too long Cathy," James said as he stared at me looking me over and up and down as if he were drinking in the memory of me and savoring every drop.

"Do I pass muster, James? I know I'm twenty years older but ..."

"But you're every bit as beautiful as you were back then. I was just noticing a few wisps of gray in your beautiful honey-blonde hair, that's all. I'm glad you didn't dye it. It looks good with your gorgeous hazel eyes. If anything you're even more beautiful now."

"Thank you James. I see you've learned how to pay compliments over the years although I'm not sure mentioning my gray hair is such a compliment, but I'll ignore that and just concentrate on the 'beautiful' part.

"I'm sorry, I guess that wasn't very gallant of me but I was just struck by how beautiful you still are, some gray hairs notwithstanding. You could be bald Cathy and still be the most beautiful woman in this room."

"Compliment accepted James. I'm so sorry about Ray though. I know how much you'll all miss him."

Nodding my head in James's sisters' direction I said "I need to go over there and pay my respects to Violet and Jean. Come with me?"

We spoke with his sisters for what seemed to me like an eternity with each of us aware that we wanted to be alone; the minutes passing slowly until we could make a graceful exit.

We picked up our conversation as easily as if time had never passed. The preceding twenty years were like a blip on the radar screen of our lives, our happiness at this reunion marred only by the reason for it.

We decided it was time to exchange the heavy atmosphere of the funeral home for the lighter feeling of the coffee house across the street. We ventured outside continuing our conversation with ease, both of us stepping into the drizzling rain with light hearts and high hopes.

Holding the umbrella with one hand James placed his arm around my waist while lovingly gathering me to him. He bent down and kissed me ever so gently; then he looked at me and gave me a loving smile but one that was laced with pure animal lust; a look that I remembered so well, and had missed so much. He then released me and guided me to the coffee house by placing his hand on my buttocks, squeezing them and urging me through the door; all the while whispering how much he'd missed my 'beautiful assets'.

Under the shelter of the building's awning James folded the umbrella and placed it against the brick wall of The Coffee Bean. Pulling me tightly to him, enfolding me in his still strong arms, he smothered my mouth with his, kissing me urgently, the pent up passion of all the bygone years released in an explosion of bliss for both of us. It was so natural, and also unbelievably unnatural; all I knew was how right it felt.

I hoped he'd mellowed in the intervening years, that he'd lost his domineering ways. I knew he never meant to dominate me per se; he just needed to assert himself in what he considered a traditional man/woman relationship. That never sat well with me. I believed, and still do, in equality, that sometimes the man takes control and sometimes the woman. He'd always point out, in his defense, that there can be only one captain of a ship. Good point. But he just never got that sometimes the captain could be female.

I tended to be a submissive person back then so I suppose I was partly to blame for giving in and allowing him to take control of the rudder. But that was then ...

The rain was coming down harder just as James's arousal was becoming harder; his desire for me seemingly more intense than ever.

Entering the coffee house we found a small table in the back of the room. The only sounds were those of a lone guitarist strumming in the background competing with the happy sounds of other exuberant patrons.

"Hi, there; what can I get you?" The server asked us.

"A nice strong coffee will do me just fine." James answered. "None of those girly coffees that are more like dessert than coffee. How about you Cathy? You still drink those girly drinks?" He laughed; a look of pleasant recollection lighting up his face.

"I suppose some things never change, James," I said, watching his smile grow broader, satisfied that he still knew my likes and dislikes – or so he thought. "But tonight I think I'll join you in having just a regular coffee."

This is the new Cathy, not the old pushover who wouldn't stand up or fight for herself.

Turning to the server, I said "but don't make mine too strong, please."

"Very good and that's a wise choice not to have any of our fancy coffees because tonight we have fresh Mississippi Chocolate Mud Pie on the menu. It's worth every sinful calorie too. May I bring you some?"

James answered before I could decline such a decadent treat. "Yes, we'll both have a slice ... if that's okay with you Cathy?"

If that's okay with me? Did he really say that? Could it be he's mellowed and doesn't want to dominate me now?

"Why not; we can both use some extra serotonin and dopamine tonight. And what better way to deliver that than in a delicious chocolate dessert?"

As the server walked away, James took my hands in his, caressing and kissing them. How I had missed those kisses! No one could kiss like James. No one could ever thrill me like he could. And no one had ever hurt me like he had.

"Cathy," James had begun, his eyes misting over. "You have no idea how much it means to me that you came here tonight. I'm sorry for how I treated you before. I don't even know if I can explain my actions, how I felt, why I wanted to end our affair even though I loved you with my life ... and still do."

He explained further: "I was too young for a serious relationship, a commitment, a responsibility to another person. I was scared and couldn't admit that to you or to myself at the time. All I cared about was sex and lots of it. I had no idea what a real relationship should be like. I guess it just took me a long time to grow up."

"Me too, I suppose. It took me a long time to learn how to be strong."

He caressed my face with his eyes. "You don't know how many times throughout the years I picked up the phone to call you, only to lose my resolve, fearing rejection."

"I understand, really I do. We were young and immature ... and randy as hell," I laughed while blushing at the same time, memories of our enthusiastic sex flashing before my eyes.

"When I heard you'd married Darren, I spiraled into a depression, finding refuge in Jack, and Johnny; Jack Daniels and Johnny Walker to be precise. They were my only companions for years - until I discovered Xanax; then I had more friends to help me get through the nights, and days. I don't understand why I'm not dead. It wasn't for lack of trying at times. Sometimes I'd drive by your office at quitting time hoping to catch a glimpse of you. Other times I'd sit in the parking lot and wait. I know – I was pretty pathetic, but that's what booze and drugs will do to you. They take over your mind and body and are in complete control."

I ran my hand down his arm, and then held both his hands in mine. "I'm so sorry James. I had no idea you were so addicted and that you cared so much. There was no way I could know. When you decided you weren't interested in continuing our relationship and we parted and you never contacted me I picked up the pieces and tried to put them back together. It wasn't easy. In fact, it was damn hard."

"I really made a mess of it didn't I, Cathy? But when I heard you and Darren had divorced I decided to straighten up and fly right. I knew there was no way I'd ever have a chance with you again if I was drinking and also adding pills to the mix. I also knew I had to be sober for some time before you'd give me any kind of chance."

"Has it been some time, James?

"One year and 25 days Cathy. But who's counting?" James laughed, reaching into his pocket and showing me one of several chips he had with him.

"That's a wonderful start. I'm proud of you James. I can only imagine how hard this is for you."

"Yes it is Cathy. It truly is one day at a time but those days will be a lot of easier if I have you by my side. I couldn't believe it when I saw you come into the funeral home tonight. I wanted to run to you and pick you up and swing you over my head. Lucky for you I'm not still drinking." He grinned; his entire face lighting up with the joy of a little boy on Christmas morning.

"I've missed you more than I can possibly say, James. I've missed how you kiss, your incredible lovemaking, your talented tongue – and other body parts," I blushed -again. My cheeks were on fire, as well as the rest of my body. "You're the only man who has ever been able to bring me to such heights of ecstasy, James. I mean that. We were great together."

"And we'll be great together again, sweetheart," James whispered in his seductive voice, touching my legs under the table, running his hand up and down from my knees to my thighs, squeezing and stroking, "if you'll give me one last chance. That's all I'll need because I promise you I will never screw up again. It was a long, hard lesson to learn. I love you Cathy. Always have. Always will."

"I love you too James. You stole my heart twenty years ago. I used to want it back but not anymore. It's yours to keep - forever."

We sat at the table a little longer, waiting for the rain to let up; drinking coffee, eating dessert, talking, listening, kissing, loving, exploring, promising, and vowing to never be apart again. How bittersweet that it had taken a funeral to wake us up to life and love.

We're older now, much wiser, more forgiving, and more under-standing of life's foibles, more in tune, and more in love with each other than ever. Sometimes life gives us a second chance. Only the prideful will pass it by.

Mississippi Chocolate Mud Pie

....

Ingredients

All purpose flour for work surface

8 oz bittersweet chocolate, coarsely chopped plus ½ ounce shaved

1 cup coarsely chopped pecans, toasted

½ cup (1 stick) unsalted butter

4 large eggs

1 cup granulated sugar

3 tablespoons light corn syrup

½ tsp salt

1 cup heavy cream

¼ cup confectioners' sugar

Directions

Preheat the oven to 375. On a lightly floured work surface, roll dough out to a 12 inch round. Fit into a 9 inch deep dish pie plate. Using kitchen shears, trim crust leaving a 1 inch overhang. Fold edge under then crimp with your fingers. Prick bottom all over with a fork; refrigerate 30 minutes.

Line with parchment paper and fill with pie weights or dried beans. Place on a rimmed baking sheet. Bake 15 to 20 minutes until edges are just beginning to turn golden. Remove parchment and pie weights, and return shell to oven. Bake 15 to 20 minutes or until golden all over. Transfer to a wire rack to cool. Reduce oven temperature to 350.

In a medium heatproof bowl, set over, not in, a pan of simmering water, melt 2 ounces of the chocolate. Brush bottom of cooled shell with chocolate and scatter pecans over.

Using the same bowl, set over simmering water, and melt butter with remaining 6 ounces of chocolate.

Using an electric mixer on high, beat eggs, granulated sugar, corn syrup, and salt until thick and batter falls back in a ribbon when beaters are lifted from bowl; about 3 minutes. Gently fold butter-chocolate mixture into egg mixture. Pour into pie shell. Bake 35 to 40 minutes or until top forms a crust and filling is just set.

Transfer to a wire rack to cool completely, then refrigerate until well chilled.

Using an electric mixer on medium speed, beat cream with confectioners' sugar until soft peaks form. Top cooled pie with whipped cream and chocolate shavings.

(www.marthastewart.com)

"Love is lovelier the second time around,

just as wonderful with both feet on the ground

It's that second time you hear your love song sung

Makes you think perhaps that love like youth was

wasted on the young"

"Class Reunion"

. . . .

"Sandy, guess who I just found on the computer? On Facebook?" Ginger giggled into the phone.

"Actually I didn't find him. He found me. I'd no sooner joined and he asked to be my friend," Ginger laughed, as she stood in the kitchen of her country home in a tony, upscale New Jersey neighborhood close to the New York State line.

"Well, you'll never guess so I'll just tell you. Tony Devito. Remember him?"

"Wow, that's a blast from the past! Of course I remember Tony. He was so sweet. Everybody liked Tony. He may have been short but he sure had a tall personality. He dressed well and if memory serves me correctly, he was voted Best Dressed guy in our senior year. I remember how the Best Dressed girl towered over him in the yearbook picture; Maureen Mc Somebody or other. I can't remember her last name now, can you believe that? I just remember she was an only child and was spoiled rotten; always had the latest fashions from pencil thin skirts to the Black Watch plaid pinafores. Boy we thought those things were so hot."

Ginger paced back and forth in her kitchen with her cell in one hand and a diet soft drink in the other as was her custom whenever she was on the phone.

Even the smallest bit of exercise counts when trying to keep in shape.

"Yep I remember her - Maureen Mitchell - and remember how jealous we all were of her and when she became a cheerleader everybody was even more jealous of her – except me of course because I was a cheerleader too. We used to argue about which one of us cheered the best but we all knew it was me. At least that's how I remember it!" Ginger laughed.

"Speaking about Tony, we'll get to see him again Sandy. He contacted me to let me know our 50th high school reunion is coming up in six weeks. Can you believe that? Fifty years! Where the hell has the time gone?"

"I don't know Ginge. Well I guess we do, really. You traveled, had a wonderful job as a travel writer, and settled down with a great man. I sold a lot of pricey real estate and had a wonderful daughter; a truly beautiful person. Too bad I can't say the same for her lying, cheating, womanizing father."

"He was good to Chloe though so I guess he wasn't all bad, Sandy. And besides we shouldn't speak ill of the dead. You did plenty of that while the rat was still alive. I'm just sayin'."

"You always make my day, sweetie," Sandy laughed into the phone. "We shouldn't complain I guess."

Ginger tossed the soda can in the recycle bin, and stared out the window watching the ominous storm rolling in. The crash of the thunder and the flashes of lightning illuminating the kitchen always evoked bittersweet memories. She and Bill had spent many happy times in this same kitchen sipping coffee or drinking a glass of wine while watching the storm and snuggling; arms about each other's waists, Ginger's head resting on Bill's chest, his head leaning down on the top of her head.

"I know, Sandy. I've had so much but what I wouldn't give to have Bill back. Sometimes I still expect him to walk through the door, even though it's been 10 years since he passed away. I miss him so much."

"Yes, it's awful Ginger. I lost Dan a long time before he died though; losing him to every available female in town. But we've grown stronger and have made new lives for ourselves. We've learned to accept what fate has dealt us. Hold on just a sec; it's Candace calling. Let me tell her I'll call her later."

Ginger continued pacing while plucking another can of diet soda from the fridge. She set it on the counter and added a few jumping jacks to her routine until Sandy came back on the phone.

"You'll never believe it Ginge, but Candice wanted to tell me about the class reunion too. I wonder why we didn't know and all of a sudden it seems everybody's talking about it. I guess we waited a little bit too long to hop on board the technology train, huh?"

"Well I'm glad we finally did and found out in time to lose a few pounds too," Ginger laughed, looking at Miss Kitty curled up on the window seat, thinking Miss Kitty could afford to lose a pound or two herself.

"We're both going, right?"

"Honey, wild horses couldn't keep me away from this event. I wonder what all the old geezers will look like today and ..."

Ginger nearly choked on her soda as she laughed into the phone. "I don't know how to break it to you girlfriend, but we're old geezers too. I know we don't think we look it but let's face it, this is our 50th reunion and not our 25th."

"Well, you're right about that Ginger. We're in the geezer class now I suppose but I really don't think we look it. That's my story and I'm sticking to it," Sandy said. "And we don't think old either. We're definitely young at heart and we're fun people. So we'll go, have a good time, renew old friendships and then meet for lunch the next day and rehash the entire night."

"Okay Sandy, it's a done deal. Gotta go. Miss Kitty has gotten up and is now winding around my legs purring her little head off. She wants her treats now. Talk to you later."

Ginger bent down and picked Miss Kitty up and cradled her in her arm while she opened the catnip treats and poured them into her bowl.

"You're lucky you're so adorable girl because you sure are one spoiled cat; and getting a bit large around the middle too. We'll have to do something about that," Ginger said as she took a few of the treats and put them back in the container. Miss Kitty delicately swiped at Ginger's hand, trying to pull the treats back to her bowl, mewing her dissatisfaction with Ginger's temerity.

❧

Ginger and Sandy spent an inordinate amount of time discussing the upcoming reunion, shopping and choosing and discarding dress after dress until each had found just the right one.

"You know, we might be what some would call 'old broads' but I'll be damned if we can't still rock a sexy silk dress," Sandy said, unabashedly admiring her reflection in the mirror, although taking care to hold her chin up as she did so. "

"Helllllllooo; I think the only thing we can rock today is a rocking chair, girl, and if we're lucky we can rock it without falling off. Yeah. That's what I'm sayin'. But without being too immodest I do believe you're right. We don't look too bad for umm, women of a certain age."

"That's one hell of a euphemism Ginge but I still say we can rock a sexy dress, no matter what age we are."

"As long as the dress's sleeves are long enough to hide these damn bat wings, Sandy. Gravity gets us in the most inconvenient places; faces, eyelids, chins, necks, arms, and of course, not to forget our once glorious most prized possessions; the girls!"

Cupping her generous breasts with both hands, and holding them up, Ginger sighed. "The elevator doesn't go up to that floor anymore. It's just straight down heading rapidly and inexorably to the knees. Even they seem to be sagging Sandy. Think we can get a full body lift in time for the reunion?"

Bursting into laughter, they both held up their breasts and pranced around the dressing room, alternately pulling their facial skin back and pulling their eyelids up. They collapsed in a heap of laughter on the chaise, much like they would do when they were young girls.

"You know what, Ginger?" Sandy suddenly said as she stood up, wiping the laugh tears off her face and eyeing herself in the mirror again.

"No. What Sandy? Are you going to tell me about something else that's sagging that I can't see? Oh, right, how could I forget; my butt. My beautiful, bodacious bootylicious butt. How's that for alliteration? Old Mrs. Jones would be proud of me for finally understanding that," Ginger laughed, recalling their 9th grade English teacher with her imperious manner, gray hair fashioned in a bun and sensible shoes.

"Yes we were all terrified of her for sure Ginger. It's a wonder we could learn anything from that, well ... from that old Geezer. Damn, we're as old now as she was then. Yikes! Anyway I just had a very sobering thought."

She looked long and hard at her breasts, gently squeezing them and feeling a sudden appreciation of them. "We shouldn't be complaining about our breasts. At least we have them! Not all of our sisters are as fortunate."

"Well buzz kill, Sandy! But yes, you're right. You're so right. I'm sorry. I should, WE should appreciate what we've got."

Embracing her best friend, whom she'd known all her life, Ginger kissed her on the cheek. "Thanks for reminding me of what really counts, Sandy. We're alive, we're healthy, and we've still got all our body parts even if some of them do jiggle and droop and look like they belong on a Shar-Pei puppy."

"Right you are! We'll flaunt what we can and hide the rest," Sandy giggled as she took the dress that she'd selected and then put her arm through Ginger's.

As they left the dressing room Sandy said "We're still gonna have fun. I think we've got a brand new appreciation of life now and nice new clothes to go along with it. But a little part of me hopes that Barb Jones has gotten fat!"

"Or looks much older than us," Ginger chimed in; laughing and hoping karma wouldn't punish them for such unkind thoughts.

They left their favorite boutique bubbling with enthusiasm and feeling like teenage girls again. They laughed as they airily walked along the cobblestone street looking in the shop windows of the colonial inspired buildings. The sun was shining, with only a few fluffy white 'Simpson' clouds overhead; could Homer Simpson be far away?

In a few minutes they found themselves at the entrance to Pete's Deli, one of their favorite lunch places.

"Hey girls," Pete, the owner called as they walked through the door. "Have a seat and I'll be right with you; your usual today?"

In unison they both said "of course," mouths watering as they anticipated Pete's famous pastrami on rye sandwiches with his secret sauce, followed by his secret recipe chocolate confection for dessert. They didn't dare ask the calorie count but justified whatever it could be because they only indulged themselves once a month.

After Pete brought them lunch the conversation continued about the reunion. "Ginger, do you think Sonny will come? I wonder whatever became of him and wonder if he still has that beautiful head of hair and those movie star looks."

Noticing the look that crossed Ginger's face, Sandy said "Oh, I'm sorry hon. I shouldn't have brought up the name of the guy who broke your heart. That was very insensitive of me."

Ginger took a sip of her wine and then placed the glass on the table, considering Sandy's question thoughtfully. "It's okay. I've often wondered the same thing, Sandy. When he took Arleen to the prom instead of me I just wanted to die. I thought we had an understanding that we were exclusive, 'going steady' as we used to call it. Apparently it was a *mis*understanding though."

"I think it all turned out for the best Ginge. I mean, if you had continued dating him perhaps he's the guy you would have married and you'd never have met Bill. I guess that's how we have to look at things. You think?"

"I agree. Yes, I definitely do agree. Bill was the love of my life although when Sonny broke my heart I never would have believed I could fall in love again. But Sonny will always be my first love. We can never forget them, can we? Even if they break our hearts they still occupy a special little place there."

"Yeah, like an oyster agitating a pearl," Sandy laughed.

"But you're right, we can never forget them."

Raising her glass of wine, Sandy said "Here's to first loves and the ones who broke our hearts. May we stay forever young and they lose the function of certain body parts."

Ginger came close to spilling her drink all over herself. "That's a hoot girlfriend! I will most certainly drink to that," Ginger laughed as she clinked her glass against Sandy's. A sly smile passed over her lips.

"I've always wondered if the rumors were true, that Arleen was pregnant and Sonny was the father. She was dating the other basketball star, Butch, at about the same time too so who knows? I think it's more than just rumor though. I mean why else would they both move right after graduation and not contact any of us again? Things were so different back then, weren't they? Today, they'd just move in together, have the baby and everything would be tickety boo."

"Ha! You're right about that. And with those movie star looks of his I'm surprised we never saw him in any movies or on TV. That was his ambition as I recall."

Sandy lifted her sandwich to take a bite but paused mid air and said "He probably couldn't get hired for any acting parts because of his cocky attitude. He always thought he was better than everybody else just because he was so handsome so he probably ticked a lot of directors off."

Tall, dark and handsome, that was Sonny; star basketball player, and captain of the debate team with a bright future facing him. Everybody was sure he'd become a pro player after graduating from college, but nobody ever heard anything about him after high school graduation.

"Yes he was cocky for sure, but he was a bit shy too. He seemed to have two sides to him; the public arrogant persona but the gentle, caring private boy who I thought really loved me."

"You give him too much credit Ginge. He was so good looking and arrogant about his looks. We can only hope that he comes to the reunion and ... he's bald," Sandy giggled, almost spitting out her wine.

"We'll see soon enough Sandy; that is if he even shows up. Maybe nobody could find him to tell him about the reunion or ... oh, I don't even want to consider the possibility. He may have broken my heart Sandy but I'd still love to see him again. We did have some great times before he so callously cast me aside. But that was eons ago."

"I know hon but I think we might have heard something if anything had happened to him. Try not to think about it. Let's pay for our food and go home. And let's hope we don't pay for it later on our hips!" Sandy laughed.

"Not funny Sandy. My new dress won't allow even one extra inch. Okay, my treat today. I've got to get home. Miss Kitty will be wondering where I am."

Sandy smiled and said "You and your cat. I don't know who dotes on whom more. Is that right, 'who dotes on whom'? Damn, where's our English teacher now when I need her? Or should I say now, when I'd actually pay attention to her? But who listened to old geezers?" Sandy laughed.

Ginger laughed along with her, knowing that Sandy loved Miss Kitty almost as much as she did. She paid the tab and they both waved goodbye to Pete, walking out the door into the welcome sunshine.

Walking into the beautifully decorated hotel convention room with their school colors of purple and gold prominently displayed and balloons and metallic streamers everywhere, Ginger and Sandy scanned the crowd searching for familiar faces. They were surreptitiously eyeing what all the other women were wearing; gauging how many pounds had been added to the girl voted Most Popular and how much older looking the girl voted Prettiest looked.

"It's a good thing they had these name badges made for everybody Sandy or I'm sure I wouldn't know half the people here. But wait a minute, look over there. That's Cassie Johnson isn't it? She's really held up well. Hmmm, what a disappointment," Ginger and Sandy laughed simultaneously.

"I know Ginge. But we also look good; and I think our bodies are better than hers too," Sandy said, hoping that others would think the same.

'Oh Sandy, you look terrific. You always do, so stop worrying about it. By the way I wonder where Tony is. I sure hope we didn't walk right by him. Wouldn't that be an embarrassment?

They headed to the buffet table, looking forward to sampling the sumptuous treats after weeks of watching what they ate. "Boy, what little piglets we are," Sandy said. "We didn't even check to see what table we're sitting at. "

"Hey Ginger! Over here. It's Tony," a loud voice boomed from a diminutive body from the other side of the table. He made his way around the end of the table, his plate of food balanced on his right hand with his left arm reaching out to hug Ginger.

"I'd know you anywhere Ginge," Tony said as he hugged her while trying not to spill his food.

"Remember we used to always call you Ginge?

"Some people still do Tony," Ginger smiled as she pointed to Sandy who was standing silently by them, watching and smiling.

"You remember Sandy don't you? She still calls me Ginge. She thinks we're still in high school."

Tony grabbed Sandy and hugged her tightly, his head almost lost in her cleavage. He looked her up and down, admiring her sexy dress. "You look wonderful Sandy; you and Ginge. You both look like you're in maybe 15th grade, no older," Tony laughed at his joke. Tony always laughed at his own jokes. Apparently some things never change, Ginger thought.

"Come on; let's go over to our table. I arranged for our old gang to sit together. Well all of us who are still around, that is. Some didn't survive Viet Nam but I'm sure you already know about that. Let's have a drink and toast them while we reminisce. Gee, you girls look terrific. And I still see you as girls."

"Hey everybody; look who I found! It's Ginger and Sandy," Tony exclaimed as they approached their table. Tony, Ginger and Sandy placed their food plates on the table. Ginger and Sandy excitedly hugged the others who were sitting there, exchanging hellos and glad that after a few moments they were able to recognize them; all except one good looking man with beautiful silvery hair pulled back into a pony tail.

"You're probably wondering who this good looking man is," Tony said pointing to the silver haired man. "I'd like you to meet Ron, my partner ... as in life partner. Surprised?"

Ginger and Sandy exchanged surprised looks. "No wonder you never asked me out Tony. It all makes sense now, come to think of it," Ginger said.

"You were always the nicest guy in school," Sandy said. "I wish you and Ron much happiness."

Sandy extended her hand to shake hands with Ron but he hugged her instead and pulled Ginger into the hug too. "Tony has been talking about you so much I feel like I know you too. I'm very pleased to meet you and Tony was right. You're both beautiful."

The band played "In The Still Of The Night" by The Five Satins and Tony asked Ginger to dance with him. "Excuse me Ron. I have to have a long-awaited dance with Ginger. It's been 50 years in the making."

As they danced around the floor, they were animatedly comparing notes; Tony explaining that he was crazy about Ginger in a sisterly way all those years ago but he was gay and afraid to come out back then. He explained that he always enjoyed her friendship and was so glad to be reconnected with her.

"I was always crazy about you too Tony but I sensed that you loved me as a sister. I'm so glad times have changed and we can all be who we are. Ron seems like a very nice man and quite good looking too."

"Well, he's taken Ginge," Tony laughed. "Hands off!"

When the song was over they walked back to their table, joining the others who were all laughing, drinking and having a wonderful time. It wasn't long before Sonny's name came up with everyone wondering what had happened to him.

"He's probably in Europe appearing in some 'spaghetti westerns,'" someone offered.

"Or playing on some third rate basketball team that nobody's ever heard of," another one said.

Smiling at Ginger was Jack, one of her good friends in school. He raised his glass to hers and said "Well, he'd have one hell of a nerve if he showed his face here tonight, after ditching you for Arlene. Nobody even knew he was seeing her behind your back. But that was a long time ago. I suppose we should just keep it in the past. Here's to you Ginger. You made a great life for yourself with a man who deserved you. I'm just sorry he's not with us tonight."

"Thank you, Jack. You're a good friend. Excuse me though," Ginger said.

"I'm going to the dessert table. I need a chocolate fix. They have the best looking chocolate confections there. Be right back."

Ginger had her eye on more than the chocolates though; she thought for sure she saw a man who resembled Sonny. His hair was salt and pepper with a decidedly generous serving of salt and it was no longer curly and full. He didn't appear quite as tall as she remembered. If this was Sonny, he'd put on several pounds, no longer the fit, trim, muscled ball player. *Is it him, or isn't it?*

Ginger casually made her way to the dessert table and reached for some scrumptious looking chocolate petits fours, feigning interest in the desserts. She summoned her courage and brought her eyes up and noticed a pair of eyes catching hers from across the table. She smiled at ... Sonny! Indeed it was him. She knew it even though he wasn't wearing a name badge.

"Ginge. Ginger Baldwin." His voice was mellow and smooth just as she remembered it; that voice that had said so many tender things to her.

"I'd know it was you even without the name badge. It's Sonny," he said tentatively as he looked at where his name badge should be.

"Sonny McNeill. I guess I lost my name badge somewhere."

Ginger popped a petit four in her mouth, savoring it and giving her time to think because she didn't know what to say to Sonny. Looking at his still handsome face she realized she had a swarm of butterflies in her stomach.

She finished swallowing the confection and gave what she hoped was a friendly smile, just friendly, nothing more. What do you say to a man who greets you with such a platonic greeting after what they'd shared all those years ago?

"Hello Sonny. You don't need the name tag for me to know who you are and you certainly don't need to tell me your last name."

Before she knew it, the words were spilling out of her mouth belying her friendly smile — "How could I forget the boy who ripped my heart out and stomped all over it? Oh and throwing in an extra dose of humiliation too. That's memorable. And by the way, how *is* Arleen?"

Sonny's jaw dropped along with the plate of chocolates he was holding. The resulting crash brought unwanted attention to them, which found Sonny averting his eyes from the curious onlookers while Ginger stood quietly with a wicked smile on her face.

"Well, that's a real ice-breaker! How do I top that? Perhaps by building a mound out of all these desserts and sitting on them practicing self-immolation? Would that help? Because if it would I think I'd almost do it. Well, almost. Maybe you have a less painful form of penance for me?"

Sonny had come around the table and was getting very close to Ginger. Too close for comfort she thought. It had been 50 years since she'd been this near to him and she had to take a deep breath. Her knees felt weak and she could feel her hands shaking.

"Sorry. I shouldn't have blurted that out but I've been holding that in for 50 years. Wasn't very polite of me was it?" Ginger stammered.

Why am I apologizing to him? He's the one who needs to apologize and that funeral pyre idea isn't too bad either.

Sonny walked even closer to Ginger. He extended his hand and grasped hers. "Ginger, there are no words to explain how awful I feel for how I treated you. All these years I've carried the guilt of what I did ... what Arleen and I did. I was such a fool."

Releasing her hand from Sonny's, Ginger cut off the rest of his explanation. She held a staying hand in front of his face and said "Well, it was a long time ago Sonny. I said what I wanted to. Let's just let it go."

"I can't let it go Ginge. Ginge. That brings back such precious memories to me, calling you by that name. I wanted to call you so many times too. You don't know it but I kept track of you all these years."

They stood at the table, looking at each other and trying to overcome the awkwardness of the situation. Sonny gently grasped Ginger's arm and led her away from the dessert table, maneuvering her to a quiet area out of earshot of the other classmates." Let's talk over there. I have so much I have to unload, so many explanations to offer you."

Ginger was speechless. She allowed Sonny to lead her out of the ballroom and into a quiet alcove off the lobby. "Please, sit down. Please," he implored her.

"Ginger, I know you don't owe me a thing … "

"You've got that right Sonny, but I'm in a generous mood tonight so I'll give you five minutes, and not one minute more to explain why you hurt me so much. I have a whole tableful of people waiting for me and most likely wondering where the heck I took off to. And they all think the world of me unlike some people."

"Oh, I suspect all eyes were upon us as we left the dessert table, watching where we were headed," Sonny laughed.

"But I'm wasting my five minutes," he said as he smiled and looked at his watch.

Ginger shifted in her chair waiting to hear a 50 year overdue apology.

This is going to be a real doozy, I'll bet. But I have to hear it.

"Go on. Time's a'wasting."

"Oh man, where do I begin? There's so much I've wanted to say to you and … "

Ginger shot him a sideways glance. "Sonny … the clock is ticking. Are you stalling? If you have something to say, please say it."

"I'm nervous. Please cut me some slack. Okay I'll start with the Reader's Digest version and then I'll answer all your questions and go into full detail ... in between apologizing profusely and begging your forgiveness."

"Well, it appears you only have time for the Reader's Digest version anyway," Ginger said. She found her lips beginning to curl up in a smile in spite of herself.

"Arleen kept calling me and chasing me. She stroked my ego big time and in short, she just threw herself at me. And you know what a jerk I could be in high school. I was so full of myself and I wanted it all. I didn't want to lose you, because believe it or not I loved you.

But ..."

"But I wouldn't 'put out' and she would. Am I right? You know I might have if you'd given me more time. But I wasn't part of the sexual revolution; I was really innocent."

Sonny cleared his throat and looked down at the floor. Rubbing his hands together nervously, he continued with his explanation. "Yes, you're right. Arleen and I got together a few times but that's all it took for her to become pregnant. I was going to break it off with her because I realized the relationship wasn't what I wanted. I wanted you. But then when she told me about the baby..."

"And you wanted to do the honorable thing, right?"

"You're wrong there Ginge. I didn't *want* to do the honorable thing but I had to. It's how my mother raised me. Besides, Arleen threatened to move and take the baby and never let me see him ... or her. She insisted I take her to the prom. What could I do? I was going to be a father and it was such an incredible feeling; me, a dad. My own dad had died when I was just a little kid and I didn't want my child to grow up without a dad."

"Which was it?"

"Which was what?"

Ginger leaned into Sonny and placed her hand on his arm, feeling his muscles and feeling stirrings of desire in her groin that she hadn't felt for ten years. She sucked in a deep breath and barely whispered, "Which was it, a boy or a girl?"

"Oh! Well my five minutes are already up. If you'll give me 5 minutes more I'll tell you." They both laughed. How easily they laughed. "A girl; a beautiful girl. You know most people think that men only want a son but I didn't care. I really didn't. I just wanted to be a dad more than anything. I wished it could have been with you Ginger, but we don't always get what we want in life, do we?"

"No, but sometimes we get exactly what we deserve."

"Ouch!"

"I don't understand why you couldn't have told me Sonny, instead of just calling our relationship off and making me wonder what I did wrong. Any explanation would have been better than nothing. Oh wait, you did give me some flimsy excuse, that you weren't ready to be serious with anyone. I almost missed going to the prom you know."

"But you did go. You went with Geoffrey, the English kid who came to our school in the eleventh grade. I watched you dancing with him wishing it were me you were dancing with. Anyway, let me hurry this up. Arleen and I went to Maryland, got married and moved in with her uncle in Baltimore. Our daughter was born there. Marielle. Marielle Marie."

"That's a beautiful name, Sonny. I'll bet she's beautiful too with such handsome parents."

The pride that Sonny felt for his daughter was evident by the enormous grin that broke out on his face at the mere mention of Marielle's name. "She was a beautiful baby and grew into a beautiful woman, both inside and out." Sonny's smile grew wider and his eyes brightened as he told Ginger all about Marielle.

"She's the shining star in my life, Ginger. She's what kept me going when Arleen left us."

"What?" Ginger asked incredulously.

"Yeah, she grew tired of being a wife to me and a mother to Marielle. She wanted to relive her glory days as head cheerleader and be the center of attention. She really just didn't want to grow up and be a responsible adult. All the care of Marielle fell upon me but I'm not complaining. I enjoyed every minute of it. In fact I think I was a bit glad that Arleen took no interest in our daughter. That way I could raise her properly and instill good values in her, which I did I'm proud to say. " A wistful look crossed his face and Ginger felt the beginnings of tender feelings toward him.

"I'm so sorry Sonny. All these years I held such resentment toward you, not knowing how you were suffering."

Sonny's eyes held Ginger's as he smiled and explained that his love for his daughter far outweighed any sadness in his life. "She gave me terrific twin grandsons to boot; Michael and Matthew. But enough about me Ginge; how are you doing? I told you I'd kept up with what was going on in your life. I was truly sorry to hear about Bill's passing."

A questioning look played across Ginger's face as she asked Sonny how, and more important, why did he follow her life. "Nobody ever heard from you again after graduation, so how could you know what was going on with me?"

"It's not true that nobody ever heard from me again. Arleen's cousin, Caryn stayed in touch with me through the years. She had always liked me and couldn't understand how Arleen could be so foolish, and downright mean. Her words, not mine;" he laughed as he recalled how Caryn would call him with the latest gossip, who married whom, which couples divorced and sadly which ones of their classmates had died.

"So Caryn was your pipeline. I never would have expected that. I hadn't talked to her since graduation but as big a gossip as she was in high school I guess it's no surprise that she kept up with everybody's doings. "

Sonny took Ginger's hand and stood up, gently pulling her up with him. "You know I would have called you, Ginger, but I could never get up the nerve, not knowing how you would treat me. And I wouldn't have blamed you one bit if you had hung up on me – or worse. Then I heard that you'd married Bill. I knew he'd be a great husband to you but I have to admit it broke my heart. All hope of being with you again vanished when I heard that news."

Ginger's heart was fluttering and her skin was becoming damp. Her breath was catching.

He actually still cared for me after all those years. If only I'd known ... but what would I have done? Would I have chosen Sonny over Bill? No, that's absurd. Sonny broke my heart. Why would I have given him a second chance?

Ginger's thoughts were interrupted by what she heard Sonny say next; "By the time I'd heard that Bill had passed away, I'd already remarried and was happy."

Ginger stood there with her hand in Sonny's and felt her throat go dry. Her heart sank a little knowing Sonny had remarried.

Why hasn't he brought his wife with him ... or did she leave him too?

"I hope your second wife is much nicer to you than Arleen was. I do mean that."

"She was indeed much nicer to me Ginge, but she passed away last year from pneumonia. We had a good marriage and she and Marielle got along almost like mother and daughter. I miss her."

Oh, that's not how I envisioned her leaving him. How terribly sad. I can so relate.

Ginger squeezed Sonny's hand and felt her throat clutch as tiny tears escaped from her eyes. "I know what it's like to miss your mate, Sonny. I will always miss Bill. He was such a huge part of my life for so many years. I loved him so much. So I understand how much you miss ..."

"Stephanie Maxwell, Steffie. She grew up in Baltimore. We lived there until she passed away. I just moved back to Woodland Hills and have kept a pretty low profile. Then I read about the reunion on Facebook and knew I had to come. I hoped that you'd be here. Again, I didn't have the nerve to call you. I also hoped that I wouldn't be shunned. But mainly I wanted to explain to you what had happened and to tell you that I'm really not an unfeeling jerk."

Sonny sighed and grinned as he said, "and I also thought you wouldn't beat me up too badly if our meeting took place in a public setting."

"That all depends on your apology Sonny which so far you haven't really given me," Ginger laughed.

"You've talked about it but I still haven't received a real formal heartfelt apology. You know - the- get- down- on- the –floor- knife- aimed -at your- chest- type apology. Sort of like the knife

45

you put through my heart. But I always did have a flair for the dramatic didn't I? So let's dance. Isn't this one of the reasons we came to this reunion, besides seeing old friends and pigging out on such good food?"

I just want to feel his arms around me again, to be close to him, to feel his warmth, smell the sexy sweetness of his cologne mixed with the musky scent of his body heat.

"No words can ever make up for what happened Ginger. But I promise you I'll do better than the knife in the chest thing." Sonny's right arm gently encircled Ginger's waist as he held her right hand in his left hand, pressing it close to his chest. He danced her around the floor, as they listened to the strains of the fifties and sixties music wafting into the lobby from the ballroom.

Ginger didn't want him to let her go. It had been ten years since she'd felt so comfortable in a man's arms. A twinge of guilt threatened to overshadow her feelings of hope and anticipation.

But it's time to start living again. Time to honor my promise to Bill; that I wouldn't suspend my life because his was ending. He loved me too much to want me to deny myself another chance at happiness. Time to ...

"A penny for your thoughts, Ginge," Sonny interrupted her silent musings.

"You're not here. You seem to be miles away ... or is it years away? Are you thinking about Bill? If you are, I certainly understand; because Steffie still lives in my heart. She'll always live there and Bill will always live in your heart. But we can't change what happened. Life is for the living. This isn't a dress rehearsal, so we have to live it to the fullest. Carpe' diem!"

Ginger ran her hand through the back of Sonny's hair and gazed intently into his deep chocolate brown eyes. "I don't know what lies ahead Sonny or even if I'll be sharing my life with anyone but I know Bill would want me to move forward. I've known it for some time but haven't found anyone I've wanted to take a chance with, that is ..."

"That is – until tonight?" Sonny asked with great hope in his eyes and in his heart.

"I don't know Sonny. This is all so sudden and confusing. But I'd like to start taking chances again. I didn't realize how much I've missed you until I saw you tonight."

"You know I've had serious doubts about there being a heaven, Ginger, but if there isn't, then how do you explain this?"

"I'd say that you danced into my dream, Sonny. As Bob Dylan said, 'I'll let you be in my dreams if I can be in yours.' That's how I'd explain it," Ginger blushed. She actually blushed.

I'm 67 years old, nearly 68 and he's making my cheeks blush. Can this really be happening at my age; at my old geezer age?

"Well then I'm so glad I did. Of all the places I could have landed, I fell smack-dab into your dream. And I'd like to stay here ... if you'll allow me. I've missed that beautiful smile, Ginger. After all these years it still gives me goosebumps. Do you think we can take advantage of our reunion and make the most of however many years we have left? Would you like to get to know each other again? Go out on a date? Stop me before I make too much of a fool of myself. Please!"

"No, don't stop. I'm enjoying it" Ginger laughed.

"Well, I hope we have many years left Sonny and plenty of time to date. I'm game if you are – perhaps. We'll see how things progress tonight. I know you must think I'm being petty and foolish but somehow an apology – a really meaningful one – would help.

What does everyone say today; closure? Not sure I know exactly what that means but I think that's the right word."

Deeply inhaling, trying to quell the butterflies that were threatening to jump out of his mouth, Sonny said "Yes, closure – for both of us. Hold on to that thought Ginge, okay? Right now there's something more important, at least I hope you think so too," Sonny said as he wrapped both arms around her. He drew her closer to him, and leaned his head into hers and brushed his lips against her lips. When she didn't resist, it emboldened him and he pressed his mouth harder against hers. She responded eagerly, kissing him in turn, with a passion she hadn't felt in years. She could feel it in every fiber of her being. She wanted him, heaven help her she desired him just as she did all those years ago, all fifty years ago. She was a mere girl then with no experience. Now she was a woman; a woman experiencing a resurgence of passion that she hadn't felt in ten years and dammit all she wasn't going to deny herself this time with Sonny.

They stood there kissing for a few minutes more, pressing their bodies to each other and swaying to the music emanating from the ballroom. Sonny's desire for her was growing and he wasn't trying to hide it. She wasn't shying away from it either. She was enjoying the feel of his maleness pressing against her while he pulled her into him, urging her closer with his right hand and then slowly withdrawing his left hand from hers and letting it slide over her right breast. She couldn't believe the intensity of her feelings. They'd been dormant for much too long and Sonny, with the merest of touches, was bringing them back to life and making her inwardly scream for more.

They danced, if it could be called that, for what seemed like forever and conversely felt like mere minutes when Sonny took a deep breath, removed his hands from Ginger, and said "now let's go and face the music. No pun intended. Well, we should wait a few minutes though, until ah, things settle down a bit. And to speed that process along Ginge, you'd better back away from me. Otherwise we'll be here all night," he laughed.

As Sonny and Ginger re-entered the ballroom, with Sonny's arm around Ginger's shoulders, they were aware they were the center of attention. "I'm sitting at this table over here, with Sandy and Tony and almost the whole gang," Ginger said pointing to a large table in the center of the room. She was so flushed and weak she wasn't sure if her legs would carry her across the dance floor. She hoped that Sonny was coming down from the experience, she laughed to herself.

Sonny flashed his famous smile and said hello to everybody, shaking everyone's hands. "I know I'm the last person you expected to see here and especially in Ginger's company, but I hope you won't be too offended by my presence. Fifty years is a long time and I'm hoping that our advanced years have dimmed the memories of events somewhat," Sonny said laughingly as everyone surprisingly laughed with him.

The song that the band was playing, "Unchained Melody" by the Righteous Brothers, was coming to an end as Sonny excused himself from Ginger and the group. "I'll be right back. There's something I have to do."

Oh my love, my darling, I've hungered for your touch a long lonely time.

The lyrics reverberated in his head as he stepped up to the bandstand.

Ginger and the gang watched as Sonny began talking to the bandleader. In a minute, Sonny exchanged places with him and was standing in front of the microphone.

As the bandleader looked at Sonny and smiled broadly, Sonny spoke into the mic. "Ladies and gentlemen of Woodland Hills

High, I have a special announcement to make. You all know who I am and are undoubtedly surprised to see me here tonight. And I know you're doubly surprised to have seen me walk into the ball-room with Ginger Baldwin."

There was a mixture of laughter and murmurings from the crowd as people craned their necks to look at Ginger.

Ginger sat at the table with her friends, her mouth agape, not knowing what to expect next. What did come next caught her totally by surprise.

"I'm here to make a public apology to Ginger for all the hurt I caused her all those years ago."

Ginger let out an audible gasp, nearly spilling her chocolate raspberry cherry martini. Her blue eyes shimmered as she listened to every word. Sandy hugged her, reveling in her best friend's long awaited satisfaction and apparent joy.

Sonny continued, looking directly at Ginger, his left hand holding the mic while he pointed to Ginger with his right hand. "I'm also here to beg your forgiveness Ginge and to ask for another chance to prove that I've done a lot of growing up these past fifty years. I've grown a bit wider too as you can see."

The crowd erupted in spontaneous laughter and Ginger laughed along with them. "So, Ginge, will you forgive me for being such a heel? Is this public admission of my cheating on you as good as putting that knife to my chest? Because believe me this is one of the hardest things I've ever had to do, but I'm happy to do it if it will help you forgive me. I'm sorry and I'll spend the next fifty years trying to atone for my past indiscretion. Well the next 10 or 20 years if I'm lucky."

Again, everyone laughed and the room was filled with applause.

"So, what do you say Ginge?" Sonny said as he fought back the tears that were threatening to spill onto his cheeks. "Can you find it in your heart to not only forgive me but to accept my deepest heartfelt and way overdue apology?"

Ginger got up from her seat and walked to the bandstand smiling, and then laughing as she held her arms out to Sonny. "Of course I forgive you Sonny. At this time in our lives, there's no point in continuing to hold a grudge." Ginger shouted, "I accept your apology. Thank you. It's way better than you putting a knife to your chest."

The room was filled with hoots and hollers, laughter and applause. Sonny held up his hand to stay the crowd and then spoke into the mic again as Ginger stood there looking up at him; her facial expression a mixture of awe and satisfaction with definite happiness that she made no effort to conceal.

"Ginger, may I have this dance?" Sonny asked. He turned to the bandleader and gave him the thumbs up. Sonny stepped down from the bandstand and took Ginger in his arms. They looked around the room, both of them smiling, acknowledging the admiring and approving looks from their friends.

Then they looked deeply into each other's eyes, holding each other tightly, relishing this second chance at ... at what? At love? Could it really happen?

Sonny said to Ginger in a low, dulcet tone, "This song is from my heart to yours Ginge, and I mean every word of it." They began to dance, slowly, rhythmically. Sonny placed his mouth on Ginger's ear. The band played the old Frank Sinatra tune as Sonny sang along ... "who can say what led us to this miracle we've found? There are those who'll bet love comes but once and yet I'm oh so glad we met the second time around ..."

Decadent Chocolate Raspberry Cherry Martini (For Two)

- 3 ounces dark chocolate liqueur

- 2 ounces raspberry vodka

- 2 ounces half and half (or 2 ounces vanilla schnapps, your choice)

- 1 cup of ice

- chocolate syrup

- maraschino cherries or chocolate covered cherries

1. Chill 2 martini glasses.

2. Using a cocktail shaker combine the chocolate liqueur, cherry vodka, half and half (or the vanilla schnapps) and the ice. Shake vigorously.

3. Squeeze a moderate amount of chocolate syrup into the bottoms of the chilled martini glasses and swish. Pour martini into the glasses. Garnish with maraschino cherries or chocolate covered cherries. Include the ice in the martini if you wish.

(The author's recipe)

"Because She Would Ask Me Why I Loved Her"

If questioning would make us wise
No eyes would ever gaze in eyes;
If all our tale were told in speech
No mouths would wander each to each.

Were spirits free from mortal mesh
And love not bound in hearts of flesh
No aching breasts would yearn to meet
And find their ecstasy complete.

For who is there that lives and knows
The secret powers by which he grows?
Were knowledge all, what were our need
To thrill and faint and sweetly bleed?

Then seek not, sweet, the "If" and "Why"
I love you now until I die.
For I must love because I live
And life in me is what you give.

~Christopher Brennan (1870 – 1932)

"And even though you feel delirious you know you really can't get serious not with those young men, that's who I mean young men, so young and green are you shocked and surprised? Are you scandalized? Or are you, admit it, tantalized?"

Sauce for the Goose is Sauce for the Gander

. . . .

The first storm of the winter had arrived earlier enveloping most of Raleigh, North Carolina in a beautiful blanket of white snow. A good foot had fallen and traffic would be slowed to a crawl. Andy would be arriving soon, although a bit later than usual probably because of the storm, and he and Susan would engage in their usual weekend pastime of good wine, delicious food, and hot sex.

Her cell rang and it was Andy. "I'm gonna be another half-hour or so Suze. This traffic's a bitch. But I'll be there. See ya in a little bit."

That's odd, Susan thought. Andy always says 'I love you' when he hangs up. It must be the stress of driving in such bad conditions.

Fifteen minutes went by while Susan placed the plates, utensils and glasses on the coffee table in the den. It was their custom to eat in the den, and then make love on the sofa in front of the TV. After sex, they'd watch a movie and then fall asleep. Sometimes they wouldn't make it all the way through the movie before they were both nodding off due to their full bellies but mostly due to the vigorous sexual workout.

Andy was not a typical male, at least not typical of any males she'd been with. Andy was a pleaser. He seemed to enjoy sex the most when she really enjoyed it. He definitely was not a 'slam bam thank you Ma'am' type.

But the relationship didn't seem to be progressing beyond a highly sexual one. As good as that was, actually as great as that was, there needed to be more to sustain it.

She checked on the dinner she was preparing, her special shrimp puttanesca accompanied by one of her great salads. The wine was a lovely blueberry port which would go great with the chocolate rum cheesecake she'd prepared yesterday.

Susan always looked forward to these weekends after her stressful week of running the city's largest multi-specialty medical clinic and dealing with spoiled and obstreperous physicians. Most of them suffered from an entitlement complex and were quite demanding of her time and attention. She worked long hours; the sex she had with Andy was her weekly stress buster and she so looked forward to it.

The doorbell rang. "Andy, I'm so glad you're here, I was beginning to worry, what with the awful weather and all," Susan said as she opened the door for Andy. She hugged him and kissed him while noting a subtle lack of interest in his response to her.

"Take off your coat sweetheart; it's wet from the snow. Dinner will be about another ten minutes. I'll open the Shiraz for now and I've got a wonderful blueberry port to go with dessert."

Andy cleared his throat and shifted on his feet, obviously nervous and ill at ease. A wan smile crossed his face. "Suze, can we sit down? I'm sorry; there's no way to say this but we need to talk. I didn't want to say this on the phone."

'We need to talk;' the four words that portend an imminent heartbreak; instantly transforming a pleasant evening to a nightmare. Susan held her breath. She could feel it coming although she wasn't as surprised as she otherwise might have been a month or so ago. Her inner antenna had been detecting subtle signals but like all subtlety she had difficulty recognizing it for what it was; that's why it was subtlety.

Andy explained that he loved her but not like he used to; he had enjoyed their time together but he didn't see the relationship going anywhere; their love life had become routine and lacked passion. Not physical passion, he explained, but emotional passion. Because of what he felt was a dead end relationship he was going to accept an offer in Maryland at a bigger medical clinic to practice medicine there.

"As you know Suze, my contract with the clinic is up in two weeks. I'm sure you've been curious as to why I haven't renewed it even though you never pushed me on it. It was a tough decision. I wouldn't be leaving if our relationship hadn't begun to fizzle. I'm sure you've felt it too. My feelings for you are strong but I think I feel more friendship than ... I don't know, I'm just so sorry, Suze."

When she thought about it Suze had to agree. She hadn't wanted to admit it but when her thoughts drifted back to the last six months of their relationship she had to admit Andy was speaking the truth. They were really in a rut and the sparks had indeed fizzled out in the last month or so. Why, she didn't know. She still loved him but she supposed she wasn't *in* love with him, nor was he with her she realized.

They had talked for over an hour, not eating or drinking; Suze's prepared dinner be damned; neither had an appetite nor a desire for anything.

"Well Andy, there's really nothing more to be said, is there? I think it would be best if you were to leave. Besides, there's no dinner. I'm sure it's all burned to a crisp. Better to end this here and now."

"Susan I truly am sorry. I don't want to hurt you but ..."

"It's okay Andy. Just go. We'll get through these next two weeks ... as friends. Enjoy your new life when you get to Maryland. I wish you well. Maybe we'll meet for a drink sometime when you return to visit your family. I know you won't be able to stay away from your nieces and nephews for too long."

Andy drew himself up to his full 5'10" height, realizing his shoulders had been slumping, looking like a little boy in trouble. His shaggy brown hair fell over his right eye and he ran his fingers through it, pulling it off his face. "Thanks Suze. I ... I guess I *will* be going now."

He didn't even make an awkward attempt to kiss her goodbye and for that she was grateful. She watched him walk out the door and out of her life.

"Drive carefully," Susan called after him.

Well, no use letting a good wine go to waste, Susan thought, or a good dessert. Her heart would mend. It had before. You don't get to be 43 years old without suffering a few broken hearts along the way.

⚜

The weekly staff meetings were less tedious the past two months since Susan and the board had hired two new doctors; Dr. Sasha Benton and Dr. Blake Morrison. Andy's presence was missed but the clinic was doing well with the addition of the two new physicians.

Dr. Benton was a young, recent graduate of Emory University in Atlanta. She had excellent credentials and was eager to begin her career at Cade Medical Clinic as an internist.

She was pretty enough and tall enough to be a supermodel. All the physicians were enamored of her; the single ones and married ones alike. She put up a fine pretense but underneath she was a man-eater with no scruples. Whatever she wanted, she got. She was outspoken, opinionated and clashed with Susan on more than one occasion; which caused the meetings to be quite lively at times.

Dr. Morrison on the other hand was an affable, highly skilled cardiologist who'd received training at The Cleveland Clinic in Cleveland, Ohio, one of the top four hospitals in the United States. He was young, tall, standing at 6'4", slim with long hair stylishly cut and possessed of the most beautiful twinkling blue eyes. He came from a wealthy family, was single, with a legion of female admirers, and was on the fast track to success.

The annual physicians retreat was coming up next weekend in Gatlinburg, Tennessee and Susan had her hands full arranging everything. It would be an intense 4 days of business with their nights free to relax with plenty of wining and dining.

❧

Susan and the doctors were eager to unwind at the conclusion of the first day. They were gathered in the main dining room of the lodge enjoying the music, the food and each other's company. Susan was standing in a small group chatting amiably with everyone. From across the room her eye was caught by Dr. Blake Morrison; he was smiling at her, rather flirtatiously she thought, as he'd been doing ever since they'd hired him. She always rebuffed his flirtations; she didn't want to become involved with another physician and especially one who was much younger than she.

She smiled back and raised her glass to him. She turned her attention back to the people in her circle and took a sip of her wine. Soon she felt a presence behind her followed by a firm hand on her waist.

"Susan, how are you?" Dr. Morrison inquired. Looking at everyone standing with her, he said hello to each of them, all the while keeping his hand touching Susan's waist.

"Hey Blake, glad you've joined us," Dr. Lassiter said.

"It sure was a lucky day when you agreed to join Cade Medical; you and Dr. Benton. You've both been a great addition to our group."

Blake reluctantly removed his hand from Susan's waist and shook hands with Dr. Lassiter, thanking him. He turned his face toward Susan and flashed a sexy smile. "It was a great day for me too when I was hired. I've been enjoying working with everyone, and working for such a great administrator."

Susan felt Blake move closer to her, their hips touching. This is ridiculous, she thought. He's being very friendly, too friendly? She wondered.

"Susan, come on, dance with me." It was Dr. Lassiter.

"Excuse us everybody, but Susan and I love this song." They walked on to the dance floor and began dancing to an oldie but goodie, 'Hot Stuff' by Donna Summer.

"You're a great dancer Susan. I don't know if I like dancing with you better or watching you shake your booty. But don't tell my wife that." Luke Lassiter laughed. Susan had learned over the 3 years that she'd been the CEO of Cade Medical that Luke was all bluff; he loved his wife and liked Susan a lot. They were good friends and Luke was her strongest ally when she needed backup in dealing with an unruly physician.

"I noticed Blake was invading your personal space a bit - again. I think he's sweet on you Suze."

"Now there's an old timey expression Luke. Are you sure you're 45 and not 65?"

"Whatever. I still say he's sweet on you. Would you rather I said he wants to jump your bones? But I think it's more than that. Yep, he's definitely sweet on you."

"Oh please Luke, he's 33 years old and ... and I'm not." She laughed but with a wisp of regret in her voice.

"Yeah, but you're hot stuff yourself." He twirled her around, thoroughly enjoying old-fashioned dancing; in the 1940s they called it jitterbugging. Luke knew that; he knew a lot of things and one thing he knew for sure was that Susan, his dear friend with the beautiful auburn hair and green eyes needed a good man; one who would treat her right. Not Andy. No, that was definitely a big mistake on her part when she'd hooked up with him. She needed a nice guy like Blake.

"Well he *is* good looking I'll give you that. And in about another five years he'll be really handsome and worldly looking, but for now he's got a baby face."

"Come on Susan, you wouldn't do him? Really?"

"Funny, but I don't recall saying *that*, Luke." They both laughed.

"But seriously I wouldn't. I just had one affair with a physician end badly and I'm swearing off doctors. It isn't good business anyway. Andy and I had already been dating before I was hired as the CEO of Cade. So nobody could have a problem with that.'

"I know. You're right too, it's not wise to date within the company; especially physicians. We tend to have a pretty high opinion of ourselves. You may have noticed."

The song ended and they walked back toward their fellow physicians who were all engaged in a lively discussion about the pros and cons of adding a plastic surgeon to their rapidly expanding group. Susan felt a twinge of disappointment when she noticed that Blake was no longer among them. She let her eyes wander around the room, feigning interest in the dancing couples while scanning the faces for Blake's.

Disappointment turned to a touch of jealousy when she discovered Blake in earnest conversation with Sasha Benton over by the doors leading to the deck. Where did that come from she wondered. She certainly wasn't the jealous type and she had no designs on a 33-year-old … did she?

She had trouble concentrating on the conversations going on around her. "Oh, what? I'm sorry. Yes, you're right. Absolutely." She had no idea what Dr. Montgomery was absolutely right about but she hoped it wouldn't come back to bite her in the butt.

Within minutes Blake and Sasha started dancing. It was a slow song, 'I Swear,' one of Susan's favorites.

Why is this bothering me so much? He means nothing to me. He's ten years younger than I am. Get a grip Susan. He definitely was flirting with me though – again!

"Susan? Suze? Hello?" Dr. Montgomery again.

"I'd give much more than a penny for your thoughts. I see you standing here but you're not really here. Everything okay?

Susan smiled her biggest smile and apologized. "I'm sorry Joe. I was thinking about our meetings tomorrow. I have so much to do and shouldn't be spending my time dancing and drinking and eating."

Raising her voice above the music Susan begged off and apologized to everyone for leaving. She'd see them tomorrow morning bright and early for a full day of discussions and planning the future of Cade Medical Clinic.

Susan exited the main dining room and then, deciding to catch a breath of fresh air before turning in for the night, she walked out onto the large deck that surrounded the lodge. She stood there thinking about Andy. She wondered how he was making out with his new life in Maryland. Did she really miss him or was she just lonely ... and missing their great sex?

"Hey Susan, enjoying this beautiful night?" Blake. Not only Blake but Blake and Sasha. They were walking toward her – Sasha's arm looped through Blake's. Sasha didn't say anything but seemed to pull Blake a little closer to her while giving Susan a smile; one that Susan could only interpret as bitchy. Men may not notice these things but women do.

"Oh, hey guys. Yes, it's been a wonderful night but I've got some papers to go over before our meeting tomorrow morning so I'm going to turn in. I'll say goodnight now. Enjoy the rest of your evening."

"Oh, I'm sure we will," Sasha said switching her gaze from Blake to Susan and giving Susan that I've-got-him-and-you-don't smile, her eyes flashing.

Screw you Sasha. I wonder what you'd think if you knew Blake was always flirting with me. Damn it. Why am I letting this bother me? They can have each other for all I care.

Susan noticed an odd look on Blake's face but she wasn't sure what it meant. She walked back along the deck heading toward her room, pondering that curious look.

She opened the door to her room, entered and then locked it behind her. She dropped her purse on the table, removed her heels and walked into the bathroom and began filling the tub. A nice bubble bath would be nice, she thought. She poured herself a glass of chardonnay, lit some candles and began undressing. Tonight she would relax because tomorrow would be another stress-filled day.

Once the tub was full she prepared to dip her feet in; her thoughts drifting to Blake. The wine was relaxing her allowing her to give into her repressed desire for him. She had to admit it, he was handsome and sexy and his flirtations flattered her. She wanted him. There, she'd admitted it. She'd love to have that lanky body draped over hers; she was fantasizing about how his lips would feel pressed on hers and how his hands would feel roaming all over her body.

Her reverie was interrupted by a soft rap on the door. She was annoyed she'd have to put her robe on and contend with whatever problem some pesky doctor was having. Not now, she thought. Just let me relax and enjoy my bath – and the wine. Tomorrow's going to be a long day and I need some 'me' time right now.

She considered ignoring this intrusion into her privacy but knew if she didn't take care of it now whoever it was would probably persist. "Just a second," she yelled while putting her robe on and then making her way to the door. She looked through the peep hole and was astonished to see Blake standing there. She craned her neck sideways in an attempt to see if Sasha was with him. She wasn't.

She opened the door, embarrassed by her state of undress. "Come in Blake. This is a surprise." Pulling the belt tighter around her, Susan apologized; "I was just about to take a bath when I heard you knock on the door. If you'll give me a minute I'll put my clothes back on and ..."

Blake walked closer to Susan, smiled and said "Well that's the opposite effect I was hoping for."

"Very funny Blake; what can I do for you anyway? Why are you here? Wait, before you tell me I really do have to put my clothes back on. I'm a little uncomfortable talking to you while I'm in my robe.'

"I understand Susan. It's not my intention to embarrass you or make you feel uncomfortable. May I have a glass of that wine while you're changing?"

"Of course; help yourself. There's an extra glass on the counter. I won't be long."

Blake poured himself a glass from the bottle of chardonnay and settled back on the comfortable sofa, a broad smile crossing his gorgeous face.

Within a minute Susan was back in the room clothed in a pair of skin tight sexy jeans and a silk blouse with the top three buttons undone; the opening of the blouse hanging loosely over her firm breasts. "There, I feel better now. So, where's Sasha?"

"Don't know, don't care, Susan. Great blouse."

"Thank you." She blushed. "So she blew you off, did she? I got the impression she really wanted you. What happened?"

"She wanted me alright. Although actually I'm not sure if it was a case of her wanting me or her not wanting you to have me. I probably shouldn't say this but she said some pretty catty things about you. Seriously, she did."

"Well, I was right then. I caught those vibes from her. But she has nothing to worry about. There's nothing between us ..."

"Not just yet, there isn't," Blake laughed as he tipped his glass to Susan.

"Blake Morrison! Where did that come from?"

"Come on Susan, you must know I'm attracted to you; very attracted to you. Ever since I've been working at Cade, I've flirted with you every chance I've had hoping to get some reciprocation. I thought I would explode tonight when I was standing next to you."

"Blake, I'm 10 years older than you. That means when I was 23, you were 13 or when I was 13, you were 3."

"Yes I've heard that argument before, but contrariwise, you gorgeous creature, that means when you're 83, I'll be 73. Not such a difference, right?" he laughed at the same time beckoning Susan to sit beside him on the sofa.

Susan picked up her glass of wine and sat next to Blake; every part of her body on fire, contrary to the icy attitude she was hoping to convey. "But this is now Blake. I'm 43 and you're 33."

"Almost 34," Blake said, "so that makes the age difference only about 9 years now. We're getting closer together."

"By a matter of months? You call that close? Good thing you aren't a math teacher, Blake," Susan said as she laughed. They spent the next half hour drinking wine, and really getting to know each other; sitting close with their legs rubbing against each others', flirting as if they were in high school. Susan was amazed at how much they had in common in spite of their age difference. Blake was more like a contemporary of hers, not her junior.

She found herself looking into his eyes and seeing a really nice, decent man looking back at her. Another bottle of wine found them loosening up even more; serious talk turning to playful sex talk. They both knew where this was headed.

Blake slid closer to Susan, putting his glass on the coffee table and cupping her face with his hand.

"Blake do you think this is wise, I mean ..."

"Shh," Blake said as he pulled Susan's face to his and placed a soft kiss on her forehead. He kissed her on the tip of her nose and then her cheeks. When she didn't resist or pull away, he kissed her on the lips, softly at first. When she responded, parting her lips and kissing him back, he kissed her harder. He traced his tongue around her lips and then inserted it in her mouth where it was eagerly met by hers.

"We shouldn't be doing this," Susan whispered.

"But we *are* doing this Susan. And admit it; it feels right. I think you want me as much as I want you. Well maybe not as much as *I* want *you* yet, but just give it time. You'll find that the age difference will just disappear. It really doesn't matter Susan. I've wanted to be this close to you and kiss you ever since the first interview."

"Blake, you don't understand ..."

"I understand this Susan – 'what's sauce for the goose is sauce for the gander,' although in this case I suppose we should technically say 'what's sauce for the gander is sauce for the goose.' Why should men be the only ones allowed to date younger people? It's time society moved past that outmoded thinking, don't you think? Disdaining women for dating younger men is nothing more than ageism ... and also most likely jealousy on the part of women who can't get a younger man."

"Oh meow, meow," Susan chuckled. "You do make good points though."

Blake put his arm around Susan's neck and his other arm on the sofa cushion and leaned her back on the sofa; still kissing her while she eagerly returned his ardor. He laid his body on top of hers, his arousal exciting her.

"Don't you wish you'd kept your robe on now, Susan?" Blake whispered with a slight chuckle.

"It would be so much easier to remove than these jeans. You can help me you know," Blake whispered in Susan's ear as he tugged on the zipper letting his hand drift down to the "V" between her legs and back up to the zipper again.

Susan pulled Blake's face to her breasts twining her hands through his silky black hair while emitting soft groans as he removed her jeans. He hastily removed his clothing, eyeing her lustily as he did so. It was then she realized she hadn't experienced this type of passion with Andy in a long time, indeed if ever.

Susan was reveling in the thrill of passion as Blake lifted her up with his hands and squeezed her buttocks. Blake might be a young man but he had a world of experience in how he handled her body, how he finessed her. He brought out the best in her too, or the devil in her depending upon how one looked at it.

She wanted to give as much as she wanted to receive. They took turns pleasing each other and being pleased, kissing and fondling and exploring each other's bodies. By the time they'd finished their coupling there was almost no body part left untouched or unexplored. They were a match and a perfect fit both physically and emotionally.

"Thank you Susan – thank you for not dismissing me out of hand. I told you we're right for each other."

"Now I'm thinking you also would have made a great salesman, Blake. You're a man of many talents," Susan purred in his ear.

"As are you, babe, a woman of extraordinary talents. I think I've met my match."

Blake stood up, grasping Susan's hand and pulling her up next to him. "I believe you were drawing a hot bath before I interrupted you. You wanna add some hot water to it and go soak for awhile? There's still Chardonnay left."

❧

The next morning found all the physicians and Susan sitting around the conference table drinking coffee or tea. They had orange juice and fresh fruit and yogurt with baskets of bagels accompanied by varying flavors of cream cheese on the table.

They had lengthy discussions about the future of Cade Medical Clinic, finally breaking for lunch from 1:00 to 2:00 p.m., and then right back at it again until dinner time signaled the end of day two.

Sasha had been unusually quiet during the discussions, not offering much input. When the meeting was finished and everyone was leaving the conference room, she sidled over to Blake and whispered something in his ear.

Blake said something back and Sasha's face turned crimson, not from embarrassment so much as it seemed from anger. She cast a glance over her shoulder in Susan's direction and then turned on her heels and stormed out.

Susan and Blake were the only two remaining in the room now and her curiosity had gotten the better of her. "Blake, what was that all about? I feel somehow I'm getting blamed for something."

Blake guided Susan to the door. "Let's go back to my room before dinner okay? We can talk along the way. I'm telling you Susan she may be a brilliant physician but she's a she-devil. She wanted to go back to my room for the best sex I'd ever have – according to her. I declined, not daring to tell her that I'd already had the best sex ever," Blake smiled.

"I'm quite serious about that too. You're all the woman I need."

"Well, I'm glad you didn't say anything to her. You turned her down. That's enough humiliation for a woman like her who doesn't like to take no for an answer. I have a question about last night though."

"Hmmm, do I want to hear this question? Does it have anything to do with my performance? Don't answer if it does ..."

"No, you big silly. Your performance was quite extraordinary last night ... and early this morning too, as you well know," Susan said as she squeezed Blake's hand. "It's about last night when I saw you and Sasha on the deck. As you were leaving you had a strange look on your face. I couldn't quite make it out."

"Did it look like this?" Blake asked as he perfectly recreated the look he had on his face last night; the look of a man who wanted to be rescued. "I didn't want to be with her Susan. She practically hijacked me onto the dance floor and then led me out onto the deck. She had me in a vise grip. All I could think about was you and how much I wanted to be with you and not her."

"I don't know if you're sincere or just full of it Blake. Whatever it is though you sure know how to make a girl feel special."

"Here we are at my room. Let's go inside and I'll show you how special you are to me. And you are Susan ... you're very special."

"She doesn't go down without a fight, does she, I mean trying to get you in her web again this morning." If she wasn't such a good doctor, I'd fire her and make her spin her web in somebody else's clinic. But having designs on you isn't really cause for her dismissal – at least not legally."

"Let's not waste another breath talking about her Susan." Blake removed his jacket and threw it on the chair. Turning his attention to Susan, he began kissing her while his hands began unbuttoning her blouse. In his haste, he lost his balance, tripping over his shoes and stumbling, knocking them both into the bedside table sending the lamp to the floor. They fell onto the edge of the bed and then tumbled onto the floor, barely missing falling on the lamp.

"This will be something to tell our grandchildren about," Blake laughed as he rolled on his back and pulled Susan on top of him. "Kiss me you beautiful woman."

They made love right there on the floor; it was every bit as exquisite as this morning and last night had been.

The next two days and nights were repeats of the same ... except ... except now Susan knew she couldn't continue the relationship. Ever since Blake's comment about grandchildren she'd been uneasy. Susan didn't want children. She felt she was too old. Blake had tried to reassure her that many women have children at her age and even older. She let it go while they were in

Gatlinburg but she knew the issue would have to be revisited and finalized once they returned to Raleigh.

⚜

It had been two months since Susan had called off the relationship with Blake. What relationship she asked herself. It had been only four passion-filled nights ... and mornings. It was a fling; merely that she assured herself.

Blake had used all his wiles and persuasive charms to try to convince her otherwise but she was adamant that she was not the woman for him. She'd insisted that he needed a woman more his age; a woman of childbearing age with fresh eggs; not ones shriveled up like old tomatoes as she supposed hers were.

The staff meetings were difficult; the air was thick with tension between the two of them with only Dr. Lassiter and Dr. Benton aware of their Gatlinburg affair – or at least that's what Susan thought, or hoped. If any of the others knew, they were polite enough and professional enough not to say anything.

Susan missed his kisses and his gentle touch coupled with his incredible passion and magic fingers. She missed their easy conversations and the laughter they shared over the silliest things. Damn it, she just missed everything about him. But she didn't want to hold him back. He loved children and wanted them. She loved them too but didn't want them. And she was not going to be abandoned by a younger man.

Truthfully, she would like children of her own, if only she were younger. She enjoyed her brother John's two daughters. She loved to take them shopping and doing girly things with them. At seven and eight years of age they were a delight and loved their Aunt Susan. They'll just have to do, Susan told herself. I love them like they were my own. And nobody ever said life is fair.

Her cell rang. "Hello."

"Susan?"

She smiled when she recognized the voice.

"Andy! Hello."

"Hi Susan; I hope I'm not bothering you. I just got back into town and thought I'd take a chance on calling you. I would have called you before from Maryland but I hoped the passage of time would smooth things."

"There's nothing to smooth, Andy. It's good to hear from you. If I were a betting woman I'd bet you arrived back in town, arms laden with gifts of every imaginable description for your nieces and nephews. Am I right?"

"Are you ever wrong, Suze? You know me better than I know myself. I feel sorry for all the other kids come Christmas morning when they find Santa didn't bring them anything; all the toys are at my sister's and brother-in-law's house," Andy chortled.

"You do spoil them Andy. I'll bet they'd be glad to see you back in town, even without toys."

"Well I was wondering Suze, if you'll be glad to see me. I know the annual Cade Medical Clinic Christmas party is next Saturday and I'm hoping to attend. Would that be okay with you?"

Susan stopped pacing and sat down on her very expensive Eames lounge chair; one of the few luxuries she ever allowed herself to purchase, besides the expensive dress and shoes she'd purchased last month while in Los Angeles interviewing a plastic surgeon.

What the hell, Susan had thought. We only live once and it's nice to splurge once in awhile on the finer things in life. And the dress and shoes are definitely fine.

"It's not only okay Andy but if you don't have a date you can be my plus one. I'm going stag. Well, Dr. Brandon is going with me but she's not a date," Susan laughed.

"Sounds great Susan. Shall I pick you up ... or meet you there?"

"Actually I'd like you to pick me up, pick both of us up, that way she and I can have more champagne than we should and won't have to worry about driving home or trying to catch a cab, or begging somebody to take pity on us or ..."

"Okay I'm sold,' Andy agreed. "I'll pick you and Karla up and take you back to your home; that is if you don't get a better offer."

"Thanks Andy. I doubt there will be any better offers. And Andy, it'll be nice to see you again. We shouldn't be enemies. Former lovers shouldn't turn into enemies, not when we once cared so much for each other."

"Ah, St. Susan; you always were too good for me. And I agree, we should never be enemies. I've never thought of you as such and I'm glad you don't think of me that way. I'll always consider you my friend. Perhaps that's all we should have ever been."

"You may be right, Andy but we did have some good times in the beginning; times that were more than friendly. I choose to remember those times."

"Well, we can talk about them Saturday. I choose to remember those times too. See you Saturday night, 8 o'clock, right?"

"Sure. See you then ... and Andy, thanks."

❧

"Wow! And double wow!" Andy exclaimed as Susan opened the door to him, with Karla standing beside her.

"Come on in Andy; as my mother would always admonish me, 'we're not heating all of Raleigh'." Susan laughed and Andy hurried inside. He gave Susan a tentative kiss on the cheek and turned his attention to Karla and kissed her cheek too.

"You both look sensational. I'd like to have half the money you each spent on your clothes."

"I don't know what you're talking about Andy. These are only Brian Atwood platform pumps that complement my little Zac Posen dress. And Karla here is only wearing Vera Wang with an old pair of Jimmy Choo shoes; just a little something we threw together at the last minute," Susan laughed joined by Karla chuckling along with her.

"Oh I'm sorry. I didn't mean to insult you ladies. How dare I imply that you're spending a small fortune on your outfits? I should say a freaking *large* fortune," Andy laughed.

"You've got that right Andy, but Karla and I donate a small fortune between us to our charities; and every once in a great while it feels good to splurge on ourselves. I think our local humane society would forgive us an occasional indulgence."

"Yeah," Karla chimed in, "and then we feel so guilty we double up on our contributions, so it's win-win."

"Well, whatever you spent is certainly worth it. You ladies are dazzling. I'll be the most envied man at the party tonight. So, shall we go now? Your chariot awaits; at least what passes as a chariot from the rental agency."

They walked outside and looked down the driveway to their right where Andy's vehicle was parked.

"A limo, Andy? You hired a limo? Are you serious?"

"Follow me. And yes I'm absolutely serious. Why should you two have all the fun tonight, I asked myself. We can all drink way more champagne than we should and who knows, we might even fool around a little."

Susan and Karla both laughed and shot Andy a look of total disbelief. It was going to be an interesting Christmas party.

◈

It seemed to Susan that all eyes were upon them as they walked into the ballroom at the Renaissance Raleigh at North Hills. The place was decorated exquisitely and the holiday atmosphere permeated the room. Everyone was in a festive mood and Susan was feeling quite special in her expensive haute couture. *Special. Blake thinks, or at least thought I was special.*

Dr. Montgomery, looking quite dapper in his tux, walked over to them and asked Karla to dance. They made a dashing couple Susan thought.

Andy took Susan in his arms and led her onto the dance floor; the orchestra appropriately playing 'White Christmas.' Susan knew the Christmas songs wouldn't go on all night but would eventually give in to some rollicking rock and roll interspersed with some slow dance songs so that couples could dance and snuggle together.

Dancing in Andy's arms felt good; she couldn't deny it. But her thoughts were with Blake. Why did she break off the relationship, she kept going over in her mind, why? Why? Because she was old ... or was it because he was young; or was it because of a previous humiliating relationship failure?

Rationally, she knew she wasn't old. For heaven's sake she's only 43 she reminded herself. That's young, but still, she was older than Blake. There was no avoiding it – she was 10 years older than him – or a little over 9 years as he tried to convince her.

Where is Blake, she wondered. He'd mentioned to Dr. Ostrosky at the staff meeting that he was coming to the annual Christmas party. He wouldn't tell her of course, but he would make sure she always heard his plans.

He'd given up trying to talk to her about anything other than business. Their red hot fling had deteriorated into a purely platonic relationship; one that did not please Blake. He found it difficult to believe she placed so much importance on a silly little age difference.

She was dancing with Andy but in her heart she was dancing with Blake. That came to a crashing halt when she spotted Blake standing by the dance floor talking to Sasha. Again? He's with her near a dance floor again?" Déjà vu.

Oh Blake, if only I hadn't been such an idiot. What's ten years? I mean, really, why did I make such a big deal out of it? Ten little, no, make that about nine little years. That's it. How did I ever get to be a CEO of a large company when I'm such a total moron?

Susan was quite aware of Blake's eyes on her. They followed her all around the dance floor while he was dancing with Sasha. Were they a couple now she wondered? And if so, why was he watching her? Why was he smiling at her when she looked his way?

Her hope faded as she caught Blake and Sasha heading toward the doors to the hallway. Where were they going? She wondered. As if she didn't know. Probably right to his room and there was nothing she could do about it. Or was there?

While she was contemplating what to do, Blake and Sasha stopped to talk to Dr. Ostrosky and his nurse who were standing by the exit door trying to make an unobtrusive exit; although everyone knew they were having an affair. Neither was married so Susan could never understand their trying to hide it. What was up with that?

Susan was surprised to see Blake say goodbye to Dr. Ostrosky, his nurse and to ... Sasha? He was walking away from Sasha?

Susan held her breath as Blake walked toward her. She wanted to run to him and throw her arms around him but of course she couldn't, she wouldn't. What would he do? It would serve her right if he walked right by her. He didn't. He couldn't.

"Susan, could we have a talk? Please? Not here. Would you take a walk with me, somewhere where it's quiet? We need to talk."

Oh no, not the 'we need to talk' conversation. This never ends well. Been there, done that.

Blake didn't wait for her answer and instead put his arm around Susan's waist and led her through a door into a private banquet room which was presently unoccupied.

Blake indicated a chair for Susan to sit upon. He sat down beside her and took her hands in his. "Please bear with me Susan. I know you aren't interested in me romantically, but that doesn't mean I'm not ... well, what I'm trying to say is ..."

"I love you!"

"You what? I think I'd better see a hearing specialist," Blake exclaimed, his eyes wide open.

"I could swear you just said you love me," Blake said as he pulled Susan to him and squeezed her until she thought her ribs would crack.

"I do love you Blake. I think I've loved you since the first night we spent in my room."

Blake looked into her beautiful blue eyes and asked her the question that had burned in his heart for months. "But if you love me Susan, why did you practically run away from me? Why did you cut me off? It can't be all about our age difference. I just can't buy that. You know that doesn't matter today."

"I know that Blake. If I were to be truthful I'd tell you that I was afraid you would leave me for a younger woman. It's that simple."

"I could never leave you – for any reason. I'm in love with you Susan. You'll just have to trust my love."

"I've been left for a younger woman before Blake. Ten years ago. I was 33 and he was ..."

"23?"

"Ha! No, he was 53! The old coot left me for a 25-year-old," Susan said half laughing but with a look of sadness on her face. "I was too old for him. Can you imagine that? I've carried the scars of that embarrassment for the last ten years. Only Luke knew about it ... and now you."

Blake kissed her hands and then her neck, feathering hot kisses up to her chin and then her lips where they were met with a welcoming passion.

"Susan, I knew there had to be more to it than a silly little 10 year age difference. You could have told me. There's nothing for you to be embarrassed about. This was all on him, not you. His loss 10 years ago has given me the greatest Christmas present now."

"I know Blake. I know you're right. But sometimes we carry an extra heavy load of emotional baggage that no amount of rationalization can fix."

"Well, we're going to put this baby to rest; maybe not right this instant but it's something we'll be working on – together – from now on. I've never been happier Susan."

Blake wrapped his arms around Susan, stroking her back and kissing her; kissing her head and her hair, letting his hands glide from her back to her breasts, rubbing his thumbs over her nipples, feeling her reaction to his touch.

"If you didn't look so sensational in that dress Suze, I'd rip it off you right now."

"The dress can be lifted up, Blake ... and it's private in here," Susan whispered in his ear, inserting her tongue in it and tracing it around the inside and outside, while lifting her dress up and moving her pelvis closer to him.

He leaned her against the silk paneled wall while she unzipped his trousers. They made love standing up listening to the pulsing beat of the music playing on the other side of the door.

"Even in my wildest imagination and fantasies I couldn't have envisioned this happening tonight, babe," Blake said when they'd finally caught their breath and their bodies had relaxed. He placed his hand under her chin and lifted it up and kissed her tenderly on the lips.

"I don't know about you Suze, but I've suddenly got a voracious appetite. Shall we go back into the ballroom and partake of that delicious food Madame?" Blake said facetiously.

"Absolutely; I'm famished. I've also got to let Tony and Karla know I won't be sharing the limo with them on the way home. I'm also hungry for answers such as why were you with Sasha tonight? And why were you two talking to Dr. Ostrosky? And why did you walk away from them leaving Sasha with them??

"You're certainly the little question box, my love. Ok; one, she cornered me again as she always does whenever she gets the chance. She's not going to give up until we're married – I mean until you and I are married, of course."

A wide-eyed look of surprise filled Susan's face as she said laughingly, "Blake, did you just propose to me? Or lay out a plan to rid yourself of Sasha?"

"Hold that thought. Let me answer your other questions. First, I mean second, Sasha wanted to talk to Dr. Ostrosky about covering for her next week so I walked over to them with her; I figured it would be easier to extricate myself from her clutches if she had something else to focus on. Worked like a charm.'

"You're something else Blake. Life with you would be very interesting."

Blake took Susan's hands in his, smiled into her face and said "will be, Susan."

"Will be what Blake?"

"You said life with me *would* be interesting. No, it *will* be interesting. And yes that was a proposal. It isn't how I would have planned it but tonight was such a surprise. If you say no I'll resort to groveling and begging. But I won't give up. I love you Susan and I want to spend the rest of my life with you."

"I love you too Blake, more than I've ever loved anyone. I want to grow old with you. We may grow old at a different rate," Susan laughed, "but we'll grow old together."

⚬✣⚬

Chocolate Rum Cheesecake

....

Ingredients

1 graham cracker crust

6 oz. bittersweet chocolate

1/4 cup rum

1 lb. cream cheese

3/4 cup extra fine sugar

1/2 cup sour cream

1 tbsp. vanilla extract

5 eggs

Instructions

Preheat the oven to 325°F. Prepare the graham cracker crust in a springform pan. Refrigerate the pan until needed. Melt the chocolate over low heat. Add the rum. Set aside.

Beat the cream cheese until fluffy. Gradually beat in the sugar, sour cream and vanilla. Beat in the eggs, one at a time. Mix well. Place the bowl over hot water and stir until smooth. Pour one quarter of the batter into another bowl. Set aside.

Mix the chocolate into the remaining batter. Stir over hot water until smooth. Take the springform pan from the refrigerator. Pour in the chocolate batter. Gently pour the plain batter over the top of the chocolate batter. Form swirls in the batter with a fork (some of the chocolate should show). Bake for 50 minutes. Cool to room temperature. Remove the rim from the springform pan. Refrigerate overnight. Serve. (www.foodgeeks.com)

"It doesn't matter who you love, or how you love, but that you love"

~Rod McKuen

"Oh, I wonder, wonder who, be do be, who, who wrote the book of love? Baby, baby, baby I love you yes I do, well it says so in this book of love, Ours is the one that's true, Oh I wonder wonder who, be do be who, who wrote the book of love?"

"Love in the Romance Aisle"

Browsing in the local bookstore, Renee was fantasizing about seeing her very own book displayed on the shelf; and not just visible by the spine but a full-on view of the front cover.

She realized it costs more to have your book displayed that way but she was a dreamer and her motto was - *If you're going to dream, dream big!*

She had been dreaming big ever since she'd left Jason and he had taken up with a woman who shared his belief that books were a waste of time. They were both TV aficionados, something which Renee could never understand. She *liked* TV but she *loved* books.

She also couldn't understand how she had even dated him, considering his take on the written word but when she forced herself to think about her attraction to him, she had to admit that it was purely physical; he was the embodiment of the well-endowed male.

Not that he possessed movie star looks, but he was definitely handsome and sexy and there was something about him that had attracted her and many other women; confidence! That's what he had in abundance and it definitely appealed to her and others who fell under his charm, if only for a short spell before they too became disenchanted with his shallowness.

But oh my, could he kiss! His lips were like firm velvet pouches that encircled her mouth pulling her lips into his. Even when his lips were pressed hard against hers, they still felt soft and yielding.

His lovemaking was nice, nothing sensational even considering his generous attributes. He may have had the goods but sometimes she wondered if he thought just possessing them was enough; that he didn't need to learn how to use what he had for the pleasure of others. If he at least had a personality ... or an interest in something other than his looks; anything, she might have stayed with him. But the only interest, besides his narcissistic interest in himself, was watching TV.

She didn't want to admit it to herself but she missed the kissing the most. If only she could find a man who could kiss like him but who could also rock her world in bed. Being satisfied was okay but she wanted to be super satisfied. She wanted a man who was attuned to her needs, someone who knew how to make the most of his body parts that most other men would pay to have if they could. And if he actually read books, well, to her that would be the whole package.

As she was standing in the Romance section, admiring the beauty of the book covers and reading the blurbs on the back, she was thrilled as usual to indulge in her passion without guilt – books, books, and more books.

"Judging by the smile on your face, I'd say you love a good old-fashioned romance story," the stranger next to her said kindly.

"What? Oh. Matter of fact, I do," Renee answered, turning to look at the smiling man beside her.

"I keep hoping that a book of mine will make it into a real brick and mortar book store one day, but so far I've found that I have two chances of that happening – slim and none" she laughed.

"Add a third chance to that: Fat."

Renee gave a little laugh and exclaimed "Oh, that's funny. Yes, three chances of not having my book in a book store. Thanks for pointing that out – not!"

"So you're an author? I know what you mean," the stranger said as he laughed along with her.

"It isn't easy to get published today unless you self-publish, and these book stores don't want to accept books unless they've been published by a known publishing house or are authored by someone well known. It's the old Catch-22" he said as he looked deeper into her eyes and decided he liked what he saw, someone as passionate about books as he was and someone very, very attractive.

Renee was immediately attracted to his looks but reined herself in, not wanting to be taken in by just good looks again. Still, she couldn't help admiring his aquiline nose, blondish-brown hair and blue-green eyes; eyes fringed with the longest lashes she'd ever seen on a man ... or on any woman for that matter. He wasn't overly tall, about 5'10", which was good because she was only 5'2"; actually 5'1 ½" but she always stretched it to 5'2".

Hey, if it were a man thinking about his anatomy he'd sure stretch it too, she smiled inwardly.

She wasn't skinny or fat. She liked to think of herself as Goldilocks; just right.

"I'm Dan, by the way" he said, offering his hand and feeling the warmth of her skin against his as he sidled a bit closer to her, hoping she wouldn't mind this invasion of her personal space.

"It's really nice to meet another person who seems to enjoy books, Dan," she practically cooed as she stood firm, not wanting to move away from this man.

"I'm Renee, freelance writer and would be world famous author," she grinned.

"Well join the club," Dan said.

"It's every writer's dream to be recognized and appreciated for their words. I hope to see one of my sister's books on display here too. Miranda's written several books, romance novels naturally, all of them quite good and just waiting to be discovered."

"Oh," Renee said rather disappointed.

"It's your sister who is the writer, then?" She was hoping against hope that this handsome man, but more importantly, a man who loved books, was a writer.

"Yes and she's a very good one too. I just popped in here on my way to a meeting to see if I could find a good book to give her for her birthday on Friday. It occurs to me that perhaps I can give her one of your books. I'd pay you for it of course and I know she'd appreciate a book by another struggling author" he said as he held back what he really wanted to tell her. That could wait until later; he felt sure there would indeed be a later because he knew he wanted to see her again. He hoped she would be just as amenable.

"Oh no, it would be my pleasure to give you a copy; no charge. We authors need to look out for each other. Besides, it's good karma, pay it forward and all that. I just happen to have a copy with me; okay I have two copies in this carry-all. I never go anywhere without a copy or two of my books; you never know who you'll run into.

"That's more than kind of you Renee. I know she'll appreciate it. I do too. Tell you what, why don't you come out to the book signing they're having here Friday night?" You'll be surrounded by people just like yourself and I'll introduce you to my sister."

"Then please allow me to give the book to her. That way I can sign it for her. Who knows, it might be worth something some day, maybe more than $15.95, signed by the famous author," Renee laughed.

"Very well then; I'm flattered that you're even talking to me given that you'll be so famous one day. I should take advantage of you right now before others discover you, which I'm betting they will."

"Dream on Dan. In the meantime you need to come up with another gift for Miranda."

"I'll pick her up some of her favorite perfume. She always tells me she can never have enough of it but I'll be damned if I can think of the name of it right now. I seem to be thinking of other things," he smiled seductively.

"Hmmm, perhaps she'd like a new perfume, one by Paris Hilton, Jennifer Lopez or Carolina Herrera? Or, I'm guessing since she writes romance novels, she might prefer old tried and true fragrances such as Opium, Chanel or Passion?"

Dan's face lit up at the recognition of the name Opium. "Yes, that's it, Opium. Yves de Laurent, right?"

"Close; Yves Saint Laurent, but any clerk at the perfume counter would know who you mean. It's actually a favorite of mine too believe it or not. In fact I love to combine Opium with Chanel #5. It's my own signature scent. Two very, very old fashioned perfumes but together they make a killer combination."

"I will just bet they do," Dan said as he leaned over and sniffed behind Renee's left ear. "If that's it, then it's very nice."

"Not wearing it today Dan; it's more of an evening scent. What you're sniffing is good old-fashioned shampoo," Renee laughed and blushed at the same time.

Dan felt a bit flushed too, stammering, "Well it's lovely Renee. Anyway, you and my sister seem to be kindred spirits; if you could autograph your book to Miranda that would be just great. And I'll get a chance to see you again and talk about my favorite topic, books. At least that's my favorite topic so far. I have a feeling that could change" Dan said with a dazzling twinkle in his eyes.

"I'd like that very much Dan,' Renee said.

"I take it you're not married or in a relationship at the moment? Oh my please forgive me. I don't know why I even said that; how rude of me."

Dan placed the book he'd been perusing back on the shelf and laughed "No, not rude at all Renee, you're very forthright. I like that; no pretense. But to answer your question, no, I'm not married, not anymore," He grinned.

"And it really pleases me to be able to say that. My wife didn't share my love of books, like you do, or anything else for that matter. I've wanted to meet a woman who loves books and here you are; and in the Romance section to boot. I take that as a very good sign Renee," he said as he winked at her.

Renee's knees turned to jelly right then and there. She was certain she was actually going to swoon. She wasn't sure she knew exactly what a swoon consisted of but she gathered it had something to do with falling to the floor and making a complete idiot of one's self.

She was a sucker for a wink. *What is it about a wink; a slight combined movement of the eyelid and upper cheek that conveys so much meaning in just a split second. It's something intimate that can be shared between friends, lovers and even strangers. It can mean so many different things. Oh, please Michael, wink at me again.*

"I'll see you on Friday then, 8 o'clock?" Dan said, offering his apologies for having to leave to tend to business.

"Do you have a business card or a scrap of paper that I can write my number on?" he inquired. "I'd like to call you Friday to make sure you'll be here. I'd rather not leave it to chance. I really do want to see you again Renee."

Renee opened her purse and withdrew her cell phone. "I'll go you one better Dan. If you'll give me your phone number I'll program it into my phone and if you'd like, you can program my number into yours."

"I'd like," Dan said and gave her a huge grin followed by, oh my god – another wink! "I'd definitely like."

Renee's hands were trembling as she slid her thumb across the cell phone screen giving her access to her list of contacts. They exchanged numbers and Dan apologized again for having to leave telling Renee he was looking forward to Friday.

She watched him walk hurriedly through the store and out the front door. She hoped that wouldn't be the last she'd see of him but she couldn't be sure. Some men are just flirts.

Friday could not arrive soon enough Renee lamented. She felt foolish but could not get Dan out of her mind. She was anxious to meet his sister too. She not only loved books but she also loved fellow authors.

The day after meeting Dan in the book store her cell rang. She smiled when she heard the announcement on the phone – 'Call from Dan'.

"Hello Dan. It's nice to hear from you. I thought you wouldn't call until tomorrow, but I'm glad you did."

"I'm glad I called today too, Renee. I just wanted to make sure you're coming to the book signing tomorrow. I told my sister about you and she's anxious to meet you; not just to talk about your mutual love of books but knowing my sister, she has an ulterior motive. I'm warning you, she's a born matchmaker."

Laughing, Renee said "Well, I think she has a pretty easy job facing her. I'm not normally a forward person Dan but I like you very much. I know we don't know each other well at all but I have a good feeling about you."

"I'll go you one further, I have more than a good feeling about you, Renee. I got good vibes from you immediately upon our meeting. I mean what are the odds that the two of us would show up in the Romance section of the bookstore? I'm usually in the Mysteries and Thrillers section."

"Good karma Dan, or good luck or coincidence or whatever you want to call it. Whatever it is I'm just glad it happened. I'm looking forward to tomorrow night, and getting to know you. I don't even know what you do for a living or anything about you."

"We'll have plenty of time to talk tomorrow night, Renee. There's so much I want to learn about you and a lot I want to tell you about me. But I've got a really important call that I have to take right now; not that talking to you isn't important but this is one call I have to take. I'll see you tomorrow night 8 o'clock at Books and Beans."

Renee loved Books and Beans. Their coffee must be made from the best coffee beans in the world, she thought. She also loved the beanbag chairs scattered throughout the store for comfy reading. It was her home away from home and apparently a lot of other people's too.

"Sure, see you tomorrow night Dan. I'm looking forward to it." Renee felt she should look down to make sure her feet were still firmly planted on the floor.

⚜

Renee walked into the Books and Beans and was immediately greeted by Dan who was standing right inside the door, obscuring a large sign announcing the book signing. He surprised her by enveloping her in a big hug. Putting his arm around his sister Miranda's waist, he introduced Renee to her. Renee felt an immediate connection to her just as she did when she met Dan.

"Happy Birthday, Miranda," Renee said as she withdrew a copy of her book from her carry-all bag. "Here you go, from one struggling author to another."

Miranda accepted the book and opened it, reading the autograph aloud – 'From one struggling author to another.' "Boy, isn't that the truth? Thank you so much. I look forward to reading it; I really do."

"Will you two ladies excuse me" Dan asked. "I have to go to the Book Signing Room and set up. See you there in a minute?"

Miranda noted the look of surprise on Renee's face. "I take it Dan didn't tell you why we're here?"

"Sort of; he told me there was a book signing here that he wanted me to attend and he wanted us to meet. Your brother is something else Miranda."

"Oh you have no idea, Renee."

They chatted for a few more minutes and then Miranda looped her arm in Renee's and led her back to the room that the store sets aside for book signings. They fell into place behind a line of people waiting to have their books signed. "There're only about 10 people ahead of us so it shouldn't take too long to get up to the table."

"And even more people streaming in behind us. Where's the big poster with his or her picture on it? And what are we doing in this line if we don't have a book to be signed? And ...Oh no! You've got to be kidding me Miranda. Miranda! I thought *you* were the author in the family, not Michael," Renee exclaimed, clasping her hands to her mouth as she spotted Michael at the table smiling, signing autographs.

"That's my brother for you. He wanted to surprise you."

"Shock me is more like it. Here I was telling him how I was going to be a famous author one day and instead he's the famous author."

"Well he's not exactly famous yet Renee, but judging by the amount of people who are here to have their books signed, I'd say he's well on his way. I hope one day people will come to a book signing for one of my books; oh and yours too!"

The line moved quickly and Renee smiled as she found herself at the head of the line. Dan looked up as he was holding out his hand to grab a book to be signed, and then smiled in recognition of Renee and Miranda.

"I'm sorry I don't have a book for you to sign Dan. I might have had you told me the book signing was for you."

"Then I'll just have to sign something else," Dan whispered as he reached for her, hesitated and then grabbed her hand and signed her palm.

"As I told Miranda, you're something else, Dan. I won't hold up the line. We'll probably be sitting on a beanbag chair in the Romance section, talking, until you can join us okay?

"Absolutely A-Ok, Renee. Don't tell my fans but the time is going to crawl by until the last customer leaves," Dan said in hushed tones.

"Sure and I believe in the Easter Bunny too. See you when you're finished Dan. In the meantime Miranda and I are going to get to know each other and gossip about you."

Calling to her as she walked away, Dan shouted, "If you only believe half of what she says about me, you'll still think I'm the god of all gods and the be all end all of everything. I think she likes me!"

Renee turned and laughed watching Dan sign a book, so happy for him and yet a bit envious that it wasn't her doing the book signing. One day, she told herself, one day ...

Renee and Miranda found a quiet corner and each settled on a beanbag chair. The server came by and asked for their order. Both agreed they'd like the chocolate pizza and a cappuccino.

About two hours later Dan joined them, a look of smug satisfaction on his handsome face. He'd signed a phenomenal 60 books and made a lot of interesting contacts.

"So this is an unusual way to spend your birthday, huh sis?"

"It's a wonderful way to spend my birthday Dan. I couldn't be happier; I'm so glad you suggested it. Renee and I are practically like sisters. And we're all authors – but one of us is on the way to being the next John Grisham or Clive Cussler. Happy Birthday to me and Happy Unbirthday to you two," Miranda laughed as she got up and gave Dan and Renee a warm hug and a kiss.

Dan explained to Renee the reason why he had to cut their phone conversation off so quickly yesterday; his publisher was calling to tell him his second manuscript had been accepted and he needed to sign some papers.

"That is so wonderful Dan. I'm so happy for you," Miranda said.

"Me too, Dan; I'm really thrilled. Now I can say *I* know a famous author."

Dan leaned into Renee, hugged her tenderly and sniffed her behind her left ear again. "Mmm, now that is definitely a delicious scent. *That* is Opium and Chanel isn't it? Oh and speaking of Opium, here Miranda; I nearly forgot to give you your gift."

Dan reached into his jacket pocket and brought out a beautifully wrapped container of Opium and handed it to his sister. "Happy Birthday little sis."

"Oh Dan you're always so thoughtful. Thank you; you know how much I love Opium. And see, Renee and I have something else in common besides books; Opium perfume. This is a good sign," she said as she gave Renee a sly wink.

Miranda stayed for only another 20 minutes or so and then excused herself, knowing Dan and Renee wanted to be alone together.

After Dan took a bite of the chocolate pizza he and Renee left the Books and Beans bookstore and strolled arm in arm through Faneuil Hall also known as Quincy Marketplace in beautiful Boston. The weather was perfect, the stars were twinkling, the boats on the Charles River were gently rocking and Renee was with a handsome, wonderful man. It had all the makings for the beginning of a perfect romance novel. Her thoughts were traveling at light speed.

"I've got a bottle of Perrier Jouet de Champagne that I've been saving for a special occasion," Dan said.

"How would you like to come back to my place where we can celebrate in style?"

"Whoa! That's very special champagne, Dan; not to mention very expensive. Are you sure you want to waste it on ... "

"Waste it? I think not, Renee. I was hoping you'd see it as an inducement, an enticement to snare you into my web. How's that for honesty? I desire you Renee; I'm not making any bones about it. I've desired you since I first stood next to you in the bookstore. I felt an immediate attraction and I inferred that you did too."

Renee stopped walking and turned to face Dan. She looked into his eyes and indeed saw an honest man, one whom she instinctively knew she could trust.

"I feel the same, Dan but I doubt I would have had the nerve to admit it had you not been so open and honest about your feelings."

"I'm glad you feel the same Renee. No sense in wasting a lot of precious time doing a waltz when we can get right into a tango."

He laughed lustily. "I want to get to know all about you, to make love to you, and not necessarily in that order."

Dan wrapped his arms around Renee and instead of kissing her immediately he stared down at her, his whole face smiling and he began murmuring sweet, romantic words to her; words he knew she'd appreciate hearing, words perhaps she'd written in her own romance novels. But they were words he truly wanted to say because he meant them. He'd fallen hard, and fast.

"Kiss me Dan. I hear tango music playing in my head and I feel the urge to throw my leg up over your shoulder as you bend me backwards while my hair hangs down sweeping across the dance floor," Renee purred.

Dan laughed. "Well, that erases any doubt about you being a romance writer, Renee. You paint such vivid scenes, scenes that I'd like to bring to life right now at my apartment."

Dan inclined his head toward hers, leaned down and engulfed her lips with his. She threw her arms around his neck and kissed him back just as eagerly. Her whole body was aquiver as it suddenly occurred to her that she was now living the life that she'd been writing about; this was real life true romance.

Renee had the beginning of her Romance novel and now she had the ending and she knew it would be a Happily Ever After.

Chocolate Pizza

....

Ingredients

2 tablespoons butter (1/4 stick), melted

1/4 cup chocolate-hazelnut spread (such as Nutella)

1/2 cup chopped bittersweet or semisweet chocolate   2 tablespoons chopped high-quality white chocolate (such as Lindt or Perugina)

2 tablespoons chopped toasted hazelnuts

Directions

Preheat oven to 450°F. Line large baking sheet with parchment. Roll out dough on lightly floured surface to 11-inch round. Transfer dough to prepared sheet. Make indentations all over dough with fingertips. Brush melted butter over. Bake until pale golden, about 20 minutes.

Smooth chocolate-hazelnut spread over hot crust. Sprinkle chopped bittersweet chocolate and white chocolate over. Bake until chocolate begins to melt, about 2 minutes. Sprinkle chopped hazelnuts over, cut into wedges, and serve.

(www.epicurious.com)

"So many days you passed me by see the tears standin' in my eyes you didn't stop to make me feel better by leavin' me a card or a letter"

Special Delivery

I've always loved writing and had spent many hours in my younger days fantasizing about being a famous romance novelist one day. I would write stories about the young maiden being rescued from her miserable existence by a knight in shining armor. Sure, it had been done in varying forms ad infinitum but that didn't deter me. I just knew that my stories would be different and bring me fame and fortune.

As I grew older and emboldened I decided to take a chance and submit my stories to every magazine on the market. I figured if I flung enough spaghetti against the wall surely some of it would stick. I had updated my stories from the damsel in distress of my youth to writing in earnest about more mature women and the difficulties of finding love after a certain age.

That "certain age" was rather nebulous but you didn't have to be a rocket scientist to understand that it wasn't twenty years of age; thirty-five was about as far as you could stretch it. The pickins' grew slimmer and slimmer with each passing year.

Thirty-five year old men aren't interested in thirty-five year old women. They want younger babes with no mileage on them. So you find yourself looking to older men, maybe a fifty year old, figuring they'll appreciate your youth and beauty. Uh, wrong again. The fifty-year olds aren't interested in thirty-five year old women. They're interested in women thirty-five years *younger* than them! Okay, maybe twenty-five but still it seems everyone is looking for someone much younger.

I was becoming an unwitting expert on this subject. I had had an outstanding career as a sales rep for a large pharmaceutical company traveling all over the country to new and fun places, meeting a lot of interesting people. But I had never met "the one," the one who would rescue me from my lonely existence, much like the heroes in my earlier writing attempts.

I often pondered why I hadn't found the right man. I'm not full of myself but I know that my vital statistics are what most people would say are pleasing; at 5'9" which most people say is all legs, I carry a healthy 145 pounds. My hair is a beautiful shade of blonde but that's thanks to Miss Clairol and not Mother Nature. The blue of my eyes complements my color enhanced hair.

So what's wrong with me I wonder? I'm kind and would never deliberately hurt anyone. Surely if there was something really wrong with my personality, Gloria would tell me. Oh, she'd tell me in a heartbeat, of that I had no doubt.

I've had my fair share of serious relationships throughout the years, even a couple that I thought had potential but for whatever reasons, they all seemed to fizzle out. Gloria always insisted it was because the man who would take my breath away was waiting for me out there somewhere; I just hadn't met him yet and I needed to have patience. I think still being single at my age proves I do have patience. Either that or I'm just incredibly picky or I've got a broken picker!

And so far this nebulous creature who will take my breath away isn't here in Colorado; at least not in the Boulder area that I can tell. I love Boulder and can't imagine living anywhere else. No matter where my job's travels have taken me, my heart is always in Boulder. I've been skiing since I was little more than a toddler and I love cold weather and snow.

I fantasize about skiing down Eldora Mountain and colliding with Mr. Right who will then lift me up off the snow and into his arms. Or sometimes my fantasies have me hiking along Boulder Creek Path and almost being run over by a cyclist who will have to swerve to avoid me and we'll end up talking and ... Oh my there's no limit to my crazy fantasies. All they're really good for is fodder for the short stories I write.

On my 30th birthday I gave notice at the job I'd held since I was 20. I decided if I ever wanted to be a successful writer, I had to do just that and nothing else. I'd saved a ton of money during my brief career and luckily I'd made some very good investments too. So I was finally financially set.

I was quite annoyed with myself on those occasions when I told myself I couldn't be happy without a man in my life. In truth I was very happy, but down deep we know that happiness shared is so much better. It isn't that I can't be happy without that little slip of paper, the marriage certificate. But it would be nice to have someone to come home to who isn't covered with fur, or hair; as much as I love my kitties and dog they won't join in on the discussion of my latest romance story. Someone I can share my day with, someone just to sit in the living room with as I read a book or watch TV, someone to have great conversations with. Company! At night; that's what I'm missing.

"Why the sad face, Kristine?" Gloria asked as I was having a little Pity Party in my head. Gloria and I are close friends and we don't need to fill every second of our time together with conversation; so I hadn't realized the prolonged silence as we stood at the window watching for the mailman to arrive.

"Oh, nothing earth-shattering, G. I didn't realize my thoughts were making their way on to my face. I was just wondering how many more days I'll be waiting for the mail, eagerly looking through the letters, hoping for an acceptance of my stories instead of the usual rejections."

Gloria swallowed the last of her coffee and paused for a few seconds before responding. "Well, maybe you should be changing your focus Kris."

"Whatever are you talking about, G? My focus is on my writing and I won't be a quitter. One day the mailman will deliver that acceptance letter. I just know it. I have to believe that," I said, but not really sure that I did. "What should I focus on then?"

Gloria walked over to the kitchen counter and poured herself another cup of coffee from the coffee maker. Walking back to the window she looked outside and said, "How about focusing on your gorgeous George Clooney look-alike mailman for instance? He's got Clooney's brown and silver hair and brown eyes and the same friendly but sexy smile. He's nice and tall too with good muscular legs."

Kristine eyed her friend suspiciously; "You don't miss much do you, Inspector G? He could be blonde with blue eyes for all I know."

"I've seen him smile at you and try to talk to you but you're too busy looking for that acceptance letter. I'm serious Kate. I watch you through the window just about every day and I notice how he looks at you. I've got great distance vision too and I noticed he doesn't wear a wedding ring ..."

"Gloria, not all married men wear wedding rings; you know that as well as anyone. Your Frankie doesn't wear one and he's madly in love with you. And besides how can you spot an empty ring finger from a few yards away even with such great vision? You'd make a great spy girlfriend."

"Well, to respond to your first comment Kris, Frankie doesn't wear one because he has a fear of his ring getting caught on something and him losing his finger or some such thing. I told him it's irrational, but the man loves me. That's all that counts." And secondly, your single man detection skills are deteriorating. I might be married but I keep those skills honed, because you never know," Gloria said as her eyes crinkled and she smiled at me.

"Well I hope you never have to use those skills, G, unless of course it's to help me."

Gloria is so sweet, stopping by every day for our daily ritual of coffee and conversation; or our daily gossip as her Frankie calls it. It's probably a little bit of both but I'd like to think that we're nice people and that it's mostly conversation.

The past two days she's been accompanying me out to the mailbox hoping to share in my enthusiasm when the acceptance letter finally arrives.

"Well, today I want you to smile and say more than hello to him without even as much as a glance at him. Engage him in some conversation. Tell him about the letter you're looking for, for goodness' sake. Just talk to him. You know, you form some thoughts in your head, open your mouth, then let the words spill forth and voila! You've got a conversation going. Next thing you know you're choosing your wedding dress and ..."

"You know what, G? You're a really pushy broad." We both laughed.

· ·

"But you're a damn good friend so if I engage him in conversation my dear, will you get off my back?"

"Promise!" Gloria said and then squealed "He's here, Kris."

"You mean the mail is here Gloria, right? Not *him*; the *mail*. That *is* what we're waiting for after all. Well at least one of us is."

Gloria practically pushed me out the door and hurried me along the few yards to my mailbox. The mailman was just putting my mail in the box. Today I didn't rush to grab the letters but instead paused and said hello.

This time I took a really good look at him and I'll be damned if the pushy broad isn't right; he really does resemble George Clooney, maybe even better looking. Yeah, like that's possible, but he *is* seriously handsome.

How could I not notice how good looking he is? What red-blooded woman would overlook a hunk for a piece of paper? Ha! A woman who's given up on any type of physical relationship, that's who. Well that stops right here and now ...

I summoned my courage and spoke to him. Introducing myself, I smiled and said "Hi, I'm Kristine. My friends call me Kris." Turning my head to the side, I smiled and said, "And this is my closest friend Gloria."

The mailman smiled back, looking at each of us in turn and shaking our hands. "It's a pleasure to meet both of you" the mailman said, flashing an incredible smile. "And I know who you are Kristine." he said in a rich baritone. "My name's Mike, Mike Palermo. And you're Kristine Harper. May I call you Kris?"

"What? How'd you know my last name Mike?" I asked incredulously. I felt G's elbow in my ribs as she laughed, giving me that *I can't believe you just said that* look.

My cheeks flushed in what must have been the brightest crimson on the color wheel when Mike handed me my mail. There it was in black and white – Kristine Harper. "Oh my, I'm so embarrassed. I can't believe how foolish that was. You wouldn't be much of a mailman I suppose if you didn't notice silly little things like names and addresses," I sputtered.

"Yes, of course you may call me Kris."

"Well I *am* your mailman Kris, and I do see your name every day." His smile broke into a laugh which actually helped put me at ease.

"I've been wondering if we'd ever get a chance to talk but you're always more interested in the mail that I bring you. I hope one day I can deliver whatever it is that you're waiting for."

Oh Mike, I'm beginning to think of something else you could deliver.

"I'm a writer" I blurted out.

"Well, not really a writer, I guess, because I haven't been paid for anything I've written yet. What I'm waiting for every day is an acceptance letter for one of the many stories that I've written. I didn't realize I'd been so single minded until Gloria scolded me for not being polite. I'm sorry if I've been rude," I offered.

"Not at all Kris; I'm just glad to know that you weren't purposely ignoring me. I've wanted to get to know you for some time but you always grabbed the mail and ran back into your house," Mike said sheepishly.

Oh my god this man really is seriously handsome and with a drop-dead gorgeous smile. Why didn't I wear something sexy, brush my hair better, and put some lip gloss on, some blush? Oh, Hell's bells I surely don't need the blush today!

We stood by the mailbox talking for what must have been a good ten minutes before either of us realized that Gloria had quietly walked away. I discovered that Mike was my age, just a few years younger – Wait, that doesn't qualify me as a cougar, does it? The thought made me smile.

I discovered that Mike also had never been married, loved traveling and had a deep interest in animal welfare. All his pets were rescues and he was a huge proponent of spaying and neutering, saving the whales and just about every other critter on the planet, it seemed.

Oh boy, can this man be any more perfect?

"I'd love to read your stories, Kris."

Bingo! That did it. I'd have stripped naked right there, done a belly dance for him and then sold all my possessions and followed him to the ends of the earth. But common sense prevailed.

"Goodness, Mike," I said, suddenly aware that I was holding him up from his appointed rounds

"I didn't mean to delay my neighbors' mail delivery. Maybe one of them is waiting for an urgent letter too. Tell you what, how about coming by on Sunday and you can read my stories; if you promise not to reject them, that is." I laughed.

"I'll be here at the same time on Sunday then Kris, and we can read your stories together. I'll bet it won't be long before I'll be delivering you that acceptance letter," Mike said reassuringly, squeezing my hand and smiling that warm smile that made me forget all about that damn letter.

There may not be mail delivery on Sunday, I mused, but there was Mike, and with luck he would be delivering some much needed smiles and excitement.

I forced myself to walk s-l-o-w-l-y back to the house, when what I really wanted to do was to run full speed ahead, or fly if only that were possible. I couldn't wait to tell Gloria my exciting news.

I ran in the front door waving the mail over my head. Pal, my faithful part Scotty, part Chow rescue, ran to greet me at the door as usual, as if I'd been gone for 10 days instead of 10 minutes. My two cats, Boo Boo and Trigger yawned simultaneously, and promptly fell back to sleep in their little cat beds. Well that's how I would recount the episode in any story I'd write but truthfully they were snoozing on the island counter; forbidden territory, thus enormously appealing to the little darlings.

"Gloria, you'll never believe it. I can't thank you enough for your advice."

Gloria ran to me, nearly being tripped by Pal who was doing his little excited dance, jumping up and down, so happy to see me again after all this time! Gloria squeezed me so hard I thought I'd expel every last bit of breath from my diaphragm.

"Oh Kris, let me see the letter. I can't believe you finally got the acceptance letter. This is so exciting. I can't begin to tell you how happy I am for you."

"Whatever are you talking about, G? I didn't get any acceptance letter!" Gloria's face slowly broke into a knowing grin. She pulled my hand and dragged me over to the kitchen table sitting us both down.

"Now spill your guts Kris. Is the mailman going to deliver, wink, wink, nudge, nudge?" Gloria laughed convulsively.

"Well I hope so, G, but let's not put the cart before the horse. Mike's coming over on Sunday and he's going to read my stories. I know it's a bit early in the day but I think this calls for wine instead of more coffee."

"Well it's the cocktail hour somewhere in the world so break out the bottle girl. This is an auspicious occasion, the day when you came out of your shell and looked at the mailman instead of the mail."

I opened a nice bottle of clos du bois and poured us each a glass. I had the feeling that the chardonnay wouldn't be far behind; and perhaps a nice Australian Shiraz. Oh lordy I was going to have a hangover tomorrow but I'd have two days to recuperate before Sunday.

"Okay, you'll never believe this G, but he's kind, thoughtful, considerate, compassionate ..."

"Always prepared? A real Boy Scout, huh," Gloria giggled as she downed her second glass of wine.

"Well, so far, so good, my friend. We only talked for ten minutes but we babbled to each other like two school kids. I found out so much about him. And I can't wait to find out more on Sunday. "

"Yeah, like is he good in bed?" Gloria laughed as some of the wine dribbled down onto her chin as she was jabbering and laughing.

"Well, you'll be the first to know ... oh wait, you'll be the second to know," I laughed as the effects of the wine were growing stronger.

"I may be getting a little tipsy Kris, but I think you mean that I'll be the *third* person to know. Mike *will* be a part of this, right? And let's hope an outstanding part of it too if you know what I mean."

"I can't wait to tell you," I laughed as I refilled our glasses. "I wonder what our mothers would think of our behavior today. I mean not just us but all the females of our generation; sex before marriage and all that."

"Don't kid yourself, Kris," Gloria said as she took a healthy swig of her wine. "They were doing the same thing back in the day. The only difference is that they didn't talk about it. Kind of makes you wonder how many babies were conceived in the back seats of cars, right?"

I giggled at the thought of our own mothers having premarital sex and perhaps even doing it in a car. That thought, in combination with the two, or was it three, glasses of wine had me in stitches.

We spent the whole day and into the early evening talking, laughing and of course drinking. Not to mention eating pizza since neither of us was in any shape to cook. Luckily I had all the fixings for chocolate mug cake and I also had chocolate fudge ice cream. We were only 5 minutes away from falling into chocolate heaven and we were having a real, honest to goodness girlfest; something that men just don't understand.

∽❈∼

Sunday finally arrived. I'd had a choice; greet Mike at the mailbox on Saturday hung over looking like the Wreck of the Hesperus of Longfellow's poem; I sure felt like it and knew I also looked like it. Or I could leave him a note telling him that I was under the weather but would definitely see him tomorrow.

There was a gentle rap on the door at precisely 1 p.m. I'd watched Mike walk up to the door through the kitchen window. I took several deep breaths and walked over to the door and answered it in my usual fashion; one foot on the floor and the other gently pushing Pal to the side.

"Well, hello there," Mike said as he bent down and petted Pal's head and ruffled his hair. "Nice dog; but then he would be, he's got a nice owner."

I hoped I wasn't blushing as I thanked Mike for the compliment.

Resuming an upright position with the little traitor Pal fawning all over him, Mike said, "Well you don't look sick to me. In fact you look downright beautiful."

Thank goodness for lots of sleep and good makeup. Not to mention many glasses of water.

"Thank you, Mike. Come on in. I'm feeling much better today. I just had a 24 hour bug, I guess."

"Really? I thought perhaps you didn't want to see me. I hate to say this but I'm almost glad you were sick and not just avoiding me." He smiled and winked at me. Like most women I find a wink super sexy.

"Umm, hung over."

"Excuse me?" Mike said with a questioning look on his face.

I put my hand on his arm and led him into the living room. "Let's sit in here and talk okay? Yes, I said hung over, as in Gloria and I had way too much wine on Friday and chocolate cake and chocolate fudge ice cream and I don't even want to think about wine or food right now! Whew! And that's the ugly truth. I'm not much of a drinker, usually just a glass of wine with dinner and that's it. I twisted the truth because I didn't want you to think I was a lush."

Mike sat down on the couch and patted the seat next to him inviting me to sit down. I sat next to him hoping he'd throw his arms around me and kiss me passionately like a scene out of a "B" chick flick. But he didn't.

Smiling at me, Mike said "I'm not one to judge anyone Kris. I've twisted the truth a time or two myself; actually this is one of those times; I've done it more than a time or two," he laughed.

"And I've sure had my fair share of benders. Now I just have a glass of wine as you do – well as you usually do." He laughed again.

"But mainly I'm a beer man and not a beer snob either. If it's beer, I'll pretty much drink it ... but not light beer."

"Well, see, that's one thing we didn't discover about each other so I'm afraid I don't have any beer, just wine. I'm sorry."

"You mean you actually have some wine left?" Mike teased.

"But I don't want to assault your nostrils with such a wicked reminder. I'll just have an iced tea if you have any."

"Methinks you're too good to be true, Mike. And thank you. Iced tea will be just fine. I'll go and get it. In the meantime I've put a folder of all my stories on the coffee table if you'd like to take a look. Be right back."

I took my time getting the iced tea and slicing a lemon and putting the pitcher and glasses on a tray, to give Mike a little time to read at least one short story.

As I came back into the living room, I found Mike quite engrossed in the first of my stories. "I'm no writer or editor Kris, but just from perusing the first story here, I'd say you have a lot of talent. I'm enjoying what I'm reading."

We sat for hours reading my stories much to my initial embarrassment. But Mike's encouraging words made me feel much better. He helped reignite hope in me that someone might actually buy my stories one day. He even made some very astute observations and offered some good constructive criticism.

We put the stories away and turned our attention to each other, talking and questioning and discovering what we liked and didn't like. There was so much to learn about each other.

We already knew that Pal adored Mike. He sat on the sofa next to him, head and front paws draped over Mike's lap. It was a scene of domestic bliss right out of a Norman Rockwell painting; Mike relaxing on the sofa, a glass of iced tea in one hand and his other hand stroking Pal's head while Boo Boo, the friendlier, or perhaps more aptly, the more obnoxious of my two cats, lying on the back of the sofa with one paw draped down just touching Mike's shoulder. Trigger popped into the room for a brief moment just to see what was going on and then headed back into the kitchen to indulge in his favorite pastime – eating.

Finally as dusk settled in I got up and lit some candles and then settled back down on the sofa, my heart thumping in my chest, enjoying every minute of this glorious night and not wanting it to ever end.

"Some music would be nice to complement the candles Kris. You like smooth jazz?"

"Another thing we have in common Mike, smooth jazz. I especially like Chuck Mangione, and Candy Dulfer. You?"

"I like them too. Absolutely. I also like the Rippingtons and ... well don't laugh but I also like Kenny G. Oh, and Spyro Gyra and Dave Koz and Chick Corea and a whole lot more. I'm a big smooth jazz fan. Music's always been a big part of my life. I play a pretty mean sax; used to have my own band called Tantrum and damn we were good!"

"Well, since I let you read my stories, you'll have to let me hear you play the sax. Alto or tenor?"

"Both ... but I prefer the tenor ... and you?"

"Oh hell I don't know one from the other, Mike. I was just trying to appear knowledgeable and impress you,' I laughed.

"Just you being you is impressive, Kris."

Mike got up from the couch much to the chagrin of Pal, and tuned the radio in to our local college station that played a lot of smooth jazz. He walked over to the couch and extended his arms toward me. "Kris, I'd like to dance with you. I'm not much of a dancer but it's a good excuse to hold you in my arms; something I've wanted to do since I first began delivering your mail."

We didn't dance so much as we did sway back and forth in one place until I thought we'd wear a hole in the rug. Mike was holding me, nuzzling his face into my neck and planting gentle kisses on me. I had my arms wrapped around his neck enjoying the warmth and firmness of his body pressing against mine. He looked down at me, his dark eyes blazing into mine and then he kissed me, a kiss of deep intensity; the kind of kiss one only reads about.

His desire for me was becoming more evident with each rhythmic movement of our bodies. His hands roamed over my body, squeezing me and caressing me, holding onto my buttocks, swaying me from one side to the other and breathing heavily into my ear. His kisses were soft at first and then hard as he pressed against my lips, parting them with his tongue. He only stopped long enough to tell me that he wanted me. The music in my head was playing along with the music on the radio.

"Kris, I don't want you to think I'm just here for a quick roll in the hay. It's not like that. I'd like this relationship to move on, to be something real, not just sexual. I'm willing to take this slow if that's what you want. Reading your romance stories has given me a lot of insight into what type of hero you're looking for. I'd like to be that kind of hero, Kris."

"Mike, I feel the same way. I'd like this relationship to evolve into something. I'd like to write a story, a true story, with a happily ever after ending or an HEA, as we call it in the romance biz."

"I think you're too good to be true too, Kris. I've gotta tell you though I really want you and it won't be easy to wait." Mike then said with a devilish look on his face and a broad grin that resembled the Cheshire cat's.

"But as the saying goes, all good things come to those who wait."

His double entendre was definitely not wasted on me. I took Mike's hands and led him to my bedroom as I said to him, "I want you just as much. I think you could really be my hero. In fact, I think you already are. Life is short, Mike. And ..." I smiled slyly, "I have to have something to tell Gloria tomorrow."

Mike stopped at the bedroom door and kissed me again. "I hope you have really good things to report to her tomorrow Kris, and not only about tonight, but maybe you'll be able to report that you finally got that acceptance letter. Let's see what the mailman delivers tomorrow."

"Mmm, that would be great. But you know what Mike," I said as I gazed up at his handsome face, "I'm much more interested in what the mailman delivers tonight."

⚬❀⚬

5 Minute Chocolate Mug Cake

. . . .

Ingredients

4 tablespoons flour

4 tablespoons sugar

2 tablespoons cocoa

1 egg

3 tablespoons milk

3 tablespoons oil

3 tablespoons chocolate chips (optional)

Small splash of vanilla extract

1 large coffee mug

Directions

Add dry ingredients to mug, and mix well. Add the egg and mix thoroughly. Pour in the milk and oil and mix well. Add the chocolate chips (if using) and vanilla extract, and mix again.

Put mug in the microwave and cook for 3 minutes at 1000 watts. The cake will rise over the top of the mug, but don't be alarmed. Allow to cool a little, and tip out onto a plate if desired. Can serve two if you want to share! (www.tndaisy1960.vox.com

"Autumn in New York, the gleaming rooftops at sundown, Oh Autumn in New York, It lifts you up when you run down ... Autumn in New York why does it seem so inviting, Autumn in New York, it spells the thrill of first-nighting"

"The Big Apple"

. . . .

"Hi Kat," my dear friend Julie bubbles excitedly over the phone, uttering her pet name for me. Julie renames everyone so I've been Kat, not Kathryn, ever since we met when we were young girls.

"I'm having a big birthday bash for Jake's 35th birthday next Saturday night and since you're his favorite girl, next to me of course, you simply must be here and I'm not taking no for an answer!"

"But Julie," I protest, "I know what you're up to. You're trying to set me up on another blind date and I've told you time and time again I'm just not ready to date right now."

It's been 18 months since I discovered the infidelity of my fiance', Kyle, the love of my life; the man I was going to marry, the man who was also sleeping with one of my co-workers. I don't know who I found more reprehensible; Kyle, for cheating on me or *her,* for knowingly dating an engaged man.

I had given him my heart completely and forever and he had returned it, broken into a thousand little pieces.

"But JW is special! JW's my name for him," Julie laughs.

"JW stands for Just Wonderful and he really is wonderful, Kat," Julie says earnestly.

"You two would be perfect together. You're tall, with a body that commands attention from everyone, and you have those gorgeous green eyes. He's tall, dark and yes, handsome; and by the way he adores redheads too," Julie says as persuasively as she can.

"Yes and JW will probably turn out to be Just Weird, not Just Wonderful, knowing my luck."

"Look Kat," Julie continues, "it's Jake's birthday. You just have to be here for it. You know you're going to give in eventually so let's just settle it now. You're coming and that's it. And besides, you know you love New York in September. It's Goldilocks weather – not too hot, not too cold, but just right."

"Ok Julie," I answer weakly.

"You know I wouldn't miss Jake's big day for all the money in the world, even though he's the one who introduced me to Kyle. But I know his heart was in the right place. I'll take the train to the city and see you next Saturday."

"Wonderful!" exclaims Julie. "We'll pick you up at Penn Station. Let me know what time you'll be arriving."

"No, Julie, I'll take a taxi to your apartment. If I'm going to have an adventure, I might as well go for the whole enchilada," I laugh.

"It's been awhile since I've done anything on my own. See you on Saturday, and Julie ... thanks for thinking of me. I love you."

❦

The train ride from Philly to New York City gives me plenty of time to reflect on my life and to ponder the future. Right now the present is pretty darn good – with or without Kyle. I just hope Julie's latest pick for me isn't another Mr. Wrong.

I also hope he's Mr. Right in bed. I don't know what's wrong with the men I've been dating lately. Not that there's been that many, just a few but it seems the concept of pleasing a woman is a totally foreign concept to them. "Female orgasms? Really, there's such a thing? Surely you jest." Well maybe they aren't quite that dunder-headed but still, they don't seem to realize that women can enjoy sex too, but besides being physical, it's also mental. We actually do like romance and to be finessed and if it takes a little longer than men to achieve that nirvana, then they should just put on their big boy boxers and deal with it.

The thrill of visiting New York City again, coupled with the excitement I always feel when riding a train has put me in an expansive mood. These past eighteen months have found me viewing the proverbial glass as half empty. Now, I'm going to view it as half full, I decide. I'll put a positive spin on my life, I tell myself. Romance may not be waiting around the corner for me but then again, this is the Big Apple. Why not be daring and take a really big bite out of it?

The steady rain beating on the street as I emerge from the railway station surprisingly does not dampen my spirits. Just another part of the adventure I tell myself as I start trying to hail a taxi.

Taxi after taxi whizzes by me, and my hair and my spirits are beginning to sag. I'll look a sight when I arrive at Julie's and Jake's place, I lament.

Another taxi drives by, slows to a stop, and backs up a bit, the cabbie beckoning me inside.

How dare some people say New Yorkers are rude? They're pretty damn wonderful

I hurriedly dash inside the taxi, shaking my umbrella profusely out the door. I'm in such a rush to get out of the rain; I haven't noticed there's already a passenger in the back seat beside me.

"Oh, excuse me," I stammer, embarrassed that perhaps I've mistaken the taxi driver's gesture to get into the vehicle. Maybe New Yorkers really are rude and he was shaking his hand at me for some imagined offense on my part. But I found that hard to believe.

"No, it's okay," the passenger offers. "I asked the driver to back up for you. You looked positively forlorn, and besides I've never been able to resist the proverbial damsel in distress. I hope that doesn't sound too chauvinistic. It's hard to keep up with the social dos and don'ts. Women are strong and self-reliant today, but I'm an old-fashioned kind of guy. I like to help people – especially beautiful young women."

I couldn't stop myself from smiling; a handsome, charming man with manners – in New York City. How great is that!

"Thank you, kind sir or should I call you Sir Walter Raleigh?"

"My turn to thank *you* for the compliment," he smiled appreciatively. "I'm on my way to my friends' place but I've got time and I don't mind sharing the ride."

"Well, this is really nice of you," I reply. "I'm not going all that far actually, just about fifteen blocks from here. I would have walked if the weather were nicer. I know these are city blocks and might seem like a long walk to some people but I do like walking and to tell you the truth, I'm not in any rush to get to where I have to go. I hope this doesn't inconvenience you too much."

"No, not at all, ah ..."

"Kathryn," I offer as I extend my hand. "Kathryn McHendry."

"I'm Jerry Weston and it is indeed a pleasure to meet you," Jerry said as he wrapped his warm hand around my fingers. "So what brings you to the city, or do you live here?"

I'm not the kind of person to open up to strangers but something in this stranger's gentle but firm handshake, his soft, soothing voice and old world charm put me oddly at ease. I find myself actually attracted to his physical looks, although he's a blonde and it's the dark-haired ones that always do it for me.

"I live in Philly, Jerry; in Bala Cynwyd, to be precise."

"So ... you live on the Main Line. Very nice. I'll bet you have a big Sycamore tree in front of your house too," Jerry smiled broadly.

"Why yes, as a matter of fact, I do. I see you're familiar with Bala Cynwyd and our Sycamore tree-lined streets.

"Very. I used to be a columnist with the Philadelphia Inquirer so I'm quite familiar with Philly."

My stomach lurched when Jerry mentioned he was a journalist. *Kyle ...*

"But I wasn't there too long before I was offered my current job here with the New York Times. There's something about New

York City that is unparalleled by any other city; the food, the theater district, the excitement, New Yorkers," he laughed.

"Other cities may have museums and great food and so on and so forth but they don't have New Yorkers."

"Well you're right about that Jerry. I love the excitement and energy of this city. It's a great place filled with great people. I wouldn't mind living here myself one day."

"And you're on your way to visit some of these great people. Any special reason? Forgive me if I'm being intrusive; it's a job hazard," Jerry said as he gave me a friendly smile.

"I'm here to attend a good friend's birthday party. That's the story, anyway. In actuality the birthday boy's wife is just using this as an excuse to set me up on yet another blind date. She never gives up trying to find Mr. Right for me."

"She just keeps finding you Mr. Right Now, right?"

"Exactly! You've got her number too and you haven't even met her" I laughed.

Jerry laughed easily, his beautiful gray-blue eyes piercing mine as we spoke.

"A blind date?" Jerry asked. "Hmm, you won't believe this. I always swore I'd never do that myself but ..."

Finding myself unusually talkative, I cut Jerry off in mid-sentence explaining this is not something I normally do either. If he knew my friend, I tell him, and her powers of persuasion, he'd understand.

"I've been on more than I want to admit, thanks to my girlfriend. You'd think she'd know what kind of man I'd be interested in if I *were* looking. But I'm not. I actually enjoy being single and being able to come and go as I please without having to answer to anyone; well anyone other than my black lab and big orange cat – Bandit and Toby. And believe me I do answer to them too. They're quite bossy. Then there's my nursing supervisor of course, Nurse Ratchett, as we affectionately call her," I laughed.

"Well if you don't want to go out on the blind dates, why do you do it? You don't seem to me to be the kind of woman who would let someone boss you – except for Bandit and Toby of course. And I understand about that – I've got one big 20 pound boss myself. Pumpkin. And no, he's not a little dog. He's a cat; a big orange and white fur ball. I think half his weight is fur."

"So you're a gentleman and you also love animals. Be careful, if my friend discovers you, she'll be trying to fix us up. But maybe not, she hasn't picked any good ones for me yet,' I laughed.

"Yes I like all animals. At one time I entertained thoughts of becoming a veterinarian but ..."

"But what? That's a noble profession."

"Well I was just a kid. I wanted to be everything; veterinarian, physician, astronaut, president. Don't laugh, when you're 10 the sky's the limit in your imagination. But I've always loved animals. We had a whole house full of them when I was growing up. Everyone seemed to know if you had an animal that you didn't want, just take it to the Weston Farm. Even as a young boy it made me angry that people treated animals as things and just discarded them like last week's news."

"Amen to that Jerry. People can be so cruel. I'm sure glad I'm not one," I laughed.

"I am too Kathryn," Jerry smiled; those eyes were drawing me in. I could get lost in them, until I heard him say, "I would have had more animals but my wife claimed she was allergic to them. Of course she didn't tell me that until after we were married. She kept up a good pretense of liking them beforehand, but by then it was too late. It wasn't long though before ..."

My heart sank. It didn't occur to me until he mentioned that he was married, that I was developing a strong attraction to him. Doesn't that just figure? I found myself thinking. I was already beginning to envision what it would be like to kiss those lips, to have him sit closer to me and place his arms around me and stroke my hair and kiss me with abandon.

Stop fantasizing about another woman's husband Kathryn. It's okay if it's Brad Pitt or somebody like that; someone unobtainable. As if this hunk is obtainable. Ha!

"I'm sorry about that Jerry," I cut him off. I didn't want to hear any more about his wife. I was being rude and I knew it but that's one four letter word I didn't want to hear mentioned again. And one thing I was not was a husband stealer.

"We just have to deal with the cards that life has dealt us and make the most of them. Excuse me," I said as my cell rang. "It's Julie and I have to take it. She's probably telling my blind date how wonderful I am and is wondering where I am. I'll just be a second."

Jerry grinned at me as I placed the cell back in my purse, a bemused expression on his handsome face. "Sorry, but obviously I couldn't help overhearing your conversation – at least your side of it. So what are you expecting from this blind date Kathryn?"

Kathryn. He says my name as if he's reciting poetry. I wonder if he says his wife's name in the same way.

"Would you like to meet a rich man about town or would you settle for a down to earth, average Joe with a good heart and a good sense of humor?" Jerry asks curiously.

"As a writer, I'm always looking at life from different angles. I hope you don't mind the inquisition," he laughs.

"Not at all," I replied, "but in response to your question, the answer is no; No, I will never 'settle' for anything or anyone. I may choose but I am definitely not the settling kind. And I would choose someone with good manners; someone who is kind and who loves animals of course, and someone who would be faithful to me" I said as I got lost in those beautiful gray-blue eyes again.

"He doesn't have to be wealthy, but he should at least have a job. Oh, and someone whose presence charges the air. That would be exciting.

"And positively someone who isn't married," I said, a look of disdain crossing my face.

Jerry didn't notice and grinned and patted my knee sending an electrical charge all through me; while I struggled with my conflicted feelings.

Oh yeah, that's what I'm talking about, just like that, but it's wrong with a capital W.

I moved away from him as unobtrusively as possible, not wanting to appear rude yet not wanting to give off the wrong vibe about myself. It was just a short taxi ride shared with a handsome stranger whom I'd never see again. No harm, no foul.

"I hope you find someone like that, Kathryn. I do believe there are a lot of good men out there and you – no, Julie just needs to meet one and introduce him to you. I have a feeling she will."

Jerry laughed while I sat there deep in thought about the perfect man and this ineligible one sitting next to me.

"Oh and I forgot – roses would be nice; yellow ones. Yes, I read a lot of romance novels, a whole lot of them. I read them to some of my patients too. They love it. It's our guilty pleasure."

"Well, I don't read romance novels – Tom Clancy and Dale Brown are more my type – but I do believe in old-fashioned romance. I may not be a knight in shining armor but I'd like to be able to sweep a lady off her feet, especially one as beautiful as you with such wonderful romantic fantasies."

Jerry sidled closer to me, leaning into me to – kiss me. He was actually going to try to kiss me!

I looked at him in shear astonishment. Another married man or engaged man who thinks nothing of cheating on his wife or fiancée. We'd arrived at Julie's apartment building and I instructed the cabbie to pull over.

"This is where I get out," I said, my voice laced with annoyance and dismay. As I fished in my purse for my share of the taxi ride, Jerry told me that it was his treat.

"Kathryn, please don't leave without giving me your number," he entreated.

Right, and maybe you could show it to your wife

I handed Jerry what I knew to be more than my fair share of the taxi ride. "Here, take this. And Jerry, I won't give you my number because - I've already got yours!"

I admired myself for my restraint in merely closing the door when I wanted to slam it full force on his hand – or both hands and feet. A whole body slam would be even better with other certain parts receiving an extra slam. It's the least the unfaithful womanizer deserved.

Jerry's wrong. There aren't any decent men anymore. They're all a bunch of callous Lotharios or greedy little piglets who only care about getting their own jollies.

I hurried away from the taxi in a rush, not looking back, trying to run into the building before I looked like the proverbial drowned rat; it didn't work. I was wet through to the bone. My thoughts were a jumbled mess. My mood was not one that would lend itself to pleasant conversation or encourage any man to seek my company again. No, this birthday party was a disaster in the making.

❦

"Kat! You're here!" Julie threw her arms around me and squeezed me silly.

"Come in, come in. Jake," she yelled," your girlfriend is here! And she looks – well actually she looks bloody awful. She's soaked. Hey Kat, I'll be right back. I have a call to make. When Jake's finished molesting you, you can go into my bedroom and dry off and do something with your hair. I think I've found Mr. Really Right this time."

Jake wended his way through all the birthday guests, a glass of champagne in one hand, and a big fat cigar in the other; unlit of course. Julie didn't allow smoking inside. Jake and the cigar would be relegated to the balcony; birthday or not.

"Come here gorgeous. Give your favorite guy a kiss and don't mind my beautiful wife ... or my tongue. Julie knows you're second in line to ascend the throne of the House of Jake. My tongue on the other hand ..."

"Your tongue on the other hand is what always gets you in trouble Jake. Tie a string around it, why don't you! As a matter of fact, tie it to your penis; that way you can keep them both out of trouble. Now Happy Birthday, big guy. You're one of the few really good and decent men in the world. Julie's very lucky. I envy her, I really do but if you ever do try to tongue me I'll tell on you. So just keep that in mind buddy."

"Okay, okay. I just thought since it's my birthday ...Yeah, yeah, I know – I'm all hat and no cattle."

"I'm well aware of that. It's one of the reasons I love you. Your devotion to Julie is an inspiration. If only I could find someone like you – don't get carried away Jake, I said someone *like* you, not you!"

"You really know how to break 'em Kat," Jake laughed. "Any guy who is lucky enough to get you had better be on his toes."

Handing Jake an expensive box of cigars, I said "Well since it's your birthday, here's a little something for you. Don't smoke 'em all at once and whatever you do, don't smoke them in here – not if you want to remain married that is."

"Indeed I do. So I'll save these for later. Thank you Kathryn. But if Julie leaves me, will you marry me? You know I love you, my second favorite person in the world," Jake laughed as he hugged me.

"And I love you and Julie. You're my two best friends."

"And Julie and I are lucky to have you here; especially my match-making wife. She never gives up when really all she needs to do is clone me!"

"Ha! I wish she could! Julie is one lucky woman. And you're faithful too. You *are* faithful aren't you, Jake? No, don't answer that. I don't want to be disabused of the notion that there are still faithful men in this world."

"Ahhh Kathryn, always the cynic. One bad apple doesn't spoil all the rest you know. Not all men are Winesap apples. Kyle was a mistake on my part. I thought he was principled. I like to think most of us are Golden Delicious. And yes – I'm true blue. Julie is the best thing that ever happened to me and she's hell bent on finding you someone just as wonderful as me, as if that's possible, right?"

"Well you *are* blonde so I suppose you *could* be a Golden Delicious. And tonight she's going to be parading another of her finds in front of me. She's on a mission – from Satan I think."

"I know. She never tires of it. She keeps thinking that one day you might actually like one of her choices for you. And I keep telling her unless she finds another Jake you're not going to be happy with her choice." Jake laughed.

"Well you would be hard to top Jake. You're handsome, not to mention oh so modest!"

"Oh, here she comes now," Jake said. "Let's put on our best No-I-wasn't-talking-about-you-face." We both laughed, watching Julie walking toward us, amazingly with no man in tow.

"He's on his way Kat. Mr. Right, that is. He had a last minute errand to do but said he'll be right here. You're gonna love him. Honest. This time I got it right. I can't wait for you two to meet. He's honest and actually he's a grown up version of a Boy Scout, but oh such a sexy Boy Scout. Your panties are going to drop right to the floor when you meet him."

"Well that should make for some interesting entertainment for Jake's birthday party, that's for sure; notwithstanding what a great first impression it would make. Now you've really got me interested. So where is he?"

"Any minute Kat. While we're waiting why don't you get out of your wet clothes and do something with your hair and then we can have some of my delicious Chocolate Pate' with Cranberry Coulis. It's to die for. I don't know what's better – JW or this dessert."

Julie was right. I changed into a slinky little dress and ran her blow dryer over my hair and then joined her at the buffet table she'd set up. The Chocolate Pate' dessert was brilliant. JW will have a hard time competing with this for my attention, I thought. Julie, Jake and I drank some champagne, nervously waiting for Mr. Right or Mr. Wrong, whichever he turned out to be. I had a feeling I knew which way this was going to go but what the hell, life is an adventure; anything can happen.

Anything - but - that! That cannot be Jerry. I won't let it be Jerry. What is she thinking? This is the Boy Scout who's so damn wonderful? The man I'm supposed to drop my panties for?

Turning around to see Jerry, Julie said, "Kat I want you to meet our friend, JW." She prodded JW toward me.

"His name is Jerry but you know me and my nicknames. And this is my dear friend Kat whom I've told you about, Jerry."

"Kathryn. I prefer Kathryn,' Jerry said as he smiled at me almost apologetically.

"Well, yes her name is actually Kathryn but I call her Kat. How did you know her name?" Julie looked positively apoplectic.

"Oh, I'll tell you how he knows my name Julie. I'll tell you all about it in three part harmony. Your Mr. Right here and I have met. Today. We shared a taxi ride here."

"And a wonderful ride it was too Kathryn until something – well something happened and I don't know what it was. One minute you were smiling and I thought we had something going on. The next thing I know you're angry with me. I'm resisting the temptation to make a sexist remark about women here,' Jerry laughed nervously.

Julie's face took on an even more perplexed look. "I don't understand. First, if you shared a taxi here then why are you just getting here now Jerry? And before you answer that - Kat, why did you get angry with him?"

I took a sip of my champagne resisting the urge to throw the liquid in Jerry's face. "I'm sorry Julie but I have to tell you that JW – Jerry – is married. I'm sorry that this little matchmaking attempt of yours didn't work out but Jerry has a wife." I glared at him as I practically spat the words out but those gray-blue eyes were still working their magic on me.

"Yes he's married."

"I am?" Jerry said as he drew in a sharp breath.

"When I woke up this morning, alone in my bed mind you, I was single. I don't recall any marriage ceremony taking place between waking up and getting into the taxi."

"Look, the music is really loud and with everybody talking and laughing, it's hard to understand anything being said," Julie uttered.

"Can we all go out onto the balcony and sort this out in private? Okay?"

"Why don't the three of you go out there?" Jake said.

"You can fill me in later but I don't think both of us should leave our guests, okay, Julie?" Jake smiled and squeezed Jerry's arm in a reassuring manner as he walked by him.

Men!

The rain had let up earlier and the air was cool compared to the hot, charged atmosphere inside; although the atmosphere on the balcony was threatening to rival that of the inside.

Jerry spoke first. "Kathryn, the only one who holds the answer to this is you. Why do you think I'm married?"

Men!

I looked at him, then at Julie and then back to those gorgeous eyes. "Because you told me so yourself, Jerry. We were talking about animals and you mentioned that your *wife* claimed to be allergic. How could I possibly misunderstand that?" I folded my arms across my chest in a *How- are-you-going-to-get-out-of-this* pose?

Jerry surprised us with his sudden laugh. "Oh man; some com-municator *I* am. I make my living with words and I can't even use them properly."

In an even, deliberate voice, I said "You didn't seem to have any problem using them in the taxi."

Jerry grabbed my hands and held onto them, not letting go. "Ah, the light dawns. As I recall now, Kathryn, you cut me off mid-sentence when I was talking about my *wife*. At the time period that I was talking about, Vivienne *was* my wife. She isn't now and hasn't been for quite some time. I was relating to you what had happened before but you didn't give me a chance to finish what I was telling you. And I never gave it another thought, not even when your mood turned sour against me."

Julie looped her arms through ours, lifting her head up to look each of us in the eye in turn. "So, that's one hell of an introduction, don't you think? It's surely one to tell the grandchildren!" Julie said then placed her hand over her mouth emitting a nervous laugh.

"Jerry, I'm, well I'm; I don't know what I am besides being the most embarrassed woman in the world right now. I'm so sorry. I jumped to conclusions which is bad enough but I didn't give you a chance to talk. I was thinking you were the creep and it turns out it's me. I'm very sorry."

Jerry gave me a tender kiss on the cheek, still not letting go of my hands. "No one is a creep Kathryn, let alone you. It was just a gross misunderstanding. I'll be certain to phrase my words more carefully the next time. There *will* be a next time won't there? And perhaps a lot more *next times?* "

I placed my arms around Jerry's neck and once again looked into those magnetic eyes that kept drawing me in. "I certainly hope so, Jerry. I've never felt so comfortable with anyone in my life. And we met almost without Julie's help."

"Hey what do you mean by that? Okay you met before I could actually introduce you but still you met *because* of me. You gotta give me that much."

We all shared a laugh and then Julie mentioned that Jerry hadn't answered why he'd arrived at her apartment 15 minutes after me.

"Oh, right. How could I forget? Wait right here. I'll be right back." Jerry hurried through the balcony doors.

Julie and I took the opportunity to gush about how handsome Jerry is and how she just knew that we were meant for each other. "But Julie, you lied to me about Jerry."

"How so, Kathryn?"

He is not a brunette. He's blonde! And you know that dark-haired men are the ones who command my attention and give me goosebumps. I don't know why but there's definitely something to the 'tall, dark and handsome' concept."

"Well I didn't lie. I fibbed."

"You lied."

"I confabulated."

"You lied."

"I prevaricated."

"You lied and you're going to run out of synonyms pretty soon."

"Very well; I work in advertising and marketing as you know. I was just plying my trade."

"And you're very good at your trade Julie; if you weren't I wouldn't be here tonight and I wouldn't have met the man who is going to be responsible for my panties dropping," I laughed and Julie laughed with me.

"I knew you wouldn't come Kat, if I told you he was a blonde and a journalist, the same as Kyle. I knew how much he would remind you of him, but honestly that's the only resemblance. Jerry is a wonderful person, not to mention he's really hot."

"I forgive you then. He *is* hot with a capital H," I laughed. Julie joined me in laughing. We were still laughing as Jerry came through the door, holding his right arm behind his back.

He gave me a sweeping bow and, easing a bouquet of beautiful yellow roses from behind his back, said "this is why I was late arriving here. I had to make a quick stop at the florist for these. I stashed them in the kitchen when I saw Julie because I wanted you to be the first to see them."

Grabbing the bouquet, I hugged them to my chest and said "You figured out that Kathryn and Kat were one and the same, did you?"

"Yep, I'm a real Sherlock Holmes, I am; the name didn't quite click at first, but that beautiful mane of red hair had me thinking and then when you had the taxi stop right out in front of Julie's and Jake's apartment after talking to someone named Julie on your cell, I almost blurted out that I was your blind date.. Oh, and gee the 35th birthday party reference might have been a subtle clue too. I may be a bit dense sometimes but I'm not entirely stupid."

"Well, why didn't you say something and get out of the taxi when I did?"

"Because of our conversation – your idea of what Mr. Right would do; the yellow roses. I wanted to get them for you. And then I forgot to give them to you. Sir Walter Raleigh I'm not!"

"Oh; that's so sweet, Jerry."

"Besides you seemed so angry I didn't want to get within ten feet of that umbrella," Jerry laughed.

Julie gave us each a long hug. "My work here is done," she said as she laughed and walked away, looking like the cat who'd just swallowed the cream.

Jerry took the flowers and placed them on the table next to us and then pulled me to him; kissing me with the softest, sweetest lips I'd ever had on mine.

Oh my god he's doin' it. He's making me quiver – ALL over

"Tell me, what were you and Julie laughing so uproariously about when I returned with the flowers?"

"Oh! I'd forgotten about that," I said blushing.

"Girl talk Jerry, just girl talk."

"Hmm, girl talk that makes you blush, huh? Now this is something I want to hear about."

"Or see," I giggled.

"Now you've really got me curious, Kathryn. I can't wait to hear *and* see what you're talking about. Tell me, do you think you might like living in the big city? There're plenty of nursing jobs here. I know that for a fact."

"Oh my, whatever you do, don't let Julie hear you say that. She'd have my bags packed and a train ticket in my hand in ... in a New York minute," Jerry said in unison with me as we both laughed.

"I'm serious Kathryn. I felt an electrical charge in the taxi tonight. I think sometimes we just know when it's right. And let's not forget Julie – she's absolutely certain we're right for each other. We have to prove her right."

"Well, my new philosophy is that life is an adventure and we should grab it with gusto. I'd really like to get to know you better Jerry. I'm not really looking for a knight in shining armor; that's way too much responsibility to place on anyone. But a man who is kind, and a gentleman and loves animals is someone I could be seriously interested in. You know anyone who fits that bill?"

"Oh yeah, I do. But there's no reason 'Knight in Shining Armor' can't be added to that list. I'm applying for the position, Kathryn and I hope I'm the only applicant."

Jerry cupped my face with both hands and stared into my eyes, smiling, and then kissed me with a desire that made me feel sexy, special and wanted. We turned and looked over the balcony, my left arm around Jerry's waist and his left arm crossing over the front of my body at the waist with his right hand softly rubbing up and down my right arm. He kissed me on the cheek lightly and tenderly; a lover's kiss.

We stood there gazing down at the sights of one of the most magical cities in the world; New York City, the Big Apple.

Yes, I could definitely live here. I could be a New Yorker and I'd have my very own Knight in Shining Armor to watch over me. Thank you Julie. You not only found Mr. Right; you found Mr. Right Now and Forever.

ॐ

Chocolate Pate' with Cranberry Coulis

Cranberry Coulis Ingredients -

1 ½ cups Ocean Spray Jellied Cranberry Sauce

¾ cup Ocean Spray Cranberry Juice Cocktail

1 tsp lime juice

Pate' ingredients –

1 ½ cups heavy whipping cream, divided

1 large egg yolk

2 cups (12 oz pkg) Nestle Toll House Semi-Sweet Chocolate Morsels

1/3 cup light corn syrup

¼ cup (1/2 stick) butter or margarine

1 tsp vanilla extract

Whipped cream

Directions for Cranberry Coulis

Place cranberry sauce, cranberry juice cocktail and lime juice in blender; cover. Blend until smooth. Refrigerate. Makes 1 ¾ cups.

Directions for pate'

Line 8 x 4 inch baking pan with plastic wrap. Combine ¼ cup whipping cream and egg yolk in small bowl.

Combine morsels, corn syrup and butter in heavy-duty medium saucepan. Melt over lowest possible heat. When morsels begin to melt, remove from heat; stir. Return to heat for a few seconds at a time, stirring until smooth. Remove from heat. Add cream mixture to saucepan. Cook, stirring constantly, over medium heat for 1 minute. Let cool to room temperature.

Beat remaining cream and vanilla extract in small mixer bowl until soft peaks form. Using a rubber spatula, gently fold chocolate mixture into the whipped cream. Pour into prepared pan. Cover with plastic wrap. Refrigerate overnight or freeze 3 hours.

To serve, spoon Cranberry Coulis on a dessert plate. Place a slice of Chocolate Pate' on plate. Garnish with shipped cream. (www.verybestbaking.com)

The Passionate Shepherd to his Love

Come live with me and be my love,
And we will all the pleasures prove
That valleys, groves, hills, and fields,
Woods or steepy mountain yields.

And we will sit upon the rocks,
Seeing the shepherds feed their flocks,
By shallow rivers to whose falls
Melodious birds sing madrigals.

And I will make thee beds of roses
And a thousand fragrant posies,
A cap of flowers, and a kirtle
Embroidered all with leaves of myrtle;

A gown made of the finest wool
Which from our pretty lambs we pull;

Fair lined slippers for the cold,
With buckles of the purest gold;

A belt of straw and ivy buds,
With coral clasps and amber studs:
And if these pleasures may thee move,
Come live with me and be my love.

The shepherds' swains shall dance and sing
For thy delight each May morning:
If these delights thy mind may move,
Then live with me and be my love.

~Christopher Marlowe (1564 – 1593)

"So baby don't you worry about growing older, those young girls ain't got nothing on you 'cause it takes some livin' to get good at givin' and giving love is just where you could teach them a thing or two"

"I'm Too Young to Be This Old"

Fiona looked at her husband, Tim, sitting in his recliner watching TV; nothing new. He's always watching TV. Never used to be that way, she thought. There was a time when the TV wouldn't even be on or if it was it would be background noise to hers and Tim's lovemaking.

Those were the days, she thought to herself, until slowly their sex life began to dwindle to where it was now – nonexistent. Not that she cared, actually. She had lost all interest in sex and in everything that used to matter to her. She'd just lost interest in life.

Tim had tried to pull her out of it, tried to get her interested in something, anything, but his efforts were to no avail. His suggestions that she visit her doctor fell on deaf ears. She knew what her problem was and why she was the way she was. She didn't like admitting it to herself because it meant facing her most dreaded fear.

She was old! And she felt it. All her talk when she was younger about age being just a number came back to haunt her. Yes, it was just a number but it was a very old number. A number she thought she'd never reach.

On her next birthday she'd be ... 60! She couldn't bear to face it – her, a woman of almost 60. Judging by how quickly the preceding years had gone by she realized in no time she'd be 70. Just shoot me now, she screamed inwardly. Where had the years gone, what had she done with her life?

She never wrote the novel that she told everyone she'd have written by the time she was 50; she never wrote the best-selling song that she always had dancing around in her head but never put to paper, she never learned another language. French! She loved the language and tried to learn it but always found excuses why she didn't have time to concentrate on it. She'd never returned to her ancestral home in Dublin, Ireland – *someday* – and she'd never learned to tap dance or ... oh hell, there were so many things she hadn't done and she could see the sand falling too quickly down through the hourglass.

But what precisely did she do, she asked herself. She graduated from Northwestern University with a degree in journalism and had utilized her knowledge to gain several well-paying jobs through the years. It was at Northwestern where she'd met Tim. Theirs was a true *love at first sight* romance.

Their sex life was good, really good. They weren't super adventurous but the sex that they had was satisfying to both of them. Each knew how to please the other, how to finesse each other's bodies to satisfying completion. And then they'd cuddle. Tim knew how important that was to Fiona. He enjoyed it too because he loved her; he lived for her.

They'd raised two beautiful daughters, Molly and Annie. Both were college graduates with husbands and children. Her grandchildren, Cathleen, Colleen, Ashlynne and Liam were the lights of her life; the only things that brought her any joy, but now even they couldn't bring her out of her – what was it? Was it a legitimate depression? She didn't think so. She was just growing old and it bothered her. How many years do I have left, she wondered; ten, twenty; or maybe only a few hours? Do other women feel this way; do they ponder such things? It was driving her mad.

The phone rang. Maria; her best friend ever since she and her family had emigrated to the United States from Italy when Maria was 10 and Fiona was the same age. She and Maria had become fast friends and had remained so these past forty-nine years.

They made for an interesting couple; Fiona with her auburn hair and green eyes, light freckles dotting her porcelain skin with the typical Irish rosy cheeks. Maria's family hailed from Sicily and Maria had inherited her parents' olive skin, dark black hair, and huge brown eyes. They were both pretty little girls who grew up to be beautiful, striking women.

Maria was tall and slender and had carved out a successful career for herself as a print model. Fiona was short with an hourglass figure and the tiniest waist Maria had ever seen. What made her waist appear even smaller were her breasts. Fiona was a buxom girl which made her the recipient of some childhood taunts from the boys but with those same boys pursuing her relentlessly as she grew older.

Now one of them was happy and content and the other a brooding, sad former shell of herself; a woman whose marriage was also just an empty shell. No amount of self-analysis helped. The only cure for her condition, she told herself was impossible; it didn't exist, to be young again. To be young and full of life and throw herself into life with new enthusiasm. Unfortunately life didn't give you a re-do. Once you'd let your opportunities slip by you, they were gone forever.

"Fiona, before I tell you why I'm calling, please understand that I'm not taking no for an answer; not even a maybe. The only acceptable answer is a resounding yes."

"No!" Fiona said. "Whatever the question, the answer is no. Put on your big girl panties and deal with it, Maria. I love you to pieces but you know, well you know ..."

"Honey, if I wore big girl panties I wouldn't have had the successful modeling career that I've had and still do. So there! Just listen to me. You know that song that you're always talking about writing; the one about being too young and old at the same time, something like that?"

"'I'm too young to be this old'. That's what the song is called, well that's what the song would be about if I could ever get past the title and a few lyrics here and there. Why? What about my so-called song?"

Fiona's eyes traveled from the patio to the living room where Tim was still in his recliner watching TV; only now he was drinking his favorite drink – Mexican Hot Chocolate Shots with Spicy Foam.

Tim isn't old looking, he still looks handsome but all he does is watch that damn TV when he comes home from work. What has happened to us? Damn it. I know that 59 isn't considered old by other people's standards but ..."

"Fiona. Are you there? You're not listening to me. Have you zoned out on me again, sweetie? I know you have so let me say it again and this time listen or I'll come over there and box your ears, as you Irish people say. Or as we Italians might say – lo box le tue orecchie."

"Get on with it, Maria but I'm going to tune you out again. Don't forget, we old people don't hear very well and our minds wander. But take your best shot before I have to take my nap."

"I do believe you just showed a bit of humor there, Fiona. That's great because you'll need it. I just found out that the annual county Dolly Parton look-alike and singing/songwriting contest is being held in six weeks. Right here, in Georgia, in 'Hotlanta'."

"So? You're not suggesting that I ..."

"No, no, of course not Fiona. Don't be silly."

Fiona let out a big sigh. "Well, I'm glad to hear that Maria. You had me scared there for a minute."

"Well get re-scared Fiona. I said I'm not *suggesting* it. I'm flat out *telling* you – we're going to do it. I've already registered us. We're going to work on your song together. You'll write the lyrics and I'll put the song to music in whatever key you want and the beat and so forth. We can do it Fiona. It'll be a gas, a real hoot. Even if we don't win, we'll have fun and that is something you've been sorely lacking for quite awhile. I just know the song will lift you up and make you feel alive again."

"I'm not making any promises Maria, but come over tomorrow and we'll discuss it. Discuss it, that's all I'm open to right now."

"Ciao," Maria said.

"Ciao," Fiona repeated. She hung up the phone and walked into the living room to discover that Tim had gone upstairs to bed without even saying goodnight. What have I done to him, she wondered. He deserves so much more than I've been giving him.

Perhaps I should put some words to paper, anything to get Maria off my back.

Fiona walked into her home office and sat at her computer. She turned it on, read some email and then finally forced herself to start typing; even if the words were nonsense, she'd at least try. Maria and Tim would have to give her credit for that at least.

❧

"Fiona? Fee? What's going on?" Tim said very concerned and relieved when she stirred.

"You haven't been to bed all night, have you?" Tim had walked into her office and found her sitting at her desk with her head resting on her arms.

"Oh gee, Tim, I'm sorry I didn't mean to worry you." Fiona began to explain Maria's proposal and that she'd been up all night writing the song.

Tim was gobsmacked. He actually saw a spark in Fiona's eyes. He couldn't quite put his finger on it but it was something he hadn't seen in a long time. He was hesitant to hope, but hope is something that doesn't die easily.

"When do I get to hear the song, Fee?" Tim asked cautiously. He didn't want to push her over the edge but he didn't want to pass up a chance to perhaps see the former Fee again; he hesitated to say, even if only in his mind, the 'old' Fee.

"Soon, Tim; Maria will be here in … good grief she'll be here in about fifteen minutes" Fiona gasped, looking at the clock. "I've gotta go brush my teeth and make some coffee."

"You brush your teeth and I'll put the coffee on. Would a good morning kiss be too much to ask for?"

Fiona stood up and hugged her husband, and gave him a soft kiss on the lips before rushing upstairs to the bathroom. She wasn't ready for anything else right now but still, some old feelings were beginning to stir. There also wasn't time for anything other than that wee kiss. The drill sergeant was on her way!

Well, that's a start, Tim thought to himself. Baby steps, little baby steps Fiona.

Fiona came down the stairs in time to see Tim opening the door to admit Maria into their home.

"Hey, Maria, come on in," Tim said.

Then whispering quickly to Maria, he said "I think she'll be cooperative. Don't ask. You'll see."

"Maria, come into my office. Have I got something to show you! Get your piano fingers warmed up girl. I think we have a hit in the making. I know you can't tell by how gorgeous I look, so refreshed and all."

"Yeah, I can tell. You're a real knockout, sei un vero knockout as we'd say in Italian. What'd you do stay up drinking all night?"

"Spoken like a true friend, my fine Italian meatball. No, I was up all night writing the song that finally made it out of my head and onto the computer. I'll sing it for you and you can do whatever it is that you do to put it to music."

"Let's go. Start singing it to me and then we'll put it all together." Fiona printed 2 copies of her song for them and they rehearsed without any piano accompaniment. Maria would take care of everything at home at her piano.

"I can't wait to see you in your Dolly wig and all that makeup. You're going to look great and even if we don't win, we'll still have fun, won't we? Fiona, it's so nice to see you being more upbeat again," Maria said as she gave her friend a big hug.

Fiona smiled at Maria and kissed her on the cheek. "Maria, writing that song last night and then hearing us singing it made me realize what an idiot I've been. I'm not old at all. Yes, I'm not young, but I'm not old either and I do still have plenty of living to do. Tim even kissed me this morning and it made me feel, well it made me yearn for the old Fiona; and the old Tim. It was like a light bulb going off over my head. I want *me* back."

⚜

The night of the contest arrived. Tim was dressed and waiting for Fiona to come down the stairs. What he saw took his breath away; if he didn't know better he'd swear he was looking at the real thing; there stood Dolly Parton before his very eyes, big blonde wig, luscious red lips and an outfit that couldn't be made of more than one yard of skin tight material, not to mention three inch stilettos.

They arrived at the venue where Maria was already waiting for them bubbling over with excitement. "Fiona, you're positively gorgeous. You *are* Dolly. And guess what, we're the last act. Can you believe that? We'll be the last thing on the judges' minds."

Two hours later, the emcee announced the last act of the evening. "Ladies and gentlemen, our last Dolly contender is Fiona Smith singing not one of Dolly's own songs but a song she wrote specifically for Dolly. Accompanying Dolly on the piano is Maria Martelli. Here they are singing an original song – "I'm Too Young to be This Old.'

The crowd applauded enthusiastically when Fiona walked onstage. She definitely had her game on and she looked like Dolly's twin, more so than any of the others. Maria sat at the piano and began playing the introduction. Fiona began to sing and danced around in her best Dolly imitation. Her voice was in fine form and she was workin' it for all it was worth.

I'm Too Young To Be This Old

"Skinny jeans and belly shirts
They tell me I shouldn't wear
'cause once you pass a certain age
some parts you shouldn't bare
But I look good for my age
So I'm often told
So why do I feel this rage?
Because I'm too young to be this old.

Too young to be this old
Too old to feel this young
And if the truth be told
I'm still havin' lots of fun
'cause women of a certain age
have many talents untold
So come on sisters sing with me
We're too young to be this old

Too young to buy new shoes

For fit instead of style

Too young to sit at home

Instead of goin' out and goin' wild

Too young to be ignored

And put into a mold

Too young to be cast aside

I'm too young to be this old

I wanna wear my clothes too tight

And skirts slit up to there

Just like I did years ago

And nobody seemed to care

But now you look at me

Like silver instead of gold

Where oh where did my life go?

I'm too young to be this old

Too young to be this old

Too old to feel this young

And if the truth be told

I'm still havin' lots of fun

'cause women of a certain age

have many talents untold

So come on sisters sing with me

We're too young to be this old

I still think and feel the same

My desires have not gone cold

A good lookin' man still turns my head

Because I'm too young to be this old

Too young to be this old

Too old to feel this young

I need more time to live my life

My song has not been sung

So come on sisters sing with me

Let's rise up and be bold

We're valuable and beautiful,

And we're too young to be this old

Too young to be this old, too young to be this old "

By the time Fiona had stopped singing it was obvious to almost every person there that she would emerge the winner. People were stomping their feet while she was singing her song. The crowd begged for an encore and the emcee allowed it.

Women were standing in the aisles looping their arms through each others' and dancing around. Shouts of 'you go, girl' resounded in the room along with 'Yes, sisters, sing it loud and clear.'

When Fiona was declared the winner it was to thunderous applause. She thanked everyone including her partner Maria Martelli, her loving husband Tim and especially Dolly. It was the most satisfying moment of her life and she was overcome with emotion; something she hadn't felt for a long time – emotion. And a deep love for her husband but also remorse for how distant she had been to him.

At the end of the evening Maria said goodnight to everybody, anxious to get home, kick her shoes off and open a bottle of wine. She left with her husband Benny. Fiona and Tim drove home; only this time Fiona was cuddling up to Tim, resting her head on his shoulder while listening to their favorite radio station. Her right hand wandered onto his thigh, massaging him hesitatingly; loving the familiarity of it, the warm feeling she got as she felt him respond to her touch. Tonight was a great night and it's going to get even better, she knew.

Tim tried his best to concentrate on driving. "I've missed your touch more than you know, Fiona. A couple more minutes and we'll be home and then we can make up for lost time but it's not going to happen if you cause me to have an accident," Tim laughed as he placed a kiss on Fiona's cheek.

"Okay, I'll be good but it's going to be hard."

"Not going to be hard Fee, it is already as you well know." They both laughed; a delicious shared laugh.

"You know Fee, that could be your song on the radio one day. Who knows what this win tonight might lead to? You were – well I don't know if I can come up with enough adjectives to describe your performance tonight. I'm so proud of you, and Fee, I love you very much. I've missed you.'

Fiona leaned her head up and kissed Tim on the neck. "Tim, I don't know what got into me. Maybe I was reading too many magazine articles about how to look young, how to stay young, how to reverse signs of aging; anything but how to grow old gracefully and accept who you are and be happy with yourself. I had bought into the whole youth concept. I'm so sorry and I'm so glad you didn't leave me. I was ..."

Pulling the car into the driveway, Tim shushed Fiona. "I'll admit I didn't know what to do, how to handle the situation Fiona. I crawled into my own little shell too because you were no longer there. But you're back. We're both back. I think it's time we got back on the bicycle don't you?" Tim said as he leaned over, gathered Fiona in his arms and surrounded her lips with his.

He murmured "Let's go in the house. Some fine champagne awaits us and a big comfortable bed. You're not old my beautiful Fiona. You're vital and alive. Who knows what you'll accomplish next in your 70s and 80s, maybe even your 90s? But let's live for now. You're just a kid of 59, and you're too young to even think about being old. Hey, that sounds similar to a great song I heard tonight." Tim smiled while Fiona's spirits soared. She was definitely back!

❧

Mexican Hot Chocolate Shots with Spicy Foam

. . . .

2 cans (12 fl. oz. each) NESTLÉ® CARNATION® Evaporated Milk, divided

1 cup water

1 1/2 cups (9 oz.) * NESTLÉ® TOLL HOUSE® Semi-Sweet Chocolate Morsels

1 1/4 teaspoons vanilla extract, divided

1/2 plus 1/8 tsp ground cinnamon divided

1/8 teaspoon ground cayenne pepper, divided (optional)

Directions

Pour 1/2 cup evaporated milk into medium mixer bowl; place beaters into mixture. Freeze for about 30 minutes or until ice crystals form around edge of bowl.

Heat remaining evaporated milk, water, morsels, 1 teaspoon vanilla extract, 1/2 teaspoon cinnamon and a pinch of cayenne pepper in medium saucepan over low heat, stirring frequently until melted. Do not boil. Set aside.

Remove chilled evaporated milk from freezer. Beat on high speed for 1 minute or until very frothy. Add remaining vanilla extract, remaining cinnamon and a pinch of cayenne pepper. Continue beating for 3 to 4 minutes or until mixture forms soft peaks.

POUR hot chocolate into eight 4-ounce demitasse cups and immediately dollop with foam topping.

162

SERVING SUGGESTION:

Serve as a rich dessert drink in 4-ounce demitasse cups.

www.alllwomenstalk.com

Milk Chocolate

....

Sweet romantic confections

(Stories of pure sweet old-fashioned romance)

"There is a supernatural universe of chocolate to discover.

Close your eyes and prepare yourself for a journey to an enchanted world of remarkable and subtle flavors: soft, spicy, sweet, aromatic, light, tender, sharp, bitter, dark, creamy and even white. These magical elements, flirting and melting with one another will bring you to higher places. Never stop tasting chocolates and by all means, never forget to offer chocolate, it is too much fun! Our love story with chocolate must continually unfold."

Pascal Caffet, World Champion Master Chocolatier

"To the Virgins to Make Much of Time"

Gather ye rosebuds while ye may,
Old time is still a-flying:
And this same flower that smiles to-day
To-morrow will be dying.

The glorious lamp of heaven, the sun,
The higher he's a-getting,
The sooner will his race be run,
And nearer he's to setting.

That age is best which is the first,
When youth and blood are warmer;
But being spent, the worse, and worst
Times still succeed the former.

Then be not coy, but use your time,
And while ye may go marry:
For having lost but once your prime
You may for ever tarry.

Robert Herrick (1591-1674)

"Some people search a lifetime for a moment like this.

Some people search forever for that one special kiss.

I can't believe it's happening to me.

Some people wait a lifetime for a moment like this."

"Never Too Late For Love"

August, 1968

"I love you Skip, and one day I'm gonna marry you and we'll live in a castle high up on a hill with a moat around it and ... I'll be happy; so happy! And we'll live happily ever after. I'll have a whole stable of ponies too."

Skip squirmed as he sat on the deck of the porch with his long legs reaching down to the next step. He loved little Bobbi Sue. She was the sweetest kid he'd ever known. And that was precisely the trouble; she was a kid. She was a ten-year-old kid who lived next door and she had a huge crush on him as little girls tend to do. He was a 20-year-old boy. She was such a typical little girl. Ten years old and she was in love with him; actually she was in love with love. That was the best way to describe little girls of that tender age.

"I love you too, little girl. I love a lot of people; my mom, and dad, my sister, Sierra, and just a lot of people. There are all types of love Bobbi Sue. One day when you're grown up you'll appreciate the difference and you'll understand."

Bobbi threw her arms around Skip's neck and squealed, "But I love you, Skip. You don't understand. I am definitely going to marry you as soon as I'm grown up. You'll see."

Skip gently pulled Bobbi's arms from his neck and shifted himself away from her. "Well, you've got a long way to go until you're all grown up Bobbi Sue. You have to graduate from school and maybe you'll even go to college. You might even meet your future husband there and ..."

"No!" Bobbi exclaimed. "*You're* my future husband. You're the only one I let call me Bobbi Sue too. See, you're special and one day ..."

Skip was saved from further discomfort by the sound of Bobbi's mother calling her from next door. "Bobbi, time to come in for dinner. Hey Skip, how're you doin?" Bobbi bugging you again about marrying her?"

"Oh hi, Mrs. Davis. No, we're just having our usual conversation about growing up, with me trying to explain to Bobbi that one day she'll find the perfect man and then *they'll* live happily ever after."

Bobbi stood and then walked away pouting. She turned and yelled goodbye to Skip with one last admonition that she was going to marry *him* one day, so there.

Skip watched her walk away and his heart swelled with an avuncular concern. He knew it was tough to be a little girl with no father.

Skip's mother, Patty, opened the screen door and joined Skip on the front porch, offering him a cold glass of iced tea. "Have you told her yet, Skip?" she asked, knowing how difficult it would be for her son to break the news to Bobbi that he'd enlisted in the army and would be leaving for basic training tomorrow.

"No, mom, I chickened out. I couldn't break her little heart. Besides, she'd probably want to kiss me and that would just be too creepy. I love her like a sister but she doesn't understand that. And don't forget school starts again on Monday and she'll meet new friends and maybe even a nice little boy. She'll be okay. I'm certain of it."

⚬✖⚬

July, 2010 – forty-two years later

Bobbi, and Sherry, her best friend of 40 years, were having their weekly girls' night out accompanied by their other dear friends, Beth, Darlene, Dolores, Joan, Maureen, and Pearl, and their newer friend, Frannie joining them. They loved their get-togethers. They tried each new restaurant that they'd heard about. They enjoyed most of the food, but mostly they enjoyed each other's company. That was the point of the girls' night out; a weekly renewal of their longstanding and abiding friendship.

They'd had fun all their lives and now in their early 50s they were still having fun. There were marriages, divorces and widowhood among them and then there was Bobbi; never married.

Bobbi had had a wonderful life; single but fulfilled. But she always wondered what had ever become of her little childhood crush, Skip, who'd later become her teen crush. She never forgot him although some of the memories had dimmed over the years.

The girls had finished their dinner and were indulging in this particular restaurant's much lauded dessert, chocolate hazelnut terrine with raspberry sauce. A chorus of "delicious," and "I wonder how many calories are in *that*?" followed by "calories be damned, girl, this is gonna go around my hips twice and I'm gonna enjoy the ride;" Joan said, laughing. Peals of laughter traveled around the table. The next day they'd all be doing laps around the pool or walking on their treadmills.

Kay arrived late. She'd been babysitting her grandchildren and was breathless as she sat down at the table. "Sorry I missed dinner, guys, but I'll have some coffee and dessert accompanied by some juicy gossip. Guess what! Tommy Womack is finally getting married."

Several voices said "No kidding. Somebody finally roped him in?"

"Well I guess if Tommy can get married at his age," Beth said, "then there's hope for my son yet."

Bobbi shifted uncomfortably in her chair. "You know, not everyone in this life gets married ... or even wants to. Some of us are happily single."

"Yeah, yeah, yeah, I hear ya Bobbi," Joan laughed. "If Skip showed up on your doorstep you'd be down that aisle on roller skates, with your wedding veil flying behind you."

The visual imagery had them all in stitches. Joan could always crack them up even if it was at Bobbi's expense.

Kay dropped another bombshell. "He's marrying ... are you ready ... Veronica Taylor."

"No!" they all seemed to say simultaneously. "You're kidding. She finally divorced that scumbag husband and ..."

"And ... she called me this afternoon and said she wants all of us to come to the wedding. It's Saturday at St. Joan of Arc, just a small quickie wedding. And Frannie, pull your jaw up; she's not pregnant – as hilarious as that would be at our age."

"Hilarious, my petite white butt," Joan giggled as she stood up and shook her booty. "That would be downright terrifying. Yuck!" Everybody laughed and agreed with Joan.

Sherry looked at Bobbi with a sideways glance. She wasn't sure how the best of her best friends would take this news. She knew Bobbi would be wondering if Skip might be at the wedding; after all Skip and Tommy had been close friends, always together. They'd even entered the military together.

"Forty-two years since I was 10 years old and had a little girl crush. But thirty-seven years since I saw him last, when I'd tried to seduce him in the park when he was home on leave but he wouldn't let me. I wonder if he ever thinks about that...

❦

Saturday morning arrived. All the girls, and yes they still referred to themselves as girls, had gathered at Bobbi's home. They were still stunning. Mother Nature and Father Time had been very good to them.

They arrived at the church and seated themselves in the back pew. St. Joan's is a small church allowing a good close up view of the altar. Within five minutes, Tommy and his best man were standing up on the altar, along with the maid of honor, looking out onto the small crowd of guests. The music was playing and Veronica walked down the aisle looking as radiant as any younger bride.

Bobbi stared at the best man trying to see Skip in him; but it didn't happen. The best man was slimmer than Skip had been and this man's hair was completely gray. Whoever the best man was, Bobbi didn't recognize him and neither did the other girls ... all except Sherry. She stared and squinted and tilted her head from side to side. There was something familiar about him, she felt certain. Or maybe not, maybe she was trying too hard to make it be Skip.

After Veronica and Tommy had said their vows, they walked down the aisle followed by the best man and maid of honor, whom nobody recognized but who looked remarkably like Sierra. And the best man ...

"Bobbi Sue?" the best man mouthed as he walked by Bobbi who was sitting on the end of the pew nearest the aisle.

"Skip?" Bobbi said although she didn't mouth the words, she said them ... loud and clear. It really *was* him.

Veronica and Tommy and Skip and Sierra lined up outside the church doors greeting the wedding guests. Bobbi and the girls had deliberately held back allowing others to greet the bride and groom first.

Veronica greeted them all warmly. She was a radiant bride and Tommy looked positively happy to have finally been caught. They talked for a few minutes and Veronica whispered something in Bobbi's ear; she told her that she had purposely called Kay to tell her about the wedding and not her because she wanted Skip's presence to be a surprise. Veronica knew if Bobbi asked her she would spill the beans. She hoped Bobbi would forgive her.

"There's nothing to forgive Veronica. Thank you for inviting us to your wedding and thank you for being so discreet. Bobbi's eyes were on Skip as she was talking to Veronica.

When Veronica and Tommy entered the limousine which would take them to the reception, Skip waved goodbye to them and then turned his full attention to Bobbi.

"Bobbi Sue, I've thought of this moment more times than I care to count. I never thought I'd see you again. How *are* you? Look at you; you're as beautiful as you were when I last saw you. You were 15. Do you remember?"

"Skip, how could I forget? I threw myself at you and you turned me away. You crushed me again just like you did when I was 10."

All the girls walked away and headed toward Dar's SUV. They knew where they weren't wanted. They were already gossiping and giggling even before the last one of them got into the vehicle. "This calls for a drink, girls," Beth shouted as Dar pulled the SUV out of the parking lot.

"The hell it does --- this calls for *many* drinks," Joan shouted to a roar of laughter.

"Oh, and also a taxi ride home from Wayne's Log Cabin because none of us will be in any shape to drive. This is a momentous day," Maureen chimed in.

Bobbi and Skip didn't even notice that the girls had left without as much as a by-your-leave. Skip re-introduced his sister to Bobbi and the four of them chatted amiably for quite some time; Sierra's husband, Joe, having joined them. Sierra and Joe then took their leave of them, leaving Bobbi and Skip standing by themselves.

Skip grabbed Bobbi's hands and ran his finger around her ring finger. "No wedding ring, Bobbi? Somebody told me you'd married Jack Kelly and moved away, that's why I never tried to look you up."

"No, Skip. No wedding ring; never has been one either. Never wanted one ...You?"

"Yeah, once; it lasted almost ten years. I didn't get married until I was thirty. I've been single ever since. She left me for another GI. Actually she'd left me long before that, emotionally. She just stopped loving me. She divorced me and then had two more marriages and divorces if rumors can be believed."

"And to think you could have married me, Skip and lived happily ever after." Bobbi smiled. Skip looked at her and was kissing her with his eyes. Bobbi's legs were unsteady.

Skip put his arms around Bobbi and held her tightly. His thoughts drifted back to that day in the park when she was 15 and he was 25. How he had wanted her then, how much restraint it had taken to push her beautiful young body away, knowing he could have every part of her right then and there.

That was then, this was now. They were both single with no encumbrances. They both still cared for each other ... deeply. There was no mistaking it. This was meant to be. Skip knew he loved Bobbi; that his innocent young friendship love for a vulnerable little girl had developed into a passion of a young man for a fifteen year old ... and now after all these years, now when they were in their 50s, he loved her with a mature love. It had always been there, waiting for the right time to surface. He knew it was now; because now it was right, and honorable.

"Whadda ya say we go to the reception and we can grab a table in the corner and play catch up. I want to learn everything about you, what you've been doing and I want to tell you all about my life and career, how I missed you when my family moved from Fairview."

"I can't think of a better way to spend a Saturday."

Or the rest of my life, my handsome Skip.

The sun was streaming down on them, wrapping them in warmth and hope as they strolled to Skip's car. "Do you still like ponies, Bobbie Sue? Does anyone even call you Bobbie Sue anymore?" Skip said after he'd dropped little kisses on Bobbi's face.

"I love ponies, Skip. You know me, I love all animals. I don't know if I could handle a whole stable of them now," she winked.

"And no, you're still the only person who calls me Bobbie Sue ... and I've really missed it."

"Well, I can't quite promise a castle on a hill with a moat Bobbie," Skip said as they both laughed, recalling little Bobbi Sue's childish wishes, "but I can promise you more love than your heart can hold in a lifetime, and then some."

"Remember the promise I made to you when I was 10 years old, Skip? Well, I never break my promises."

"Music to my ears, Bobbi Sue, sweet music to my ears," Skip murmured as he put the car in Drive, happy that they were finally driving into their future together.

Bobbi snuggled against him and all the love she'd held in her heart for 42 years was finally released, out into the open, for all to see, like a burst of butterflies, and it was reciprocated.

Bobbi Sue was now happy; so happy.

෧෪ඏ

Chocolate hazelnut terrine with raspberry sauce

DARK CHOCOLATE LAYER

- 2 cups (12-oz. pkg.) NESTLÉ® TOLL HOUSE® Semi-Sweet Chocolate Morsels
- 1/3 cup butter, cut into pieces
- 1/4 cup hazelnut liqueur
- 1 1/2 cups heavy whipping cream

MILK CHOCOLATE LAYER

- 1 3/4 cups (11.5-oz. pkg.) NESTLÉ® TOLL HOUSE® Milk Chocolate Morsels
- 1/3 cup butter

RASPBERRY SAUCE

- 1 pkg. (10 oz.) frozen raspberries in syrup, thawed, puréed and strained
- 1/2 cup water
- 1 tablespoon cornstarch
- 1 teaspoon granulated sugar

Directions of Chocolate Hazelnut Terrine With Raspberry Sauce:

1. Line 9 x 5-inch loaf pan with plastic wrap.

2. FOR DARK CHOCOLATE LAYER:

3. Microwave semi-sweet morsels and 1/3 cup butter in medium, uncovered, microwave-safe bowl on HIGH (100%) power for 1 minute; STIR. Morsels may retain some of their original shape. If necessary, microwave at additional 10- to 15-second intervals, stirring just until morsels are melted. Stir in liqueur; cool to room temperature.

4. Whip cream in small mixer bowl until stiff peaks form. Fold 2 cups whipped cream into chocolate mixture. Spoon into prepared loaf pan. Refrigerate remaining whipped cream.

5. FOR MILK CHOCOLATE LAYER:

6. Microwave milk chocolate morsels and 1/3 cup butter in medium, uncovered, microwave-safe bowl on MEDIUM-HIGH (70%) power for 1 minute; STIR. Morsels may retain some of their original shape. If necessary, microwave at additional 10- to 15-second intervals, stirring just until melted. Cool to room temperature. Stir remaining whipped cream into chocolate mixture. Spread over dark chocolate layer. Cover; refrigerate for at least 2 hours or until firm.

7. FOR RASPBERRY SAUCE:

8. Cook raspberry puree, water, cornstarch and sugar over medium heat, stirring constantly, until mixture comes to a boil; boil for 1 minute. Cover; refrigerate.

TO SERVE:

Invert terrine onto serving platter; remove plastic wrap. Cut into 1/2-inch-thick slices; serve in pool of Raspberry Sauce. (www.all-womenstalk.com)

"She Walks In Beauty"

She walks in Beauty, like the night
Of cloudless climes and starry skies;
And all that's best of dark and bright
Meet in her aspect and her eyes:
Thus mellowed to that tender light
Which Heaven to gaudy day denies.

One shade the more, one ray the less,
Had half impaired the nameless grace
Which waves in every raven tress,
Or softly lightens o'er her face;
Where thoughts serenely sweet express,
How pure, how dear their dwelling-place.

And on that cheek, and o'er that brow,
So soft, so calm, yet eloquent,

The smiles that win, the tints that glow,

But tell of days in goodness spent,

A mind at peace with all below,

A heart whose love is innocent!

George Gordon, Lord Byron (1788 – 1824)

"Through the years, through all the good and bad
I knew how much we had,

I've always been so glad to be with you
through the years

It's better every day, you've kissed my tears away

As long as it's okay, I'll stay with you
through the years"

"Love Restored"

. . . .

San Francisco, California May, 1985

It was a perfectly wonderful day on that Saturday in May, 1985; a perfect day for a wedding … to your sweetheart … on a hill overlooking the city by the bay. Sharron Rose Smith was marrying her college sweetheart, Kenny Matthews. Their vows were short but heartfelt.

"I give myself to you completely and forever. We are one in two bodies. I promise to love and respect you for who you are today and who you will be in the future."

Sharron and Kenny looked out into a sea of smiling faces. Their deep devotion to each other radiated from them, spreading out and enveloping everyone in a rainbow of their love. Later at the reception they danced to *their song,* Kenny Rogers's "Through the Years."

"I can't imagine anyone in this world being happier than I am today, my love," Kenny whispered to his bride, tracing kisses along her ear, and vowing to always be there for her, loving and protecting her.

"If anyone's happier than you are Kenny, it's me," Sharron said as she smiled at this man who would be by her side forever. Kenny was honest and true. She knew he'd never give her reason to doubt him. She felt the tears pouring out of her eyes and knew if she didn't stop she'd look like a raccoon. Why do brides wear mascara on their wedding day, she asked herself.

Theirs had been a storybook romance growing stronger every day since they'd first met at the University of California Berkeley. It was what most people would call love at first sight.

Sharron and Kenny were introduced to each other by Jackson Phillips. Sharron was in one of Jackson's classes and he knew she would be his best friend Kenny's type; tall, curvaceous, long straight ash blonde hair and the biggest blue eyes he'd ever seen; and smart and environmentally conscious. Oh yeah, he mused to himself, if he wasn't already madly in love with Barbara, he'd be falling all over himself trying to date Sharron.

Sharron surprised Jackson by accepting his invitation to double date with him and Barbara. Kenny was exactly as Jackson had described him; tall, sandy blonde hair, handsome, athletic, intelligent, kind, and one hell of an all around nice guy. They were all amazed by the chemistry that had instantly formed between Sharron and Kenny, like potassium and chlorine. Their bond was that immediate and that strong. That first double date soon became solo dates between them, followed not long after by their engagement and then the wedding.

They were besotted with each other. If they could have lived in a vacuum, just the two of them, they would have. They were in the throes of new love and they both knew it would last forever.

❧

Isla de Margarita, Venezuela May, 1985

They arrived in Porlamar on Isla de Margarita, a short hop, skip and a jump from Caracas after such a long trip from San Francisco to Miami and then finally to Venezuela. A friend owned a timeshare there and had given them a free week's stay as a wedding present. Their wedding had been perfect and now their honeymoon promised even more perfection, a free stay at a beautiful resort, surrounded by beaches and mountains and some of the most verdant scenery they'd ever seen.

Sharron had brushed up on her high school Spanish so she could converse with the locals and ask directions and order their meals. Kenny was never good with languages so it fell to Sharron to be their guide. She loved it. "Donde hay un buen restaurant?" Where is a good restaurant? That was one phrase she knew they'd need to know because they loved fine dining and wanted to experience the best that this lovely little island had to offer.

The week flew by as all vacations and honeymoons tend to do. They were reluctant to leave this island paradise with its near perfect weather and charm. They would miss the days spent in their room with the balcony doors open allowing the island breezes to enter and waft over them as they made love.

"Well, Mrs. Matthews, my beautiful Rose of Sharon, are you ready to begin our married life together? Have you had enough of the honeymoon?" Kenny laughed as he took her in his arms and feathered her face and neck with kisses, and then kissed her deeply and lovingly while caressing her as if he were holding the rarest of all jewels in his hands.

"I am ready indeed, Mr. Matthews, my wonderful, handsome husband. But our honeymoon will never be over. We won't let it be over. I love you. That will never change."

They arrived back in San Francisco, loaded down with souvenirs and tchotchkes and trinkets for everyone and almost completely divested of their cash, but that was okay, they agreed. It was their honeymoon and worth every Bolivar that they spent.

❧

Marin County, California, April, 2010

They'd moved a few years ago from San Francisco to Marin County. They'd been happy, every bit as happy as they'd promised themselves they would be on their wedding day nearly 25 years earlier.

They both had satisfying jobs and good friends and family. They never had children and didn't feel the need to; they had each other. They satisfied their maternal and paternal instincts by being a Big Brother and Big Sister. They didn't want to bring more children into the world; they just wanted to do their best to make the lives of the ones who were already here, happier. It was a win-win situation they agreed.

"Sharron Rose, what's wrong?" Kenny asked. "You look worried or something."

Kenny always called her by her full name. The Rose of Sharon was her mother's favorite flower so when Sharron was born her mother added the extra 'r' to her name and reversed it to Sharron Rose. Her name sounded so beautiful when Kenny uttered it.

"Nothing; I'm just a little tired I guess. But not as tired as you with all that work you're doing restoring Bella. Go on. Don't worry about me. Bella awaits you.'

Sharron knew how much Kenny loved restoring his 1955 Chevy BelAir. She wondered what would happen if she gave him a 'Sophie's Choice' between her and that damn car. She wanted him to use those hands to rub over her body, at least she used to want and enjoy that. Now she didn't even want him touching her. Why would he even want to? She asked herself.

She walked into their bedroom and sat at the vanity in her spacious dressing room staring at the reflection in the mirror. When did she get so old, she wondered. It seemed like yesterday when she was young and vibrant. She knew she had a beautiful face; at least she used to be beautiful. But that was before the attack of the giant caterpillar feet that had taken up residence around her eyes and lately it seemed were extending their route farther down her face. Crow's feet. Ha! She *aspired* to crow's feet. At least *they* were *fine* lines. These lines were big and deep and seemed to be growing as fast as her expanding waist line. At least that's how she saw them, looking at her face with a critical eye.

And what was so cute about puppets? Sure, they were cute on children's hands but they took on a whole new dimension when they were wrapped around one's mouth like huge parentheses, emphasizing the pucker lines around the lips. Who'd want to kiss those lips! And the beginnings of a crepey neck – well don't even go there! She admonished herself. Just shoot me now!

She could see the handwriting on the wall and it was writing 'You're old, old, old.' It also said 'You're fat.' That was some nasty writing, for sure. She could go on. And she did, counting off the other signs of advancing age; her once beautiful chestnut hair now had sprinklings of silver and don't kid yourself kiddo, she ruminated. This isn't that beautiful silver color that some lucky women develop, this was icky gray. You wouldn't see this color on any drugstore shelf sitting next to Miss Clairol Silver or L'Oreal Shimmering Silver or, oh wait yeah there it is; Brand X Super Icky Gray. Yep, that's what all women want. Let's take it home and slather it all over my dull chestnut hair, at least on the hairs that aren't falling out yet. And why don't I see any gray hairs in my brush, why are they all the dull brown ones? Why can't I lose the gray ones? What's up with that? She asked herself.

Well the color will go so well with my uneven skin tone now and the droopy eyelids that are threatening to hide my blue eyes, she thought. Well, maybe this is a good thing. Maybe this is a good silver lining, she said to herself, laughing at the absurdity of it. It might distract everyone's attention from her thickening waist and, burgeoning thighs.

Yep, she was a real package now she told herself. What man wouldn't want her? She'd been distancing herself from Kenny and he couldn't understand why. Their 25th wedding anniversary was approaching and she dreaded it. Kenny would want to take her some place nice as he always did. She'd have to go through the ordeal of buying clothes, looking wistfully at all the hot dresses in size six and then having to face it; that ship had sailed long ago. The LBD, the little black dress, had now become the BBD. She couldn't even bring herself to say the word.

She stared at the myriad bottles of creams and lotions lined up on her vanity like good little soldiers waiting to perform an impossible task; make her look young again ... or at least younger. She was amazed by the amount of money she'd been spending not only on creams and lotions but little instruments that you held against your neck while they supposedly vibrated your neck to a more youthful look. Hell, she'd hold her neck against the handle of a jackhammer if she thought it would do the trick.

But what did she do? Went straight to the kitchen for some chocolate tofu cheesecake. Only another woman would appreciate that irony and sympathize with her to boot. So she called her older sister, Meghan and began pouring her heart out, in between sinful bites of the decadent dessert.

She always felt better after talking to Meghan especially now that she'd packed on those extra pounds. Meghan understood because Meghan was her sister … and a woman; a very slim woman who couldn't gain weight if she had an IV of a thousand calories pumped into her veins each hour. Meghan understood what it was like to have a poor body image, to have people make comments about her weight as if it were unacceptable to comment on fat people but it was perfectly okay to comment on their skinny counterparts.

"Sharron, have you told Kenny how you feel about being neglected? Knowing you, you probably haven't said anything. I know you don't like confrontation but Kenny isn't the sharpest knife in the drawer when it comes to reading the female mind."

"Ha! You're right Meghan. Kenny's more like a spoon when it comes to that! But he's smart, kind, lovable, and I know he's faithful. We've loved each other for 25 years and I hope we have at least another 25. I don't know what I'd do without him and yet I've been rebuffing him because I know I must be disgusting to him. I mean come on Meghan, how many hours can you spend restoring a car? It's just strange that I've gained weight and suddenly Kenny only has time for Bella. Even I don't like to look at me so why would Kenny?"

"Sharron, you're being as silly as a dime store watch. Kenny adores you. He wouldn't care if you've gained 50 pounds; he really wouldn't, and you know that. And don't think I'm being patronizing but I think the small fine lines around your eyes and I emphasize the word small ..."

"Give me character, yeah yeah that's what everybody who doesn't have wrinkles or these damn caterpillar tracks says."

"Caterpillar tracks? That's too funny, now I know you've lost it Sharron. You're a beautiful woman and one day, not now, but one day you'll be a beautiful *old* woman. Take it from your older sister, I think I still look hot but I don't have caterpillar tracks, mine are more like millipede tracks; that is the ones you can see that aren't obscured by the bags under my eyes."

"Thanks sis," Sharron said laughing. Meghan was always so sensible and knew how to put things in perspective.

"But there's something else ... something that has me even more concerned than what we've been talking about. You know Kenny handles all of our bills. I never have to worry about anything or even look at our bank account. If I want to buy something I just buy it so I don't know what prompted me to look at the bank statement today. I don't know if you'd call it a premonition or just chance but I looked at it and you won't believe what I discovered Meghan."

"Oh no, Sharron; please don't tell me ... don't tell me you're broke or ..."

"No, Meghan, in fact it's quite the opposite. I discovered a ten thousand dollar deposit over and above our paychecks, deposited on March 1st."

"Well gee, that's really bad news, sis. Who would want an extra ten thousand dollars? Sharron, it's a deposit not a withdrawal. Most people would get excited to discover that. But I guess I know what you're saying. Why wouldn't Kenny tell you that? I'd be very concerned too. Promise me you'll talk to Kenny about this right now. Those wrinkles and the extra pounds don't seem so important now do they?"

"No; boy talk about putting things in perspective this sure does. I'll call you later after I've talked to Kenny. I've been so worried about Kenny ignoring me that I started to overeat and now I'm so anxious that I can't eat, except for chocolate of course. But chocolate has feel good properties in it so there you have it; another excuse to eat chocolate."

They both laughed remembering how many times through their lives they'd turned to chocolate to help them through a crisis, real or imaginary. Now had been one of those times and she was feeling better.

Sharron hung up and began humming. She was humming 'Through the Years' and reflecting on the last two months and looking at her face and body now in a different perspective. She looked up and caught Kenny's reflection in her vanity mirror, a broad smile spreading across his sensuous lips. She turned to him as he said "Sharron Rose, you're humming our song."

"Kenny, I didn't think you remembered."

"How could I forget our song? We danced to it at our wedding. It's been true and will continue to be true through the years," Kenny said as he smiled at Sharron, cupping her face with his strong hands, and wiping away the tears that were beginning to trickle from her eyes.

"I've wanted to take you in my arms and sing our song to you for quite some time but ..."

"But what Kenny? Why haven't you? I thought we had the all time greatest love affair, and we truly have but these last two months all you've done is work on that damn car. Sorry, I know how much you love it so I shouldn't say that. But there's something else ..."

"My sweet flower, I haven't been ignoring you. I've been giving you your space. You've been keeping me at arms' length for some reason. I figured you'd work it out and then let me know what's going on."

"What's going on, Kenny, is, I'm starting to show signs of age and I got my panties in a wad about it, which I know is stupid. The wrinkles are getting deeper but ... we need to talk ..."

"Wrinkles? You've got wrinkles?" Kenny interrupted. "I guess it's a good thing I require glasses to see things these days because I don't see any wrinkles."

"Oh and I suppose you haven't noticed the extra twenty pounds I've put on either?"

"Oh no, sweetheart, you're wrong. I *did* notice that" Kenny said as he laughingly ducked an imaginary punch from Sharron.

"But sweetheart the extra fat helps to fill out the wrinkles. Uh oh, I guess I went too far with that one," Kenny said as Sharron really did playfully raise her hand to him, but then broke into a laugh. Kenny could always make Sharron laugh.

"So this is what this is all about, the avoidance of me, the tears? Why didn't you tell me? You know I think you're the most beautiful woman I've ever laid eyes on and if I haven't told you that enough lately, then I'm truly sorry."

"With you spending so much time away from me and my gaining all this weight I thought you had lost interest and didn't find me attractive anymore and then the wrinkles and then something else..."

"What? Are you insane; has your brain gone walkabout? I love you more than air and if I had to give up my breath for you to live,

I would, with never a second thought. I love you Sharron Rose and I always will. I meant those wedding vows – I promised to love and respect you for who you are today and who you will be in the future. This is yesterday's future and I'm still here for you and always will be."

"How did I ever get so lucky? You are truly the love of my life and I've missed you, I've missed *us*. And I want us back. I've been so silly and self-absorbed. I need a fresh start, something to get me out of this funk. I really do but first …"

"Hmmm, how about Tahiti; or Bora Bora? Maybe a little side trip to Moorea? Something like that?"

"I'm serious Kenny."

"And so am I my love."

Kenny's lips curled into a grin, a big goofy grin. "I've got a buyer for Bella!" Not only a buyer, but a very motivated buyer who offered me ten thousand more than I was asking, if I could deliver it on time; that time being Friday. I just finished her with two days to spare! He already gave me a huge deposit which has cleared our bank. This is why I've been working so feverishly on the car and ignoring you so shamefully."

"What? That's what that deposit was! I just discovered it. Are you serious? But why didn't you tell me? Why couldn't I know?"

"Because my love, my beautiful flower – I wanted to surprise you."

"Surprise is a gross understatement sweetheart. But what are we going to do with the money?"

"I just told you – We're going to fulfill your fantasy and go to Tahiti, Bora Bora and Moorea. Seriously!"

"Kenny, I don't know what to say. I seriously don't know what to say. This is all overwhelming."

"I think 'yes' would be appropriate. Oh, and you could say 'I love you'" Kenny murmured in Sharron's ear as he leaned his body into hers.

"But what about Spot? I can't bear to put him in a kennel. It's bad enough you gave him that silly name." Sharron was glad to be laughing again, and to be in Kenny's arms laughing. She was already envisioning them making love in a thatched bungalow, the kind that she'd read about, in Tahiti.

"No worries about Spot, Sharron Rose. Jackson and Barbara are coming to stay at the house, 'Spot sitting' I suppose you could say. I called Jax last month and he and Barbara are looking forward to it. I swore them to secrecy. They love us and they love Spot, but nobody loves anyone more than I love you.

I've felt so bad about ignoring you, and not telling you what's up, but I really wanted to give you the best gift I could for our silver anniversary. I know how much you've dreamed about going to French Polynesia. Oh honey; I love you Sharron Rose. Forgive me?"

"Forgive you for what, for making me deliriously happy and bringing me back to my senses? Then yes I forgive you, Kenny, my sweet, thoughtful Kenny."

Kenny took Sharron's hands and kissed each one and then placed both of her arms around his neck while putting his hands around her waist and hugging her to him. He kissed her. And then he kissed her again.

"You've only got a couple of weeks to brush up on your French mademoiselle. Hey! See, I'm speaking French already. Maybe I'll be the one to order our meals in Tahiti. 'Ahh waiter I would like to order some marbres.' How's that for a beginner? I think I just read that somewhere, they're eggs, right?"

"Well they'd be very hard eggs, Kenny since you just ordered marbles!" Sharron laughed, a really good laugh and Kenny laughed with her.

"Leave the ordering to me sweetheart and you can just pay for it with your newly acquired small fortune."

They stood locked in their embrace, smiling at each other, appreciating each other, looking at each other anew. Then Kenny led Sharron to their bed as he began singing to her – 'Through the years'.

◈

Ingredients of Decadent Chocolate Tofu Cheesecake:

- 1/3 cup chocolate wafer cookies (about 10-12), finely crushed

- 2 bars (4 oz. total) NESTLE® TOLL HOUSE® Unsweetened Chocolate Baking Bars, broken into pieces

- 3 pkgs. (24 oz. total) cream cheese, softened and cut into pieces

- 1 container (16 oz.) silken tofu, drained

- 1 cup granulated sugar

- 1 tablespoon NESTLE® TOLL HOUSE® Baking Cocoa

- 2 large eggs

- 2 teaspoons vanilla extract

Directions of Decadent Chocolate Tofu Cheesecake:

1. Preheat oven to 325? F. Lightly grease 9-inch springform pan; sprinkle cookie crumbs over bottom.

2. Microwave baking bars in small uncovered microwave-safe bowl on HIGH (100%) power for 1 minute; stir. The bars may retain some of their shape. If necessary, microwave at additional 10- to 15-second intervals, stirring just until melted.

3. Place melted chocolate, cream cheese, tofu, sugar and cocoa in food processor; cover. Process until smooth. Scrape sides of container; add eggs and vanilla extract. Process until smooth. Pour into prepared pan.

4. Bake for 60 to 70 minutes or until edge is set but center still moves slightly. Cool completely in pan on wire rack. Refrigerate for at least 4 hours or overnight.

www.allwomenstalk.com

*Love is but the discovery of
ourselves in others, and the delight
in the recognition.*"

Hot Chocolate

(SENSUALLY ROMANTIC STORIES OF SWEETNESS
WITH A COMBINATION OF SPICE AND HEAT)

"Love is like swallowing hot chocolate before it has cooled off.

It takes you by surprise at first, but keeps you warm for a long time."

Anonymous

"Love many things, for therein lies the true strength, and whosoever loves much performs much, and can accomplish much, and what is done in love is done well."

Vincent Van Gogh

"I never knew the charm of spring, never met it face to face. I never knew my heart could sing. Never missed a warm embrace 'Til April in Paris whom can I run to, what have you done to my heart?"

"The Chocolatier and the Maitre Patissier"

"Life is short. Eat dessert first" Angelique heard the waiter say in perfectly French accented English. Not heavy at all. It was a wonderfully charming accent. She hoped her own meager French sounded just as lovely in her American accent. "What would you like today?"

She raised her eyes from the menu and stared into the face of an angel, a tall, slim, curly haired blonde angel with eyes almost the color of turquoise.

You!

"Would you like a little more time to decide what you'd like Mademoiselle?" the waiter asked as he flashed a beautiful smile at her and waited patiently for her response.

Oh definitely you! On this table, right here. Right now. Oh yeah.

"Excusez-moi Monsieur. I was just thinking of something and got lost in my thoughts. I think I'd like some crepes, S'il vous plait."

Before I've had you; after all life is short. Eat dessert first.

The angel smiled. "You are an American? Or Canadienne? Forgive me but I can never tell the two apart. To us - the French - the accent is hard to differentiate. But my money is on American, n'est-ce pas?"

Angelique smiled what she hoped was a beguiling smile, as she responded "Oui. Vous avez raison." *Yes. You are correct.*

The angel smiled and said "Your French is quite good. And you speak it with an authentic sounding accent. Are you fluent?"

"Oh, Mon Dieu, most definitely not. In fact I'm quite disappointed that I've only learned pretty much what I need to know to get through school and get through daily activities. I do practice every day but the other students are busy with studying and can't devote as much time to me as I'd like."

The angel's heavenly blue eyes brightened as he blurted out the thought that had just occurred to him. "It would be my pleasure to help you with your French, mademoiselle ...?"

"Angelique. Mon nom est Angelique. Et vous?"

The angel replied, "Please forgive my bad manners. I am Philippe. And I find I must apologize again. I have neglected to put your order in for your crepes. I shall do that immediately. The patisserie will be closing shortly. Perhaps after you've finished your crepes we can have a French lesson or two," he offered with a questioning look on his face.

Oh Philippe, you've no idea what I'd like to learn from you.

"That would be wonderful. C'est magnifique, Philippe. I hope I don't choke on the crepes in my rush to begin the lessons. I do have a lot to learn you know" Angelique said quite flirtatiously and brazenly as she traced her tongue over her lips and smiled seductively.

Angelique forced herself to eat slowly and daintily lest Philippe think she were a *petit cochon,* a little pig. When she'd finished eating, Philippe cleared her table and then returned and sat down next to her, his body lightly touching hers while his beautiful, unusual blue eyes bored right into hers. She was surprised at first that he didn't sit opposite her but she intuited that he'd picked up on her not so subtle hints that she wanted more than language lessons. She wanted the language of love.

❧

Oh shoot. How much wine did I consume after leaving the Patisserie Michele last night? I'm in the city known for love, not tramps for heaven's sake. Whatever came over me?

Angelique recalled very quickly what had come over her as she looked at the sleeping form of Philippe lying in bed next to her in her grandmother's Pied-A-Terre. This was her home away from home while she'd been attending Escoffier L'ecole Patisserie. In five days she would graduate and return home to New Orleans as a master pastry chef, a maitre patissier. She would open a patisserie or perhaps Cristophe would have changed his mind by now and would sell his successful business to her.

Her musings were pleasantly interrupted by Philippe's stirrings. The bed sheets had become entangled around his ankles at some time during their exuberant love making during the night, revealing his deliciously buff body; the body that had given her so much intense pleasure last night. He was possessed of the longest legs she'd ever had wrapped around her. His curly blonde hair enhanced his angelic looks; but he was no angel in bed. She'd wanted French lessons and Philippe had not only complied, he'd taken her right to the head of the class ... twice.

What had started out as lessons in the French language had quickly turned to lessons in l'amour; Angelique, the eager student and Philippe, the willing teacher; although the roles reversed several times during the night.

Philippe didn't make her feel self-conscious about her generous body size even though she outweighed him by a good twenty-five pounds. She had one of those faces that for some reason encouraged people to comment how pretty her face was and how much prettier she'd be if only she'd lose weight. She was quite comfortable with her body image and was a healthy size 14/16. Her figure might be considered large by some but it was curvy in all the right places. She lifted weights and she was toned. She kept her brunette hair cropped short with stylish blonde chunks throughout which highlighted the gold flecks in her dark brown eyes. She had no self-esteem issues like some of her thinner counterparts.

Rolling over on his side and placing his beautifully muscled arm over Angelique's chest, Philippe asked "What are you doing awake so early, ma cherie? I thought with all those lessons last night, you'd still be sleeping. Could it be that you need extra credit?"

He smiled as he inclined his head and kissed her lips, his tongue exploring her mouth. She kissed him passionately in return, feeling the hot moisture of his mouth on hers. She ran her left hand over his hard chest, massaging and stroking him.

Enjoy it while it lasts Angelique. Soon you'll be back home and this will all be a memory; a wonderful out-of-this-world memory of sweet, sensual, spectacular sex. Nothing more; just sex.

Soon, they were re-energized with arms and legs curling around each other, bodies moving rhythmically, undulating slowly and then increasing the tempo until finally each experienced exquisite release and satisfaction.

They rested for a little while until Philippe's appetite overtook him. "I am tres faim cherie. How about you? You are hungry too? How about some profiteroles au chocolat? I will run down to the patisserie and obtain some. Then we can sit here, have a lovely breakfast and get to know one another. That sounds good, yes?"

Oh Philippe, anything sounds good with you. Who was I kidding when I said I just wanted to remember the super sex? I want to remember everything about you Philippe. Could I be falling for you? I don't even know you.

"I am tres faim too Philippe, most definitely. I'm looking forward to delicious profiteroles but more important, I'm looking forward to getting to know you. The only thing I know about you is that you're a waiter at Patisserie Michele; oh, and that you raise the bar unfairly high for other Frenchman to live up to – and Americans or Canadians for that matter." Angelique said coyly as she smiled at this man with the angel's face.

Philippe kissed Angelique, smiling at her with affection and then eased his lanky body out of bed. He dressed quickly so that not a moment would be wasted getting to and from the patisserie. He wanted to learn everything about this femme magnifique who had entered his life; he also wanted to tell her all about himself. She would be surprised to learn of his profession and his dreams and plans.

"So, Angelique, breakfast was delicious? You enjoyed it? I know I did. In fact I've enjoyed everything since about 7 p.m. last night," Philippe said as he gave her a sly smile but one that also exuded warmth and kindness.

Angelique poured them a cup of coffee and then settled down on the divan next to Philippe. "Oui, the breakfast was wonderful; delicious. But it paled in comparison to the events of last night ... and this morning."

Putting his coffee cup on the coffee table, Philippe leaned back and enfolded Angelique in his arms. "I'm a chocolatier, Angelique. Surprised?"

"Surprised? No. Not surprised at all. Shock would be a better word; 'choc'. Are you kidding me?"

"No, I am not kidding you at all. I know you think I am just a waiter at the patisserie but I recently graduated from the DCT Swiss Hotel and Culinary Arts School in Lucerne, Switzerland. I graduated at the top of the class with the flying colors as you Americans would say. I took a full program which afforded me a paid internship and now I will begin teaching others how to be a chocolatier at the famous Les Roches School next week. Je suis si hereux, Angelique."

"Yes, I agree; you are fortunate indeed, Philippe. I am very happy for you. You know, I don't always believe in the Fates or anything like that but it's so ironic that we should meet and I discover that you're a chocolatier; because I'm a maitre patissier. Or at least I will officially be one in 5 days when I graduate. This is unbelievable."

Philippe picked up his coffee, sipped it and looked at Angelique over the rim of his cup, his beautiful blue eyes sparkling. "Well I do believe in the Fates and I do believe we were meant to meet and perhaps go beyond that, to become more than lovers. But somehow we must overcome the distance that will be separating us. You could settle with me in Switzerland. I don't like to meet you and then poof! Lose you as quickly."

Oh, I'd like to lose you in my body right now. Frenchmen! They move so quickly. We just met and he wants me to move with him to Switzerland? Mon Dieu!

"But if you're a chocolatier with such a promising future, what are you doing working as a waiter at Patisserie Michele?

"It is not such a mystery Angelique. There is a very simple explanation. I came back home to Paris to visit with my family before I begin working in Switzerland. My aunt, who is the 'Michele' as in Patisserie Michele asked if I would help her by waiting tables for just one night when one of her employees called in sick. I didn't want to leave her short-handed and I thought it would be good fun."

Philippe's face broke into a smile which crinkled around his eyes. "So you see it was the Fates, Angelique. The gods were conspiring to bring us together." He leaned over and kissed her lightly on her breasts, nearly spilling his coffee on them.

Angelique took Philippe's coffee cup from his hand and placed it back on the table. "So, would you like to take advantage of the time we have left mon amour? I have a feeling we can burn those profiterole calories off and then some."

She lay back down on the divan pulling Philippe down onto her body. His body's agreement with her suggestion was immediate and very evident. Philippe's insistent murmurings of 'Je veux que vous' warmed and excited her.

I want you too.

❧

The next four nights floated by in a sex-filled haze; sometimes slow, sensual love, with Angelique lying on her side with Philippe spooning her and making love to her gently, his body pressed firmly against and into hers with his arm free to caress her breasts while he kissed her neck softly and lovingly. At other times they were sexual athletes romping all over the bed and each other, laughing and totally giving into unbridled hedonism. They were thoroughly in tune with each other's needs and desires.

Her days were spent trying to concentrate on school work. She was determined to pass the final exam with 'the flying colors' as Philippe would say.

They made love, they talked, they dined, they strolled the streets of Paris, they drank fine French wines, they squeezed in a museum or two, and ate wonderful French desserts made with the very best chocolate, of course. The one thing they didn't seem to do much of was sleep. There was precious little time for that. The few hours they did manage to steal each night were spent with their bodies snuggled against one another's, face to face, torso to torso, sleeping the sleep of the sexually sated.

Somehow she managed to get all her bags packed; a chore that both saddened and excited her. She didn't want to leave Philippe although she knew there was no real future for them. They lived worlds apart and each had their own lofty ambitions which were not to be denied. Philippe had spent years at school perfecting his craft and could not, and would not, throw it all away. Angelique's life was back in New Orleans.

It was a longtime dream of Philippe's to one day participate in The World Chocolate Masters. Now he dreamed of having his name mentioned alongside such Master Chocolatier luminaries as Shigeo Hirai of Japan, and Yvonnick Le Maux of France, and other such notables. One day he hoped the name Philippe Yves Marchand would be mentioned in the same breath.

Angelique was excited to be returning home to New Orleans to begin her new life as a maitre patissier. She would have her own patisserie, hopefully Cristophe's, but if he wouldn't sell, then she would open her own. There would be plenty of room in New Orleans for another patisserie, she assured herself. Meanwhile she would have to be content with the memories of a heavenly love affair with an angel.

She graduated on the appointed day; her long apprenticeship finally over and having passed the written exam. She knew all about tempering, molding, sculpting and decorating chocolate too which would forever remind her of her angel, Philippe, Master Chocolatier – and Master Lover.

❧

They spent the last night before Angelique was scheduled to leave Paris lying in bed, embracing each other, loving each other, reminiscing about their chance meeting, and rueing that they hadn't met when Angelique had first come to France.

There would be no sleep for them that night just as there had been no time for sleep the previous four nights. They didn't want to waste any of their dwindling time together sleeping. Angelique would sleep on the plane. Philippe would go home to sleep at his apartment.

C'est la vie

They had arrived at the most difficult decision of their lives, but the only one that was right for both of them, they knew. The affair would end now. There would be no phone calls between them, no letters exchanged, no emails and definitely no texting. It had to be a clean break if they were to go on with their lives and find lasting happiness elsewhere and with someone else. To do anything else would be to prolong the agony and to delay the inevitable outcome.

Perhaps Atropos of the Three Fates will smile upon us instead. One can hope.

There had never been any utterances of 'I love you' between them. They had both recognized their liaison for what it was; a highly charged sexual, albeit romantic affair. In their heart of hearts they knew that if they lived in the same city or even on the same continent, their couplings might have blossomed into a full-blown romance. But this time the Fates were not on their side.

Their parting at Charles de Gaulle airport was anticlimactic; nothing theatrical, no histrionics, no long embraces or embarrassing kisses in front of onlookers. They'd said and done it all the night before.

"Tu va me manqué toujours, Angelique," Philippe whispered in her ear followed with a warm embrace and a brief kiss. "Au revoir, mon amour."

"I will always miss you too, Philippe. I will think of you often and hold a special place in my heart for you. Au revoir." The urge to smother his mouth with one last wet hot kiss made her body tremble and caused her throat to constrict.

She turned and quickly walked away knowing his eyes were trailing her. She dared not turn around lest she change her mind and go running back to him like an actress in some B movie.

⚜

Patisserie Philippe
"Felicitations Angelique"

The banner hanging over the Patisserie Philippe on Royal Street near the famous New Orleans restaurant, Court of Two Sisters brought a bittersweet smile to Angelique's beautiful face. Cristophe had been surprisingly eager to sell his place to Angelique, explaining that he'd wanted to retire while he was still young enough to enjoy it. His offer to stay on for several months to help Angelique through the rough spots was met with much joy by a grateful Angelique.

Philippe, I wish you could see this; my one year anniversary of the patisserie that bears your name. My Philippe. What are you doing today; probably making some woman amazingly happy. No, probably making a lot of women amazingly happy!

"What's put that smile on your face Angelique; besides that big banner proclaiming the one year anniversary of the patisserie?" her best friend, Amy, asked. "It's half-way between a smile and a frown though, I think."

Amy and Angelique had been best friends since ninth grade, some 16 years earlier. Whereas Angelique was already developing into a tall and fuller figured girl, Amy was rail thin and of short stature. She had long blonde curly hair and pretty green eyes. They were as different as chalk and cheese as Amy's mom would often comment. But they were identical where it counted; they thought alike and had exactly the same values; both loved animals and volunteered at the local humane society. They both loved to dance and travel. They could finish each other's sentences. They shared a passion for cooking and baking. They couldn't have been closer if they were twins.

"You know me, girlfriend. I'm smiling because I'm happy that my dream came true; my very own patisserie and I should say my very own *successful* patisserie! But yes, I was just thinking about Philippe and wondering what he'd think; what he'd say if he saw his name up there. I know one thing for sure – if he were here we'd have one hell of a celebration - several times!"

She and Amy shared a wicked laugh as they stood in the hot sun, drinking in the atmosphere of this city that they both loved so much and anticipating the rowdy celebration that would begin in a couple of hours.

Amy was genuinely happy – make that ecstatic – about her best friend's success. She just wished she'd make up her mind about marrying Zack. They'd been seeing each other quite steadily since about 6 months after Angelique's return from France.

"Ange, how many more times do you think Zack will ask you to marry him? There are plenty of women in this town – including me, I might add – who would marry him in a New York minute. And I'm not kidding," Amy laughed.

Grabbing Amy by the arm, Angelique ushered her into her shop. "Come on. It's too muggy out here. Let's go inside, sit down and cool off and we can talk all about Zack."

"Honey, if we talk about Zack neither of us is going to cool off. He's hot, hot, hot. I'm just sayin'. I'm already beginning to feel the effects of just mentioning his name. Oh, I'll burn in hell for the thoughts that are going through my head."

"Well you can't have him ... at least not now anyway. I need to give it a little more time to see if these feelings are strong enough for marriage. I'm beginning to think they might be heading in that direction but ..."

"But you don't want to marry him and then have Philippe miracu- lously reappear into your life. I get it but I really don't think it's gonna happen. I'm not trying to jinx you and maybe those Fates that you always talk about really will make it happen but ..."

"Amy you're way off base; seriously. If I really wanted Philippe back in my life I'd have been on a plane back to Paris a long time ago, or Switzerland actually. It just wasn't meant to be. I could never live on *the continent*. I mean, it's a fantastic place and all that but my heart is right here in New Orleans. I love the French architecture and the Spanish influence and architecture. I love all the jazz clubs, the delicious beignets at Café Beignet right across the street from here."

"Don't let the people at Café Dumond hear you say that. After all, their name is synonymous with beignets."

Yes, I know the beignets at Café Dumond are legendary but the ones right here on Royal Street are every bit as tasty in my opinion. Well, you name it; I love just about everything that's New Orleans. It'll come back in all its glory one day too and I want to stay here to help it happen. "

The decorators were bustling about filling each table with beautiful flower arrangements and inflating helium balloons, while others were setting the tables. Her dedicated staff was in the kitchen working on a chocolate fountain and making sure the chocolate desserts were up to Angelique's standards. Angelique was a much loved boss but she was exacting when it came to anything concerning chocolate. It was her own little homage to Philippe, Master Chocolatier.

"Well I wouldn't keep him dangling for too long Angelique. I mean I'd take him in a heartbeat but you two really do make a lovely couple. I wouldn't want to see you lose him because you couldn't make up your mind."

"Excuse me Angelique," the decorator, who was also Angelique's cousin, interrupted, "I just wanted to let you know that everything's on track for tonight and you won't have to do a thing. We're taking care of all of it so you can just enjoy the party."

"Thank you Yvette, but you just try to keep me out of that kitchen. It's my life! I promise I won't interfere but you know I'll have to do something."

"Well perhaps just a little something, but mainly I want you to enjoy the party and spend time with that gorgeous Zack. Consider yourself lucky that I'm married or I'd be all over him like white on rice."

"Hey, hey," Amy called out. "I've got first dibs on him. You've got a husband. Don't be greedy."

They all laughed and Yvette made her way back to the kitchen leaving Angelique and Amy discussing the possibility of Angelique marrying Zack.

"You know Amy, I really do care for Zack; very much. I love him. I really do. I'm just not sure if I'm *in* love with him. And if you really want to know why I've been hesitant to accept his proposal, if you want to know the down and dirty reason, I'll tell you. There is no passion! I know I shouldn't compare him to any other man, especially one as gifted in the art of lovemaking as Philippe – and believe me it *is* an art, but the passion is missing lately. No bells are ringing now; no whistles are … whistling I guess. It's like sex you have after you've been married for 40 years.

"Gee, now there's something to look forward to. Old age, wrinkles, poor eyesight, bad hearing, bad hips and boring sex," Amy laughed. "But you know what? At least we'll still be having sex; and probably a lot more than I'm having now."

"That's funny Amy and I suppose you're right. Zack is a great guy and he really is a good kisser. But actually I've felt like lately he's pulling away from me a bit. Maybe that explains the lack of passion. Maybe he's not that into *me*."

"Notwithstanding what you just said about his sexual prowess, or lack thereof, I'd still like to give him a chance if you ever decide to stop seeing him. Or maybe you're right; maybe he's getting bored with you. How great would that be?"

"Amy! I might hold on to him now just to spite you. Or we could share him, we've shared everything all our lives," Angelique giggled.

"But actually I do believe you're on to something. I think Zack is ready to move on, and I don't blame him either. You have my permission to make a move on him."

"Oh, I'm sure he'd love to hear us talking about him like that."

"Well, he's a great guy and he deserves a great girl. You're a great girl Amy. I think I'll just come out and ask him tonight if he's lost interest in me. You know, come to think of it, he hasn't asked me to marry him in over a week. Hmm, food for thought."

"Speaking of food, Ange, I know you want to check out what's going on in the kitchen so I'll let you go. See you tonight. We're going to have one hell of a good time. This is your night Angelique. One whole year has flown by and your patisserie is even more successful than when Cristophe had it."

They stood up from the table and Amy prepared to leave. She turned and said, "You promised you'd have profiteroles tonight, Ange. You talk about how great they were in Paris but you've never served them. So they'd better be on the buffet table tonight or I *will* steal Zack from you."

"That gives me a thought. I should expand the business. There's plenty of room to enlarge the kitchen. I could hire a chocolatier and sell my own exquisite line of chocolates. What do you think?"

"What do I think? I think it's great. You could hire Philippe and ..." Amy stopped short when she heard Angelique make what could only be described as a cackle.

"Amy, you are so gullible. I love you to death but I swear you'll believe anything. Having my own line of delicious chocolates is a great idea, but that's all it is; a great idea. I don't have the time or enthusiasm for anything other than being the best maitre patissier in New Orleans. Now get going. I'll see you tonight."

The door closed behind Amy leaving Angelique to her thoughts.

Good thinking though Amy. But I don't need a Master Chocolatier right now. What I need is a Master Lover.

She turned around at the sound of the opening door; her senses alerted to the scent of the familiar cologne wafting into the room.

"Zack! I wasn't expecting you quite so early."

Zack inched closer to Angelique, his always smiling face replaced by the concerned look of a little boy lost. He looked at her, not knowing how to start. The beginning was always the hardest.

"What's wrong, Zack? You look so sad. Do you feel ill? Something I can get you?"

With a sharp intake of breath, Zack responded, "I'm not asking you to marry me anymore Ange."

"Okaaay. What brought this on? You *are* feeling ill aren't you?"

"No. Well, yes; but not physically ill. I mean, not; oh hell, this is harder than I thought. You know how I feel about you Angelique. I think everybody knows."

214

He took Angelique's hands in his and said "But I don't want to get married anymore. I'm sorry. I didn't want to continue the dishonesty. I've been feeling this way for a couple of weeks. I was sure you could tell. Can you ever forgive me, or at least not hate me?"

Angelique's reaction to Zack's bombshell surprised her; relief. She placed her arms around Zack's neck, pulled his head down and kissed him tenderly on the cheek. "Thank you Zack. Thank you for your honesty. You've shown more courage today than I have."

A questioning look passed over Zack's face. "What exactly do you mean, Ange? Are you saying what I think you're saying?"

"Yes Zack, I think I am. I love you but not like a woman should love the man who keeps asking her to marry him; or at least the man who used to ask her to marry him. I'm sorry too. You're a wonderful person and I'd like to think that I'm a good person too."

"You are, Angelique. Your name means 'angel' in French and you really are an angel."

"I'd never want to hurt you Zack and I'm glad I haven't. I think we were meant to be just friends, good loving friends."

"Give me a kiss, a real kiss and then I'll be out of here." Zack took Angelique in his arms for one last time and kissed her gently on the lips.

"I'll miss your soft lips, Ange. Thank you for being so understanding. I'll never forget that. I'll pop back in later tonight to help my good loving friend celebrate this auspicious occasion. I think we'll both enjoy it more now; no more tension."

Angelique was strangely happy. Zack was right; there would be no more tension. There would be no more conflicting emotions. She and Zack could be good, loving friends. The proverbial weight had been lifted from her shoulders. A smile crept across her face as she anticipated Amy's reaction to this news. She would tease her first; make her wait for it. Oh, it was going to be fun. And she hoped that her best friend would make a love connection with Zack. Life has a way of taking its own direction in spite of us, she reflected.

☙❦❧

Angelique was sure everybody in New Orleans was in her patisserie tonight to help her celebrate. The wine was flowing and the music was playing; Angelique's favorite; genuine down home Dixieland. In another city, classical music might have been the appropriate choice for the opening of a patisserie or lively French music but this was New Orleans, she wanted the feel of this marvelous city to surround them; she wanted joyful music in the air and in people's hearts. Sounds of laughter and conversation permeated the room and the compliments and felicitations were flowing as freely as the wine.

She was reveling in the celebration, dancing with good friends and enjoying the delicious food and confections prepared by her staff. Something was missing though. And it wasn't just the profiteroles which Angelique couldn't bring herself to serve. She'd promised Amy but something prevented her from honoring her promise.

Angelique took a break from the festivities and walked into the kitchen. She was standing in there deep in thought. She knew why she couldn't serve them; they were a reminder of her torrid affair, an affair to rival the affairs of Romeo and Juliet, Tristan and Isolde, Antony and Cleopatra. But hers and Philippe's affair had ended in a different kind of tragedy; not with physical death but with the emotional death of two hearts; or at least her heart. She wasn't sure how Philippe's heart had been handling the demise of the affair, and she wasn't sure she wanted to know.

Oh Philippe, I've tried so hard to forget you but the truth is I haven't been able to move on. Everything reminds me of you. Why did I name my patisserie after you? Not as an homage to you; I lied to myself. It's because I love you. I've tried so hard not to face it.

Yvette interrupted her thoughts. "You okay Ange? Tonight has been a howling success, capping a whole year of success and yet you look forlorn. What is it?"

Angelique managed a weak smile and hugged her cousin. "It's nothing Yvette. I was just thinking about how much work it will be if I expand the business. Don't let me hold you up. I know you want to get out of here early. Most of the guests will be leaving soon and as soon as we're finished I'm going home to crash. I don't have energy for anything; well just a small reserve to play with Bette and Beau."

Bette and Beau were her rescue kitties; the two most adorable kittens in the world – les chatons. Angelique's smile broadened from weak to beaming as it always did when speaking about her beloved companions; her furry family who'd been helping her get through the past year.

"Well they're approaching one year of age now Angelique so I guess they're not really kittens anymore, they're becoming les chats."

"I know Yvette. But they think they're still kittens. I wish I had their energy because I'll surely need it when I get home tonight. Ok you've got work to do and so do I; otherwise I could talk about my babies all night – as you well know."

Angelique turned her attention to the left-over food; thankful that the majority of it had been consumed and not only consumed but consumed with gusto. She was appreciated here. Her food was appreciated. As much as she wanted to be with Philippe she knew she could never leave her beloved New Orleans. Her heart may be in Paris but her home was here.

"Excuse me Angelique," Yvette said a few minutes later as she re-entered the kitchen; she was holding a folded piece of paper in her hand which she gave to her cousin.

Angelique looked at Yvette questioningly; wiping her wet hands on a tea towel, she then took the note from Yvette's hand and unfolded it. Her face paled and her lips trembled when she read the words written on the note. She wasn't sure her legs would continue to support her.

La vie est courte. Mange premier dessert.

"Yvette, where did you get this note?" Angelique gasped. "Do ... do you know what this says? 'Life is short. Eat dessert first.' Is this a joke?"

"Not at all Ange. An incredibly gorgeous hunk gave it to me, asking if I would pass it on to you. He's waiting right outside the kitchen door. Look through the window in the door and you'll see him. I'm really not kidding. He's an ..."

Angelique quickly peered through the window and found herself looking into the eyes of ... "An angel, Yvette. It's Philippe; my angel!"

Angelique propelled herself through the door with lightning speed, nearly knocking Philippe over on the other side.

"Philippe! Can it really be you? What are you doing here? I'm ..."

"Angelique, my love," Philippe whispered as he pulled her to him hugging her tightly and kissing her with a year's worth of pent up passion.

"First, tell me; are you glad to see me? I need to know that you've been pining for me as I have for you. Are you happy I'm here Angelique?" he questioned her with pleading eyes.

"Philippe, mi amour, I'm dreaming. I'm certain of it; because this can't be happening."

Philippe laughed – "Don't you want it to be happening Angelique? I'm really here and I'm not a figment of your imagination. I've missed you so much and I have so much to say to you, so much to tell you ... so much I want to do with you."

Angelique leaned into Philippe's body and kissed him ... and kissed him until she was sure her lips would be quite sore tomorrow.

"How long will you be here Philippe? How did you find me? Where are you staying? Why are you here?

Why don't you tell me you love me?

Philippe stood there holding Angelique, gazing deeply into her eyes, smiling, depositing little kisses on her lips while trying to discreetly conceal his erection. It was pointless. His desire for her was threatening to burst through his expensive trousers. He pulled her to him even tighter, allowing her to feel his need for her.

"Philippe is that a beignet in your pants or are you just happy to see me?" Angelique laughed as she rubbed her body against Philippe's, pressing into him, delighting in the hardness that greeted her in return.

"I am thrilled to see you my love, but to answer your first question – I hope, forever. Second question – Your grandmother, Chandelle, told me where you are. I visited her at her pied-a-terre where you and I had spent such wonderful days and nights. I groveled like a dog to get the information from her and she took pity on me. Third, for now I'm staying at the Hotel Maison de Ville. Actually I haven't stayed there yet, I'm just booked in there. I only arrived from Paris this evening. My plane was late or I'd have been at the patisserie earlier. By the way I love its name, Angelique. "Fourth, I'm here because I can't live without you for another day and I'm hoping you feel the same. And fifth, yes I know you didn't ask me a fifth question, but the answer to it is I'm here because I love you Angelique."

"Is it possible you can read my thoughts, Philippe? I've wanted to hear those words from you for such a long time."

"Well?" Philippe asked. "Do you love me?

"Of course, my darling Frenchman. Je t'aime. Je t'aime de tout mon coeur. I love you with all my heart - and also my body. Let's go to my place. We have so much to talk about, so many plans to make, and ..."

Philippe's arm encircled her waist as he led her to the door kissing her as they walked. "First things first mi amour," Philippe interrupted.

"I do not want to wake from this dream Philippe because I'm sure it must be a dream. My eyes see you and my heart hopes that it is truly you, that it's real. But how can it be? How ..."

"Shh," Philippe whispered as he placed a finger over her lips and then kissed them. "There is tomorrow and many more days after that to talk and to plan. Tonight is pour l'amour; a lot of l'amour; as much love as you can stand ma cherie. Je t'aime. I hope you will never grow tired of me saying that because I intend to spend the rest of my life telling you. I love you."

Angelique suddenly realized she'd been holding her breath. She expelled the air from her lungs and then took another deep breath. "But what about Switzerland and ...?"

"I have bigger plans," Philippe declared.

"Would those plans include helping me expand my business and hiring a chocolatier?" Angelique asked, not quite believing the words that had just come out of her mouth. She smiled as she pondered the possibility of the Fates intervening in their lives again.

"I happen to know an excellent chocolatier, Angelique; one who will work for l'amour. We will work together to make both our dreams come true. We shall be partners in business and in life, never again to part. Je T'aime Angelique, Je T'aime."

"Je T'aime Aussi Phillipe. I love you too!"

"We'll close the shop. Don't you two worry about it. Go and enjoy yourselves," Yvette called after them as Philippe placed his hand on the door knob.

"Assurement, Yvette," Philippe said. "Assurement. How could we not?" he grinned.

"Apres vous, Mademoiselle," Philippe said as he led Angelique out the door and into what he now knew would be a wonderful future with his precious Angelique, his gift from the Fates.

❦

Profiteroles au chocolat

....

Ingredients for the choux buns –

4 fl. oz water

Pinch of salt

2 oz butter

2 oz plain flour

2 eggs, beaten

Ingredients for the filling –

10 fl. oz double cream ** OR 1 pt. vanilla ice cream

Ingredients for the chocolate sauce –

6 oz plain chocolate

1 oz butter

2-3 tbsp water

Preparation –

Preheat the oven to 425 degrees F and lightly oil 2-3 baking sheets. Place the water, salt and butter into a medium saucepan, heat slowly until the butter melts, then bring to a boil.

Remove from the heat and add the flour all at once and mix well.

Return to a medium heat and continue to mix briskly until the mixture forms a solid ball and leaves the sides of the pan.

Remove from the heat and allow to cool slightly.

Add the eggs a little at a time, beating well to incorporate the egg thoroughly then continue to beat until the mixture forms a stiff, smooth shiny dough.

Drop spoonfuls of the pastry (16-20 in all) onto the baking sheets spaced well apart then bake at 425 degrees F for about 20 minutes or until golden and well puffed.

Once cooked, remove from the oven and make a small slit in the side of each one and cool on a wire rack.

Whip the cream until it's quite firm, then slit the puffs in half near the base and fill with the cream. Pile in a pyramid on a shallow serving platter and refrigerate until ready to serve OR use vanilla ice cream instead of the cream.

When ready to serve, break the chocolate into small pieces and place in a small heatproof bowl together with the butter and water.

Place the bowl over a pan of simmering water and heat, stirring, until the chocolate has melted and all the ingredients are mixed well.

To serve, drizzle the chocolate sauce over the profiteroles and serve immediately.

(www.justfrance.org Note: The author prefers vanilla ice cream and recipes using vanilla ice cream can also be found at www. cooks.com)

(www.justfrance.org Note: The author prefers vanilla ice cream and recipes using vanilla ice cream can also be found at www.cooks.com)

When I get home, babe Gonna light your fire

All day, I've been thinkin' about you,
babe you're my one desire

Gonna wrap my arms around you
Hold you close to me

Oh, babe, I wanna taste your lips
I wanna fill your fantasy, yeah

"The Doctor and the DJ"

It was nearly five minutes past midnight on a Friday night/Saturday morning. The next six hours are what he waited so anxiously for all week; to hear her voice; silky smooth, breathy, uber sexy with a touch of cognac. That's how Dr. John Kelly always thought of her voice.

Even her name, Jade O'Day, is sexy he thought although he was sure it was just something invented for her radio show.

It wasn't only her sexy voice that turned him on so much but what she said with that voice. Reading from the copy for the station's biggest sponsor, Luscious Lingerie, describing their teddies, thongs, edible panties, corsets and other sexy garments, he visualized her wearing them as she spoke. And he visualized removing them from her.

He varied his fantasies. Sometimes he'd picture her in the radio station control room wearing a black thong and black lace bra peeping out not so discreetly from a silky blouse which was tucked into the waistband of her black leather mini skirt. He'd lift up her skirt and pull her thong aside letting his fingers roam all over her hot, moist naughty bits. He'd be penetrating her mouth with his tongue while caressing her down there, listening to her moans of pleasure. That was Friday night's fantasy.

Saturday night found him envisioning her in another sexy outfit only this time it was a siren red pushup bra and garter belt with no panties. He'd make love to her with her clothing on. In this fantasy she'd have a neatly manicured landing strip; he didn't care for the bare, little girl look. He wanted his woman to look like a grown woman.

He just knew she was beautiful and oozed sex from every pore. How could that not be true? She had that maddeningly distracting voice, the voice that drove all the male callers crazy, each beseeching her to give them a chance, to let them explore her hot body. They weren't shy about expressing their desires either; what they wanted to do to her and what they wanted her to do to them, some of which would be illegal in certain parts of the country.

Her admirers weren't limited to male callers either; she had her share of female callers who wanted to introduce her to the joys of girl-on-girl delights. It pleased Jade that she could turn on members of both sexes but her chemistry was positively geared to male/female sex. She loved women, after all how could she not? She was one. But when it came to sex she wanted to feel male parts, male lips kissing hers, male hands squeezing and caressing her body parts, male parts entering her. She had nothing against lesbians; her sister was a lesbian but she felt that everyone had to be true to whom they were and who Jade was, was a man-loving female. There was no denying it.

He was loathe to admit it but he was jealous. Jade belonged to him. At least in his fantasies she did. He had to meet her, had to find out if she was everything he envisioned but what if she wasn't? What if she was a mere mortal with plain looks but an incredible voice? That thought is what had prevented him from going to the station to find out once and for all.

❧

Monday found Dr. John Kelly making rounds at Palmtown Community Hospital where he was the chief resident in cardiology. He'd been called in to work early because one of his patients, actually his favorite patient, Mr. Ted Donne, had arrested.

Having determined that Mr. Donne was stable and would be fine he decided to go to the Doctors' Lounge to dictate some long overdue charts. All doctors dislike dictating charts but in John's case he had a dislike bordering on hatred. He loved treating people and helping them get well but sitting in a little room dictating into a microphone was not why he became a physician. He loved the hands on and interaction with the patients.

The downside to his job was when one of his patients didn't recover. He was truly empathetic and cared for them. Dr. Kelly was undoubtedly the most admired and respected physician on staff.

Various sets of adoring eyes always followed him, especially his fine glutes, when he walked through the Transcription Department en route to the Doctors' Lounge to dictate.

His 6'1" frame carried his lean 185 pounds quite nicely. His green eyes complemented his jet black hair, which he wore in a casually tousled style, but one which took the considerable skills of his stylist to achieve.

He didn't have a great voice as Jade had and the transcriptionists were forever complaining about his dictations, how he garbled his words and fired them off rapidly. But they all forgave him because he was so nice...and so handsome.

He knew he was handsome, had known it since he was about sixteen when all the girls at school fawned over him. But he was never one to brag or boast about his looks. He accepted them with equanimity, knowing they were a genetic gift from his parents and nothing with which he had anything to do.

Saying hello to all the transcriptionists as he walked through the Transcription Department, his eye was caught as usual by the voluptuous redhead with the emerald green eyes sitting at her desk by the Doctors' Lounge, offering only the quietest greeting hello.

She intrigued him; her figure similar to what he imagined Jade's to be. She had what appeared to be at least size DD's sitting pertly under her lavender low cut cashmere sweater. He judged her to be about 5'5", maybe 130 pounds give or take.

His Jade was buxom and had womanly curves; she was not a skinny little anorexic. She'd have a full, generous mouth that was just made for loving.

This transcriptionist – what was her name? – was sexy in a full, bountiful way that always made him hurry by her desk before she could become aware of the growing erection threatening to stand at full attention and perhaps embarrass her. He wasn't one to brag but he knew he'd been blessed in that department.

Today would be different he decided. Today he would get to know her, at least find out her name. Jade was his fantasy but this woman was real.

"Hello there" he said, as he walked by, pausing at her desk to say, "I'm John Kelly and..."

"I know who you are, Dr. Kelly," Jane interrupted. "I hear your voice in my ears every day," she laughed in a breathy voice that bordered on husky – not tramp-like but a sophisticated sexy voice.

"I do your transcription. It's nice to say hello to you in person. I'm Jane."

"Jane is it?" he said quizzically, arching his eyebrow, feeling an unmistakable sense of familiarity to the voice, his mind racing, wondering. He was deep in thought, staring ...

"Dr. Kelly? Hello? Perhaps you were absent in medical school when they taught anatomy. My eyes are up here" Jane motioned with her lovely fingers pointing to her pretty, smiling face.

"Oh my god, I'm so sorry Jane," Dr. Kelly stammered while blushing like a schoolboy. "I wasn't really staring at your, well at your chest so much as I was concentrating on your voice. I swear you sound so much like someone I know."

"Someone you know, Dr. Kelly? Or perhaps someone you'd like to know?" Jane whispered seductively while standing up and leaning over her computer offering him a view of her generous breasts encased in a lacy midnight blue deep plunging bra.

"Yes, someone I've wanted to know for months now; a DJ on WSDM with the sexiest voice I've ever heard. Her name is Jade. Sounds very much like Jane, does it not?" Dr. Kelly asked coyly while smiling into her lovely eyes.

"It's my little secret, Dr..."

"John, please call me John."

"Ok John. It's my part time job on the weekends. I don't do it for the money heaven knows, but for the thrill of being on the air, and titillating my listeners. Some of them are lonely and I'm their fantasy girl. I can be anything they want me to be without being a prostitute."

"Well I'm a little lonely too Jade, I mean Jane. I fantasize about you day and night. I've had many a nice dream, actually many sexual dreams. You're quite the contortionist in them. Sorry but Jade is my fantasy girl too, only I'd much prefer now to get to know Jane."

"I'd like to get to know you too, Dr...I'm sorry, John. I just hope that I don't disappoint. Seeing your fantasy woman in person can be quite a let down if you've built her up too much in your mind. That's why I don't use my real name on the air. I don't want anyone to find out that Jade O'Day is really Plain Jane, transcriptionist" Jane said, looking at Dr. Kelly from under her long, thick lashes.

Seating himself on the edge of Jane's desk, with the charts placed strategically over his rising manhood, John leaned in closely to her, breathing into her ear, ignoring the muffled sounds of the other transcriptionists' girlish giggles.

"You're certainly not a disappointment Jane. In fact, you're even lovelier than I had imagined. Although to tell the truth in my fantasies you're wearing either a jet black or hot red bra. That Midnight Blue color that you're wearing today though is lovely. I'm sure it will be appearing in my next fantasy," John laughed with much ease as his eyes devoured her body.

Jane sat back down on her chair crossing her arms in front of her and leaning them on her desk; her breasts being more prominently displayed now exposing her beautiful cleavage.

"Oh man, I'm sorry. I truly am, not just for what I said, which I had no right to say, but also because my actions could bring a big sexual harassment suit against the hospital; and me too. I just got carried away, thinking I was talking to Jade and forgetting where I was. Can you please forgive me?"

"There's nothing to forgive John. I'm a big girl. You were being honest and quite flattering. There's no one in the Doctors' Lounge now. All the doctors have finished their dictations for the day leaving the room free and clear for...well free and clear for anything I suppose. Any thoughts come to mind, John?"

"Actually too many to count Jane! We could go in the lounge and you could give me a private showing of the Luscious Lingerie Collection" John chuckled.

"I assume that sexy bra is one of their collection."

"I see you're a man of good taste, John. They make sexy thongs too" Jane whispered in that sexy as hell voice, as she gave him a knowing smile and a wink.

My God she's so easy to talk to. It's as if I've known her forever.

Taking Jane's hand and guiding her in front of him, he let her lead the way into the lounge. A low whistle pierced the air behind them followed by an even lower chorus of "You go girl."

John looked over his shoulder and gave the small enclave of transcriptionists his most engaging smile, knowing they'd all be tittering about what they presumed was going to take place between he and Jane.

They'll just have to live vicariously through Jane. I'm not sharing myself with anyone else now that I'm this close to getting to know my fantasy woman.

Closing the door behind them, Jade led John to the farthest cubicle in the lounge, the one that all doctors avoided because of the poor lighting and that the electricians never seemed to fix. Jane was pretty sure she knew why this particular cubicle never received the needed repairs. No one wanted to work there, but playtime after hours was quite another thing.

"I believe this will suit our purpose quite nicely, John" Jade said teasingly. The look of surprise and anticipation on John's face caused Jade to giggle.

"The 'purpose' to which I'm referring, Dr. Kelly, is to get to know each other. We can sit here and chat privately without a dozen sets of eyes upon us. I hope you didn't have any bad boy thoughts going through your head."

"Yeah a whole lot of them Jane, as you well know, you temptress."

Jane took the initiative and kissed John; a sweet kiss that was both tender and sultry. "I hope my kissing you was one of the thoughts you had, John."

He smiled at her and said "That was definitely one of them. I can't believe I'm kissing Jade, my fantasy woman."

"I'm Jane but if you need me to be Jade, I understand. I'm not one to destroy a fantasy," Jane murmured as she smiled into John's kind eyes.

"Jane, Jane, Jane. I'm so sorry but I've fantasized about you – about Jade – for so long that it's going to take a bit of getting used to – calling you Jane. And by the way you're definitely not a plain Jane at all. You're definitely a Jade O'Day."

"Thank you but contrary to my radio persona, John, I'm not easy. I haven't been with anyone in over a year since my fiance' and I broke up."

"If I told you it's been the same for me too Jane, you'd know I was lying, and I don't want to lie to you. I've had a few women in my life since my wife divorced me two years ago but nobody serious. In fact, you've been my only serious romantic involvement. You, Jade I mean. That voice of yours has gotten me through many a lonely weekend. That and the sexual fantasies I conjure up of both of us."

Wrapping his arms around her, and stroking her beautiful long ginger red hair, he kissed her deeply, not wanting to let her go. He felt like a school boy again when the most popular girl in school let you kiss her. He couldn't believe his luck.

She had the most beautiful clear skin with a sprinkling of freckles scattered across her pert nose with eyes the color of cornflowers. She stood about 5'2". His doctor's eyes estimated her weight at about 110 pounds and he wanted every one of those pounds rolling around on top of him.

Removing herself from John's embrace, Jane said "Wait here John. I'll be right back. I was so excited to talk to you I forgot to log out. I don't want anyone to accuse me of canoodling on company time. Oh, and are you carrying, John?"

"Carrying ... Oh! Oh! What a shmuck you must think I am," John laughed; a boisterous yet embarrassed laugh.

"But never fear; I was a Boy Scout and you know what our motto is."

"Now don't go away. I'll be back before you can conjure another fantasy of us."

John found himself peeking out of the cubicle, staring at the closed door, blinking, wondering if he was hallucinating or had he actually just kissed Jade. He still couldn't think of her as anyone but Jade O'Day. But that would come in time he smiled to himself.

Removing his jacket, tie and shirt he smiled, hoping he hadn't misread Jane's intentions. Was she really into him or just teasing him?

Striking what he thought was a sexy pose he waited in the cubicle for Jane's return. He hoped she'd appreciate his muscled back, trim waist and strong arms. His slacks were all custom fitted and hugged his body emphasizing his generous bulge. His back was to the door when he heard it open. He knew none of the other doctors would come back there so he relaxed and waited for Jane to enter the cubicle.

"My, my, Dr. Kelly. Is this cubicle too hot for you?" the female voice purred as she walked closer to him.

Tell me I'm dreaming for God's sake. Please tell me I'm dreaming. Oh man, this isn't Dr. Williams. No, no, no!

Quickly sitting down behind the desk to cover his arousal, he immediately realized the need to do so no longer existed; he was deflated quickly and completely. He turned to face the hospital administrator, Vivian Williams, a former beauty queen with brains to match her looks. He hoped she hadn't gleaned why he was there but there wasn't much you could put by her. She didn't rise to the top of her profession by being stupid.

"Dr. Williams. Hello. I, ah, thought I'd be alone in here and get some dictation done and you're right, it is indeed hot so I took off my jacket and tie and..."

Oh my God I'm stammering. Somebody shut me up please.

234

"Dr. Kelly, you look like the little boy caught with his hand in the cookie jar, or somewhere equally as exciting and forbidden," Dr. Williams laughed as she unabashedly admired his physique. As men's physiques go, his was certainly right up there with the best of them, not that she was all that interested.

"I don't care what you wear, or don't wear to dictate as long as you get these finished" she said handing him a stack of past due charts.

"Take off your pants too if you think it'll help you get them done quicker," she said as she winked at him.

Exiting the cubicle, she turned around, giving Dr. Kelly a sly look as she said "It's a good thing I'm gay or you'd be in big trouble doctor. Try not to let too many things come between you and your dictation, if you catch my drift." She chuckled to herself as she walked out the door hoping she hadn't completely ruined his day, or his hoped for assignation.

A minute later he heard the door open again. This time the lovely Jade O'Day was smiling at him.

"John, what's wrong? You look like you've seen a ghost...or a hospital administrator," Jane said, laughing, as she walked behind the desk and sat on John's lap.

"I saw Dr. Williams come in here so I waited a bit until she left; in the meantime I was hoping you hadn't turned her over to the straight side. I think I'd like to keep you for myself, Dr. Kelly," Jane said as she laughed.

"She almost ruined it Jane. You should have gotten here before she did. I'm telling you, I looked sexy as hell, posing in my best muscle pose and..."

"You look pretty damn sexy to me just the way you are John. I like the little boy lost look. It makes you vulnerable in a sexy way. Kiss me John. Kiss me all over and over again."

"I want to do more than kiss you Jane. I want to make love to you. But before that ..."

"Before that, what, John?"

Smiling shyly, John practically stuttered as he took both of Jane's hands in his own. "Before anything happens between us, I'd really like to get to know you Jane. I need to get Jade out of my head and fill it instead with Jane. You're the person I really want to get to know, to learn all about you."

"Oh my god John, I think that's ... no, I *know* that's the sweetest gesture anyone has ever made to me."

"I know it makes me look like a real shmuck Jane. Any other guy, or even me at any other time would just jump your bones without a second thought. But you're different and you've made me feel different. I can't believe it myself."

Jane sat down on the desk and ran her eyes over John's face and body, wondering if this man could really be as nice as he seemed.

Either I've been transported to another universe or this is the nicest man in this universe or any other. Could I possibly be this lucky?

"Dr. Kelly - John," Jade said smiling, "you are quite possibly the worst dictator in this hospital and possibly the worst one in the state of Arizona but that's more than offset by your gallantry and gentlemanly ways. I don't know what to say."

"Well you could say you didn't really mean what you said about my dictating skills or lack thereof; but I know it's true," he laughed.

"Believe me, I've heard it before. Tell you what; I'll try really hard to do better, on one condition."

"And what would that condition be, John? Please don't make it too hard because I'd really like to get to know you better too."

"Well, you could say you'll go out with me and give us a chance to discover each other."

"What? That's it? Boy you sure drive a hard bargain John. I still think you're too good to be true but I'd love to find out."

⚬❦⚬

Before he knew it, it was Friday night again. Their one date had turned into an every night occurrence except on weekends when Jane had to do the overnight shift at the radio station. They had certainly gotten to know each other – physically, and emotionally. He knew every square inch of her voluptuous body, all the ins and outs of the lovely Jane or Jade O'Day.

It was no surprise to either of them that they were falling in love.

All week John had been dictating his charts much to the amusement and appreciation of Dr. Williams. He was a frequent visitor in the Transcription Department now and actually enjoyed the welcome he received from all the transcriptionists.

He also knew they were all looking at his fine butt as he passed their desks. He wished he could clone himself to make everybody happy but as long as there was only one of him, that one would be for Jane exclusively.

⚬❦⚬

He poured himself a neat Scotch from his outside bar, as he settled on his chaise longue on the back deck of his home; a home he was proud of both for its beauty and its minimal carbon footprint. He was proud of himself for being 'green' before it was cool to be so. He stared up at the brilliant deep blue Arizona sky that was bursting with diamond-like stars, as he inhaled the heady scent of the numerous desert flowers in bloom.

Five minutes to go and his precious Jane would be on the air; no, not Jane. His precious Jade O'Day would be on the air purring to all her faithful fans, lulling them into their own personal fantasies with that voice of hers. That voice that he knew would always drive him wild; Jade's voice, his Jane's voice.

He took a sip of Scotch and settled himself in taking in all that the desert had to offer, and listening to the voice of the love of his life; the beautiful precious Jane; his Jade. More precious than any gemstone.

I wonder what she'd think of a jade engagement ring. A beautiful gold band with a jade stone set in it or perhaps many jade stones, to commemorate her radio name. That's what I'll...

❧

"Good morning sweetheart. Have you been out here all night?" It was Jane purring in his ear, ever so gently, not wanting to startle him.

"You mean now that you've got me, you don't have to listen to my show anymore?" she teased while settling her body down onto his lap, straddling her legs over him writhing with pleasure and definitely waking up all parts of his body.

She lifted herself up, removed her panties and opened the fly of his pajamas and smiled at how eager he was to see her. She eased herself back down and lowered herself onto his arousal, leaning over his chest and kissing him tenderly.

"Oh my God, Jane, I can't believe I fell asleep. I've never done that before while you were talking. I was just listening to you and having great thoughts for a surprise for you and..."

"And? What kind of surprise John? No, don't answer. I don't want you to spoil it. If it's from you I know I'll love it. I've got a surprise for you too, sweetheart," Jane purred as she unbuttoned her blouse revealing a black lace bra trimmed in red barely holding her ample breasts in.

"This is for both your Friday night and Saturday night fantasies John. The red is for Friday and the black is for Saturday. Now you don't have to choose. Oh, and I've also got a sexy new thong, compliments of Luscious Lingerie. You like it?" She murmured as she held it in front of him. "They love how I sound when I do their commercials. Their rep said they think the thongs may make me feel even sexier, and therefore it'll come through over the mic. Don't you just love his choice of words?"

"Yes I like the thong but no, I don't like what he said. He's coming on to you. But I do choose, Jane. I choose you. I love you. Do you think you could choose to be with me, now and forever?

"I chose you that first day we made love, John. I knew you were the one. And if that's a proposal the answer is not yes, but Hell Yes!" Jade cried out, her heart bursting with love for this gentle man with the old world manners and charm and the body that brought her to such ecstasy.

They looked at each other and smiled with all the love that was in their hearts. "If you liked that Jane, wait until you see my surprise that I have for you. Well you won't get to see it right now. But by Saturday for sure" John whispered in Jane's ear as he put a hand on each side of her waist and began lifting her up and down, matching her thrusts with his.

"Well I don't know exactly what you've got in mind John but I'm a pretty good guesser and I'll bet it has something to do with jade; right? Am I right? You're blushing John. I love it when you blush."

John gave her a loving smile, and then claimed her mouth, kissing her again and again, before she had time to really think about his surprise. Instead she thought only about this wonderful man who loved her and was making sweet love to her as the morning sun was rising over them.

Damn, she's a pistol. She's going to be a hard one to stay one step ahead of but she's my love, my life and with that voice of hers everything will be okay...always. My precious gem, my Jade.

❖

Chocolate Raspberry Cheese Fudge

··

Ingredients –

6 oz unsweetened chocolate

6 oz cream cheese, softened to room temperature

2 tsp evaporated milk or cream

4 cups powdered sugar

2 tsp vanilla extract *** OR 1 tsp vanilla extract and 1 tsp raspberry extract

1.5 cups chopped nuts (optional) i.e., hazelnuts, almonds or your own choice

Preparation –

Prepare an 8x8 pan by lining it with aluminum foil and spraying the foil with nonstick cooking spray.

Chop the chocolate into even pieces with a large knife. Place the chocolate in a microwave-safe bowl and microwave until melted, stirring after every 30 seconds to prevent overheating.

Place the softened cream cheese and the evaporated milk in the bowl of a large stand mixer and beat with the paddle attachment until smooth. (Alternately, a hand mixer can be used.)

Stop the mixer, add the melted chocolate, and beat until well-mixed. Stop the mixer again and add the powdered sugar and vanilla extract (or add raspberry extract in addition to the vanilla), and mix until the fudge is smooth and well-combined. Stir in the nuts by hand, if you're using them.

Pour the fudge into the prepared pan and spread it in an even layer. Let it set at room temperature for 2-3 hours, or in the refrigerator for 1 hour.

Once set, cut the fudge into small squares and serve at room temperature. Fudge may be stored in an airtight container in the refrigerator for several weeks.

(www.candy.about.com – Note; the author added the raspberry extract to the recipe)

"A Red, Red Rose"

O, my luve is like a red, red rose,
That's newly sprung in June,
O, my luve is like the melodie,
That's sweetly play'd in tune.

As fair art thou, my bonie lass,
So deep in luve am I,
And I will luve thee still, my dear,
Till a' the seas gang'dry

Till a' the seas gang dry, my dear,
And the rocks melt wi' the sun!
And I will luve thee still, my dear,
While the sands o' life shall run.

And fare thee weel, my only luve,
And fare thee weel a while!
And I will come again, my luve,
Tho' it were ten thousand mile!

Robert Burns (1721-1784)

"Changes in Latitudes, Changes in Attitudes"

"So many nights I just dream of the ocean
God I wish I was sailin' again

yesterday's over my shoulder So I can't
look back for too long

There's just too much to see waiting in front of me
And I know that I just can't go wrong"

"The Metal Detector That Found a Broken Heart"

The waves came barreling in, crashing at my feet and causing them to sink into the soft sand nearly toppling me over. They'd no sooner arrived than they'd left, taking with them any hope I'd harbored of finding that damn ring; the ring that I'd just so hastily and angrily tossed into the incoming tide.

I felt so utterly alone and stupid. What was I doing out here by myself on this windy isolated stretch of beach on this lonely island in Down East, Maine? The seagulls had even deserted me it seemed, leaving only the occasional terns darting back and forth in between the incoming and outgoing waves. They pecked furiously at whatever the sea had just deposited.

Did I really think I could find the ring; the ring that I'd worn so proudly until a week ago? Why had I held onto it? I clutched at my ring finger, rubbing my thumb and index finger around it in a back and forth motion, trying to massage away the memory of it. But all I felt was a cold emptiness where a symbol of love had once been.

At least I thought it was love. I had felt certain Cale loved me. Ours had been an instant attraction like a magnet slamming into steel. We'd met on the beach in Florida where we both live. We had literally slammed into each other.

It was an exuberant game of beach volleyball. As I tried to hit the ball I reached for the sky and in my enthusiasm slammed into Cale, knocking him to the ground, with me falling on top of him, my long auburn hair tumbling onto his shocked face. When I pulled my hair back my eyes were met by the bluest blue eyes I'd ever seen staring right into mine.

That had been our joke from that day forward; that we'd fallen for each other at exactly the same moment.

At 5'9" Cale wasn't much taller than my own 5'7" frame. We both had bodies to be proud of; Cale weighing a solid 180 pounds, all muscle and my weight of 120 pounds that fit perfectly into a tiny bikini.

Cale constantly showered me with gifts and attention; those beautiful boxes containing long-stemmed roses delivered to my door for no particular reason; *just because I love you.* Romantic dinners at the best restaurants followed by visits to the theater or opera; all the things that little girls dream of and here I was being treated to it all. I was living the dream.

The marriage proposal at midnight on our favorite beach, under an achingly beautiful starry sky was the thing that dreams are made of; no, this was no ordinary dream. It was a fairy tale. Cinderella should have been so lucky.

And then I saw them; together. Her arm looped through his, exiting a restaurant; his head inclined toward hers, smiling at her. Looking at her like he always looked at me.

Then he kissed her, long and lovingly; that's the moment my world came tumbling down on me, just like the waves that were now crashing around my feet. I never knew a heart could be so broken and yet keep on beating. A sucker punch to the chest could not have taken my breath away more.

Not believing my eyes, I just stood and stared, trying to craft his image into a stranger, someone I did not know; someone who perhaps just resembled him. But I'd know that handsome face anywhere, the strong, angular face, the jet black hair, the height, the build; everything about him just screamed Cale.

I didn't remember walking back to my car. I didn't remember anything after *the kiss!* That kiss that had once rocked my world; how ironic that it had such a different meaning now; it had rocked me nearly off my feet.

It started making some sort of sense to me; the times he cancelled our plans with a flimsy but somehow plausible excuse. Or was it just that I was too blinded by love to see him for who he really was?

And just who was he anyway?

The flame that had burned so brightly in the beginning had started to dwindle ever so imperceptibly; so slowly that I couldn't, or wouldn't, see it happening.

I had expected the inevitable confrontation to be volatile, explosive, followed by his begging my forgiveness and promising that it was just a momentary lapse in judgment. But it wasn't that way at all; Cale freely confessed his infidelity and admitted that he just loved the thrill of a new romance and had always had trouble sustaining relationships. No big deal! No big freakin' deal.

The marriage proposal was an impulse he explained, telling me that he'd intended to break off the relationship. He even asked if we could continue seeing each other on a casual basis; that he still cared very deeply for me but didn't want to be monogamous. I almost felt sorry for him – almost. He was a very disturbed man.

When he told me I could keep the ring I nearly laughed in his face. Of course I was keeping the ring. I might have been heartbroken but I wasn't crazy. It would bring a good price on Ebay! But I couldn't bring myself to sell it. Hope doesn't die easily. It's a long torturous process with many ups and downs like a wild rollercoaster ride; maybe he could benefit from professional help, maybe he really does love me, maybe, maybe, maybe.

I had to face the awful truth though. He seriously needed professional help and he didn't love me. Well maybe he did; the problem was that he loved not just me, but apparently all women. He'd never adjust to monogamy. I knew I had to get away for awhile to clear my head, to just get away from him.

✎✲◉

And now here I am, on a beautiful but lonely beach on Mt. Desert Island, Maine, where I'd fled in a feeble attempt to distance myself from Cale and everybody else who knew us as a couple. Far off Maine had seemed like a good idea at the time; a month of being by myself, recharging my emotional batteries, eschewing all men and relationships. But while my physical being was in Maine, my mind and heart were still back in Florida; although the pull was beginning to lessen somewhat helped by the distance and not seeing or hearing from him in a week. And of course, the realization that he wasn't a one-woman man.

Kneeling down, staring at the water, running my fingers through the wet sand, digging and clawing with both hands I wasn't aware of anything else. The tears were falling threatening to obscure my vision.

This is so hopeless. It's gone forever, just like my chance of my ever finding love again.

In my frustration I stood up too quickly and backed right into ... what? There was nothing here but me. But that *nothing* caused me to lose my balance nearly making me fall.

Catching me before I actually did fall was an extraordinarily tall man, roughly 6'5" as best as I could estimate in my startled frame of mind. His hair was dark brown and windblown hanging down over a craggy face with the deepest, darkest eyes I'd ever seen. He was holding a long strange instrument in his left hand which I knew was a metal detector but I was surprised he wasn't wearing a headset; the absence of which gave me a bit of concern.

Is it a weapon?

"Whoa! Look out. I'm sorry. I wasn't looking where I was going." The words startled me making my heart race and my hands shake. My throat immediately went dry and I couldn't swallow. I instinctively backed away trying not to scream; trying not to lose my footing.

"Why did you bump into me? I don't know what you're up to but ..."

"Please, relax. I'm not here to hurt you. Honest. This instrument that I'm holding, that you're staring at is not a weapon. It's a metal detector. And not a very good one either. Or it could just be my bad luck lately."

"Well I don't have any metal on me so there's no reason for you to have been so close to me. Sorry, but I'm not buying your story."

"No, I'm the one who's sorry. This is all my fault; well, mostly my fault. I was so intent on finding buried treasure that I honestly didn't see you; that is until you backed into me. I swear; *you* bumped into *me*! So maybe we're both partially to blame? Will you agree to that?"

"I will as long as you don't come any closer to me. I'm still not sure you wouldn't use that as a weapon and it's quite a formidable looking one too. If you're metal detecting where are your headphones?"

The stranger smiled; a quite disarming smile and then backed up several steps. Pointing to his ear, he said "This isn't a Bluetooth; it's actually the receiver for the detector. Headsets are too big and bulky."

"Okay, sounds plausible, I suppose," I said warily.

"I'll stand right here if it'll make you feel more comfortable. Here, I'll even put my metal detector down. It hasn't done me much good today anyway."

"I'm sorry. I haven't been myself this week and my nerves are frayed. I thought I was alone on the beach except for the few birds here and there."

"Keith."

"Excuse me?"

"Keith. My name is Keith Palmer. Normally I'd offer my hand when introducing myself but I don't want to give you any further cause for alarm." He flashed that disarming smile again.

"JessicaLynn. All one word. But my friends call me Jess," I said as I tentatively offered Keith my hand. But he didn't take it. Instead he placed his left arm in front of his waist with his right arm behind his back and then gallantly bowed. He actually bowed. What century was this, the fifteen hundreds?

"It's a pleasure to meet you Jess, if you don't mind me being so familiar."

"I don't mind at all Keith. And are you sure your name isn't Sir Walter Raleigh? All you need are pantaloons and a hat with a large plume on it. That bow was lovely and I appreciate your concern for my feelings. I'm not normally such a silly girly girl."

"Well we can pretend my metal detector is a wooden cane or a staff or whatever it was that he carried," Keith laughed.

"And I promise you I won't use it as a weapon."

"Well thank you for that. That's a wise choice too. I've got my brown belt in karate, soon to have my black belt. I'd hate to have to take you down."

"Oooh, I'm so scared Jess," Keith said as he raised his arms in front of his face in a defensive position, feigning fear.

"Sorry, I was being patronizing. Forget I said that. I'm usually quite the gentleman."

"Ok. I forgive you. You can lower your arms now. You look more silly than threatening," I said with a laugh in my voice.

"So what kind of treasure are you searching for Keith? Have you ever found diamond rings?"

"Ha! Nothing as grand as that Jess; I wish. So far though I've found some old coins. Nothing going back as far as Sir Walter Raleigh's time but some pretty rare coins nonetheless. It's just a hobby; something to take my mind off my troubles. But enough about me. What are you doing here? And why are you here by yourself?"

"I'm here because I'm an idiot Keith. I just threw a beautiful and might I add quite an expensive ring into the water. Don't ask me why. I don't have a good reason, other than what I just told you; I'm an idiot."

Taking a few steps toward me he reached his hand out and took mine and shook it, holding on to it a little longer than I'd expected he would, or should. "You're not an idiot Jess. I can tell. One doesn't have to be psychic to know you're suffering from a badly broken heart."

"I'm not so sure it's a broken heart as much as it's an angry heart now. I can't believe I was so taken in by such a, a scoundrel. Yeah, that's the perfect word for him, a scoundrel. Well that's the only polite word anyway."

"If you don't mind my picking up my detector Jess, I'll help you look for that ring. No promises though. I'm pretty certain it's on its way to the bottom of the ocean somewhere. But we metal detectors, I mean we metal detector people, don't give up because we never know what we'll find."

"Well I threw it right here," I said, walking to the water's edge. "I keep hoping the tide will bring it back in. But now I'm not so sure. I think it would just make me angrier looking at it, and yet not wanting to sell it would anger me too. I'm just totally confused."

As Keith moved the detector back and forth, listening earnestly for the ping that would alert him to something, I said "Oh, and did I mention that I'm through with men? Now and forever! You're all nothing but trouble. I'm sorry, I don't know you but you're a man so enough said."

Keith removed his earpiece, placed it in his shirt pocket and eyed me with a curious look on his face. He placed his hand on my shoulder and looked at me square in the eyes. "Tell me Jess. If you bought a carton of eggs and then discovered that one of the eggs was broken, would you throw the whole carton away? Would you assume they were all bad because one of them was? Hmmm?"

"Point taken Keith. But all the others would have to prove to me that there was nothing wrong with them before I tried them. They might look okay on the outside but inside they could be hard boiled just like men's hearts."

"Oh man, talk about hard boiled eggs Jess. Seems like you're the hard boiled one." His smile was so broad it didn't allow me to give in to indignation. We were dodging the cold waves that were rushing at our feet, smiling at each other, running back and forth like our little tern companions.

"Let me give it another shot Jess. Walk with me while I listen. Maybe we'll find that ring and if not maybe we'll find something else worthwhile."

We walked along the beach back and forth for a couple of hours, Keith listening and moving the detector sideways to and fro with me looking, searching. Every so often he'd stop, reach down and poke in the sand with his trowel, bringing up pull tabs from cans, a coin or two and one time a little silver necklace; but alas no ring.

We walked and talked getting to know each other, discovering many commonalities and very few differences. We both love coffee ice cream, big salads with Ranch dressing, and cheese omelettes with blueberry pancakes drowning in blueberry syrup – a local delicacy thanks to the abundance of blueberries growing all over the island - for Saturday breakfast. Our biggest difference is that Keith loves steak and I prefer veggie burgers. One passion that we both share is a love for animals.

I couldn't believe it when I found myself thinking *'Cale who'?*

"Let's sit down Keith. I don't think we're going to find any treasures today, least-wise my ring and I'm actually a bit tired. Walking on the sand is no ... well it's no walk in the park," I laughed. Keith looked at me and laughed along with me.

We moved away from the water, walking several yards to where I'd previously placed my blanket. We sat and stared out at the sea watching the little birds catching their dinner.

"I hope they have better luck than we did today Jess. I guess finding dinner is more important than finding any treasure; although I did find a whopping twenty cents." He laughed and rested his hand on my knee, giving it a playful squeeze which sent little tendrils of excitement up and down my spine.

"And don't forget the little silver chain. We could make a fortune on Ebay with our finds today. Maybe a whole dollar or two," I said as we both shared another laugh.

The hours were flying by as the conversation flowed as smoothly as the water that was puddling around our feet. The sky was beginning to exhibit deeper shades of pink streaked with orange and deep blue. I was falling in love with Down East Maine and falling in deep like with this gorgeous man sitting next to me.

Keith tentatively put his arm around my waist and leaned his head in close to mine. I could feel the heat of his breath on my cheek, while my heartbeats threatened to drown out the sound of the waves. He kissed me lightly on the cheek and nuzzled me.

"Have you given any thought to extending your vacation, Jess? A month isn't nearly long enough to explore all the beauty of this island and to appreciate its charm. You said you haven't even chartered a sailboat yet. I don't like to toot my own horn but I *am* one of the best, if not *the* best, captains in these parts. I have a thriving business, taking tourists out on my 32' DOWNEAST sailboat and suddenly I'm in need of a good First Mate."

"You don't already have one, Keith? How can you handle a boat of that size without a First Mate?"

Keith looked out over the water, his eyes twinkling, then turned his head toward me and said "my sister's my First Mate but she's expecting twins in about four months and she has to give up sailing now. I mean right now. I'm looking for someone capable and experience is not a prerequisite. I'm a good teacher. Know anyone who might fit that description?"

"I don't know Keith. I know someone who might be interested but she'd have to return home to Florida for awhile to tie up loose ends, pick up her two cats from her sister's house, resign from her job as hostess at a fancy restaurant and a couple hundred other things, but sure, I think she might be interested. It would be quite an adventure, I should think, but it's just a nice fantasy."

"Well, there you go Jess. You already have some of the qualities I'm looking for; being a hostess shows that you have people skills. And if you don't mind my saying so you look to be in top form too. I think you could really handle the job."

"I'm sure I could but how about the pay and the bennies?" I smiled at him.

"I'd need at least cat food money," I laughed while seriously contemplating his offer; all thoughts of Cale vanishing like a plume of noxious smoke.

"As I told you Jess, I have a very successful business which means I can afford to pay you top dollar and that includes enough money for the very best cat food for what I perceive to be two very spoiled cats. Am I right?"

"Gee, whatever gave you that idea Keith; the fact that I told you they get a saucer of whipped cream every morning along with their canned food, the very best kitty kibble and catnip treats?"

"Wow! I had no idea, but I'll match you food for food when it comes to spoiling pets. Lucky, my Heinz 57 mutt eats his kibble of course but he also eats whatever I eat. I know the experts advise against that but he had such a rough start in life I like to spoil him. He deserves that and a whole lot more."

I couldn't help smiling at this wonderful, kind man, not to mention looking into his drop dead gorgeous eyes. "You're a kind man, Keith. You certainly named him right. Lucky is certainly one lucky dog."

"We're both lucky Jess. He's given me as much as I've given him. Nah, he's given me a lot more. He's taught me trust and unconditional love."

I thought my heart would burst right then and there. I think that's when I realized I was falling for him, falling hard.

Keith moved even closer to me, boldly reaching his arm around me, asking me with his eyes if it was ok. "I'm a good egg, Jess. I promise. My heart was broken too, but I've found that you do get over it; it just takes time – or meeting a new person, a nice new person." His smile spoke volumes and I was an eager reader.

I grabbed his arm that he had draped around my shoulders and squeezed his hand. The smile that he gave me was warm and genuine. "I'm sorry to hear that Keith. If you feel comfortable telling me about it I'll be glad to listen. I'm a good listener and a good egg too," I said as a smile spread across my lips.

Keith leaned into me and brushed his lips lightly against mine. The wind had died down and dusk was settling in. The little terns had flown away and we were alone and it was the best 'alone' feeling I'd ever experienced.

"I'm going to kiss you Jess, a real kiss, not a peck on the cheek. I'm telling you so you don't ..."

I reached over and grabbed his head, pulling him to me as I covered his lips with mine. He leaned me back on the blanket and returned my kiss with an intensity that threatened to take my breath away; running his hand down along my hip, gently squeezing and kneading my buttocks, and then bringing his hand around to the front of my body caressing me, and gently massaging my breasts. He lifted my bikini top up over my breasts and encircled my nipples with his fingertips and then began planting kisses on my breasts. He trailed hot kisses down to my navel, where he playfully tugged on my belly ring sending tingling sensations down to my groin.

Removing his lips from mine, Keith gazed down at me, stroking my hair, and gently winding a long strand around his forefinger. He surprised me when he whispered "I'll stop now. We'll take this slow JessicaLynn. I don't want to scare you off. I want you to know that not all men are bad."

I cupped his face with my hands and kissed him on his beautiful, long, perfect nose. "And not all women are heartbreakers, Keith. We may be a bit hardboiled sometimes but I think most of us are pretty good eggs. And any woman who would break your heart would have to be a bit cracked. Yes, I know. That was a terrible, terrible joke ... or yolk if you will," I said as I groaned my face flushing.

"You're not only incredibly kind and beautiful Jess but you've got a great sense of humor. I like that in a woman. As for those benefits, I'd like to sign you up for them now," Keith said, his breath hot on my neck, dropping little kisses all over it and down to my breasts again.

Keith slowly traced his hands along my thighs easing my bikini bottom off as he hungrily climbed on top of me and began to deliver his promise of sweet benefits.

oxXo

The next morning I was awakened by the gentle rhythmic rocking of the sailboat and glorious sunlight streaming in through the porthole. Keith was not in the cabin. I called his name but there was no answer.

I suddenly realized I was naked and looked about the cabin for my clothes. I didn't have to look far; they were folded neatly on the bedside table. Lying on top of them was a neatly handwritten note.

"First Mate Jess, I assumed this would be the first place you'd look so I put this note here. I didn't want to wake you. You were sleeping like a baby, a beautiful baby I must say. I'll be back by 9 o'clock and I'll be bringing breakfast. Make yourself comfortable. I put fresh towels next to the shower for you and a fresh bar of soap. But you don't have to feel compelled to dress afterwards. (smile) Your Captain, Keith – but you can just call me Keith ... or sweetheart if you'd like. I know I'd like."

This man is unbelievable, but then I thought Cale was unbelievable when I first met him too. Oh my god I can't believe how wonderful he was last night on the beach. I can't believe we even did it on the beach. I can't believe I'm here in Maine, thousands of miles from home forgetting all about Cale and giving in to pure carnal lust with a man I've just met.

This was not what I envisioned when I fled Florida for Mt. Desert Island, Maine. All I wanted was solitude and to get away from Cale and any man and to give myself some time to heal, for my broken heart to mend.

Yet here I am lying naked, being gently rocked to and fro in a magnificent sailboat belonging to a man who had shaken the earth for me last night. And I'm damn glad I'm here; damn glad to be away from Cale and also wondering what in the hell I'm doing.

Rationally I realize I'm setting myself up for disaster; emotionally I say what the hell. Life is short. Carpe' Diem and what the hell, carpe' nacht.

I got out of the bed and walked into the shower. I took my time, washed my hair, and then dressed, and all the while thinking; thinking about what brought me here, what am I doing here and more importantly where am I going from here? And what do I really know about Keith? Is this really his boat? Is he perhaps a serial killer? What do I know?

Don't go there. It's too late. At least we used a condom. That's one point in his favor. Well, it's too late for regrets now. I'll just stay for breakfast and then go back to the inn and make some hard and fast decisions.

A few moments later I heard voices outside the stateroom door. It was Keith and he wasn't alone. Before I had a chance to panic, conjuring all kinds of scary scenarios with crazed cult killers, Keith yelled "Jess I've got company with me, are you dressed?"

Considerate; another good point in his favor.

I walked over to the cabin door and opened it, finding Keith and a striking couple standing there smiling. Keith grabbed me, and gave me a long kiss. "Good morning gorgeous. You look beautiful."

Turning to the couple, Keith said "Robert and Julia, I'd like you to meet JessicaLynn. Jess, meet my brother Robert and my sister-in-law Julia. We ran into each other as I was picking up breakfast and I invited them here to meet you. "

We shook hands and I felt a surge of relief, a feeling of calmness or actually it was an absence of dread most likely. He brought his family to meet me. That has to be good.

Keith invited Robert and Julia to have breakfast with us and we had an enjoyable time. The blueberry pancakes with choco-late covered blueberries and blueberry syrup were delectable. I learned a lot about this man who had asked me to be his First Mate. I couldn't believe I was seriously considering it.

"Well Jess it was so nice to meet you. I hope we get to see a lot more of each other." It was Robert speaking.

Julia echoed his sentiments and said "If you take Keith up on his job offer, then we'll definitely see a lot of each other. And we'd like that Jess. This is a wonderful place to live and Keith is one of the really good guys. You'll find that out if you choose to stay."

"It was wonderful to meet you too and believe it or not I'm giving consideration to Keith's proposal. His business proposal I meant to say." I could feel my cheeks flushing as soon as the words escaped my mouth.

As soon as the door had closed behind them Keith wasted no time in removing my blouse. I wasn't wearing a bra so his hands were able to cup my breasts in record time. I pulled his shirt off him and began unbuttoning his fly.

In seconds we were fully undressed and on the bed and Keith was kissing me, feathering kisses all over my face, kissing my breasts, fondling me all over, and pulling me to him clasping his hands on my buttocks and rocking me to ecstasy.

Afterward we nestled in each other's arms while being gently rocked and falling asleep listening to the waves lapping against the boat.

An hour or so later I awoke and found Keith lying on his side, looking down into my eyes, his head propped up on his right hand with his left hand gently playing with my hair. "You know, if you agree to stay and be my First Mate, I'll look for your ring every day," Keith promised as he gave me a beaming smile.

I took his hand and kissed it and said "I don't want that stupid ring anymore, Keith. A week ago it meant the world to me and now it means nothing. Just like that – nothing. Life is so strange isn't it?"

"Indeed it is Jess. A week ago I wouldn't have believed I could ever be happy again. Hell, yesterday morning I didn't think I could ever be happy again. Now I can't imagine not having you in my life. Please stay Jess. I think we both know we've got something good going on and it can only get better."

"Aye aye Captain; I look forward to being your First Mate. I truly do. And the benefits are awesome." I gave him a smile as big as the one he'd given me. He was right. This can only get better.

"You know what Jess? You're the best treasure my metal detector has ever found ... and I intend to keep you ... forever."

❧

. . . .

Chocolate Covered Blueberries

. . . .

Ingredients –

1 cup semi-sweet chocolate chips

1 tablespoon shortening

2 cups fresh blueberries rinsed and dried.

Directions –

Melt chocolate in a glass bowl in the microwave, or in a metal bowl set over a pan of simmering water. Stir frequently until melted and smooth. Remove from the heat, and stir in the shortening until melted.

Line a baking sheet with waxed paper. Add blueberries to the chocolate, and stir gently to coat. Spoon small clumps of blueberries onto the waxed paper. Refrigerate until firm, about 10 minutes. Store in a cool place in an airtight container. These will last about 2 days.

(www.allrecipes.com)

The first time ever I saw your face,
I thought the sun rose in your eyes

And the moon and stars were the gifts you gave
to the dark and the empty skies, my love,
to the dark and the empty skies

"The Wonder from Down, Down Under"

"Russell, sweetheart, I have a wonderful birthday surprise for you," Nikki whispered breathlessly into her sweetheart's ear as she stroked his very masculine jaw, dipping her fingers into his mouth as he slowly sucked each one. She allowed her hands to travel from his jaw down to his neck and chest and beyond. She stopped short of touching him where she knew he wanted to be touched and where she wanted to touch him. There would be time for that later.

Russell knew immediately that this would be the kind of birthday present that would knock a man's socks off. He knew it because his name wasn't Russell; it was Jack. But Nikki swore her beloved of nearly 10 years looked just like an older Russell Crowe, if not more handsome.

Russell Crowe was her fantasy man and Jack enjoyed hearing Nikki relate all the salacious encounters she dreamed up in her head about her and this sexy movie star.

"But I'm not telling you about it now Jack. You have one more day to wait until your birthday and your surprise," Nikki giggled.

"You know how I like to draw out the suspense."

"You're my little vixen and I know how you love to torture me is what you really mean. So now you have to pay the price." Jack's tongue found Nikki's as his right hand played over her breasts.

"Jack honey, you're driving me crazy as you always do. Oh, what the hell, come here. I haven't been able to resist you in ten years; I'm not gonna start now."

Jack stroked Nikki's hair and her neck, his fingers splayed across her back rubbing her up and down, then pulling her dress up around her waist, his hands feeling her hot naked flesh. He pulled her body onto his; lowering her onto his hardness, their bodies moving in unison; making love as only people who are truly in love can, with passion and enthusiasm balanced by tenderness and sweetness.

"I love you so much. I don't tell you that often enough. And babe, you really do knock my socks off. "

"I know. And I love you too." Nikki smiled as she kissed Jack on his cheek. Jack curled his arm around her as she rested her head on his shoulder and made a sound akin to purring. They laid in bed in comfortable silence and in no time, they had both fallen into a contented sleep.

⚘

The next day was a long one with Jack devoting the morning to business and the afternoon to his charitable endeavors. By 4 o'clock he needed a break. Removing his tie and unbuttoning the first two buttons on his shirt, he poured himself a neat scotch, and rested his long muscular legs on his office desk. His phone rang. It was Nikki.

"Ok babe, I'm ready. Lay it on me" Jack said, breathing into the phone held in place on his neck by his rugged jaw, while cradling his drink in one hand and fondling himself with the other.

One of the things that he loved about his Nikki was her ability to give great phone sex. He knew that she was fantasizing about Russell while talking dirty to him on the phone but that was fine with him. Jack had his own fantasies.

His fantasy woman wasn't a famous movie star. He would just envision some knockout blonde or redhead or a raven haired beauty with mocha colored skin. All his fantasy women had big double D cups, full luscious lips, a slim waist and legs up to there. Sometimes he'd envision Shelley, Nikki's best friend and his own lifelong friend.

Sometimes his fantasy woman would speak with a charming French accent or a titillating Italian one. Jack knew a few phrases and words from both languages and he would use them in his fantasies even if he did mix the languages up from time to time; *Oh, ma cherie, ciao bella.*

But who cared? These were his fantasies and he could say or do whatever he wished.

"No phone sex today, Jack, sorry. I know you're working late tonight so when you're finished I want you to drive to the marina and go directly to berth 10. Do not pass go," Nikki said in that seductive voice of hers.

"Lucky for you I'm a patient man, Nikki because the suspense is driving me crazy. It's driving Little Jack crazy too. You're one hell of a woman."

"And you're one hell of a man Jack but let's face it, we're not young kids anymore and we have to keep our strength for the really good times, not just little quickies now, ok? And Jack, I don't know why you call him 'Little Jack'. We both know that isn't true," Nikki giggled.

"You're right as always my love. Also, I never thought I'd find love again at my age, but meeting you has proven to me that there can be great times and great sex past the age of 50. Not that I'm past that age yet. I still have a few more hours to go before I exit my 40s. In spite of our little fantasies and age difference, I think we make a great team and are really happy together. You agree, right?"

"I'll show you just how much I agree ... tonight" Nikki purred into the phone.

"Now get back to work and be at berth 10 at 8 o'clock ready for your birthday surprise or birthday fantasy perhaps I should say."

"Oooo, this is really going to be a special treat Nikki. Who will you be tonight, a member of the French resistance during World War II, and you don't want me to know who you are?"

"Jack, stop thinking about it or you'll get yourself worked up again and ruin my surprise. I'll see you at the marina. Berth 10. I've rented this incredible yacht for the weekend. Not a Jack Jameson yacht of course, but still a beautiful one. Joe, the marina manager will be expecting you so he'll let you onto the dock."

Standing up, Jack said "Nikki, wait. Why would you rent a yacht anyway when I make the damn things?"

"Gee, I don't know Jack, maybe because you make custom yachts and it wouldn't be right to use them before the customer gets the chance to do so. Ya think?"

"Right as usual, my love. Always so considerate. Just another of the millions of reasons why I'm so crazy about you. See you soon. I love you."

"I love you too love of my life and Jack – get your hands off Little Jack. Ciao, my love."

Jack hung up the phone and took a swig of his single malt scotch. He let it slide down his throat, savoring the exquisite taste of it while he reminisced about all the out-of-this-world sexual escapades he'd had with his beloved Nikki. God he loved that woman. And tonight he was going to show her just how much he loved her. He had his own surprise in mind for her.

I wonder which one of us will be the most surprised.

Jack was so glad that he was rich and not just rich but Rich with a capital R. He knew that money didn't matter to Nikki because she was enormously wealthy in her own right, but she wasn't rich like he was. He could buy her the moon and the stars and not even put a dent in his wallet.

Nikki didn't squander his money either and that's one more thing that he loved about her. She was sensible with excellent taste and she loved to buy things for him with her own money. Still, there was one thing that Jack wanted more than ever now. Tonight he would find out for sure if he could have it.

He still had several hours to go before the appointed hour. Switching to ice cold water now to slake his thirst he leaned back further in the chair and let his thoughts flow to when he'd first met Nikki.

He'd been a 40-year-old entrepreneur who owned his own yacht building business. His family had been in the boating business for years and Jack had grown up on boats of all sizes. The sea was in his blood. He loved Mother Ocean. And he loved working with his hands.

When he was 15, he'd built a small rowboat all by himself, christening it Mother Ocean. Never mind that he couldn't take it out on the ocean, rather he'd use it for solitary sojourns along the inland waterways. But he knew this boat was merely a stepping stone to bigger boats that he would build one day; boats, and then small ships that would be seaworthy and make his father proud.

With the backing of the family fortune, money was no object to his goals and dreams. His family, however, insisted that he go on to higher education and become a well-rounded person, not just a boat snob.

So during the intervening years, he graduated from high school, then on to college for his Bachelor's degree in Oceanography with a minor in Marketing and then an MBA degree. If his parents wanted a well-rounded son he damn sure gave it to them. During this time he had just one passion though; boats, and the bigger and more luxurious the better.

His younger sister, Jillian, a natural-born altruist, had recently returned from working in the Peace Corps, in Malawi, Africa. Coming from a privileged family fueled her desire to help those less fortunate than she. Like Jack, Jillian had inherited the Jameson family stunning looks and generous nature. Everyone loved Jack and Jillian and all resisted the impulse to refer to them as Jack and Jill, at least not since grade school. Neither would have minded though given their good natures.

Smiling to himself, Jack reminisced about his success in building small crafts for the other local rich boys who had plenty of daddy's money to throw around. It wasn't any time before he had a thriving business with many good employees and a long waiting list for one of his creations. People were discovering if you wanted a superior yacht you contacted Jack Jameson. His yachts were regarded in as high esteem as any Berger yacht, a fact of which he was extremely proud.

By his 39th birthday his company was taking contracts for small yachts with luxe interiors, and superb craftsmanship for a fair and reasonable price. One thing Jack could never understand was greed. He was an honest and decent man with strong principles.

The women loved him, from the young 18-year-old movie starlet types to their equally attractive and horny mothers. Jack loved them all back. He was an equal opportunity lover and all around good guy. Not only did the women love him, but the men wanted to be him. He was so good natured, people found it hard to resent him, much as some tried. Jealousy does strange things to people. But Jack won everybody over with his charm and genuine honesty.

He was possessed of the most magnificent mane of jet black hair that fairly glistened in the sun. It came down to just above his shoulders and had a slight rakish wave to it. Now that he was turning fifty though, he'd cut his hair shorter. It was now a salt and pepper color though still with more pepper than salt. His eyes were a tantalizing combination of blue-green and favored either shade depending on which color shirt he was wearing. Thanks to incredibly good genes he had perfect skin, a long aquiline nose, and perfectly formed teeth; well that was thanks to a lot of orthodontia as a young boy, and a beautiful, luscious but masculine mouth.

At 6'4" with those long, muscular, well tanned legs, amazing biceps, and taut abs, he could have chucked the boat business and gone to Hollywood and been a movie star. Everybody knew that and Jack knew it too. But he wasn't interested in glitz, just boats.

He was a player for sure but had never found that one person with whom he wanted to spend the rest of his life ... that is, until he'd met Nikki.

His closest friend, Marcus, was throwing him a not-so-surprise 40th birthday party at the Warratah Yacht Club a few towns south along the beach. The Warratah had the prettiest location of any marina within miles, with its luxury yachts lined up along the piers featuring a backdrop of beautiful, swaying palms, huge ferns and a myriad of bougainvillea and hibiscus.

The inside of the club was magnificently appointed with crystal chandeliers, highly polished wood beams, brass and gold everywhere it seemed and stunning photos of Australiana adorning the walls.

The new owner of the club was an Aussie transplant; Nikki Robertson, 29 years old, with long, flaming red hair and emerald green eyes with gold flecks; endowed with flawless skin and teeth with naturally plump lips that all the women envied and paid their plastic surgeons handsomely to duplicate. She was neither too short nor too tall, standing at 5'6" but could appear much taller when wearing 3 inch spike heels which she loved to wear to emphasize her slender legs and well toned calf muscles. A generous size bosom along with a waspish waist, and firm derriere made her the object of many a man's desire, not to mention some bored housewives who wanted to add some sizzle to their lives.

She'd had her share of boyfriends and in fact had left the man she'd intended to marry back home in Australia. After a nasty drinking binge on his part where he beat her in a jealous fit, Nikki had walked. She was no man's fool or chattel and there would be no second chance given, as much as he'd begged her for one.

Longing to visit America and other parts of the world, she'd tidied up some business affairs and headed out on her big adventure. After three months of travel to exotic places and some not so exotic, she'd made her way to the east coast of the United States settling in West Palm Beach, Florida. It was there that she'd first seen the Warratah Yacht Club although it was known as Ocean Palm Yacht Club at the time. The owner had fallen ill and had no family and was desperate to sell.

Rumor had it that Nikki had inherited her money from a wealthy sheep-rancher father. Another rumor had her divorced from an oil baron, taking most of his money in a nasty divorce settlement. Neither was true. In actuality, she was just a working girl from the island state of Tasmania, located south of the state of Victoria on the mainland, down under, down under...until she won the Tattersall's lottery or Tatts as everyone called it.

Parlaying her winnings into rich investments thanks to the advice of her brother Ian, a wealthy, shrewd investment counselor, Nikki eventually found herself the richest woman in Tasmania. She was pretty high up on the list of the richest woman in Australia too; all this by the ripe old age of 29.

Nikki had become a shrewd businesswoman since her miraculous luck in winning the lottery and had negotiated a fine but fair deal for the club. Within a remarkably short amount of time, Nikki had put her own personal stamp on it, changing the name to the Warratah Yacht Club. She had settled in nicely, being accepted by the locals who all fell under the spell of her beguiling personality.

The Warratah, named after a beautiful Australian flower, was Nikki's pride and joy. She delighted in hand picking everything from the furniture to the fine wines, keeping a generous stock of Australian wine from the McLaren Vale wine country to the Barossa Valley. Nikki enjoyed a nice glass of "cab sav" as the Aussies call Cabernet Sauvignon and she was becoming quite the oenophile.

The first time he saw her he was smitten; that face; the face of an angel that he intuited belied a devilish side to her. Rumors of the sexy new owner of the newly named Warratah Yacht Club had piqued his interest; enough for him to drive down there and see for himself. He liked to think he came, he saw, he conquered. The truth is the attraction was mutual and immediate.

❧

The ringing phone brought Jack out of his reverie. "Hi there, handsome" Nikki's and Jack's best friend, Shelley, purred into the phone. "What's up?"

"Not a damn thing Shelley and that's the way it has to stay or I'll suffer Nikki's wrath. I'll ruin her surprise that she has lined up for later tonight, she said, if you catch my drift."

"Oh she doesn't want you to wear it out beforehand, huh? I get it. Then I won't talk dirty to you, Jack. Don't want Big Jack and Little Jack getting worked up before the big event."

Jack laughed, mentally recalling the harmless flirtations that he and Shelley always engaged in. Jack and Shelley had been good friends since childhood, and where you found one, you found the other. But no spark had ever ignited between them. They were just good friends, nothing more, who liked to indulge in innocent sexual bantering, knowing it would never lead to anything. Still, there was always the secret thrill of *what if.*

"So, what's on your mind, Shelley? You gonna tell me what Nikki's surprise is? Huh? Please?"

"Jack you know I'd never do anything to ruin your surprise or ruin anything for Nikki. She loves you with a passion and she'd do anything for you...and I do mean anything. So be a good boy, keep it in your pants and just have patience."

"But Shelley ..."

"But Shelley, my eye. I'm calling to ask you what you would like for your birthday and don't say a ménage a trois with Nikki and me because you know you could never go through with it. You'd feel like you were cheating on Nikki. So let's be realistic. What's your second choice for your birthday?" Shelley asked, as she fumbled around her purse, seeking her ever-ready pack of gum. So far it was helping her keep her no smoking resolution.

"What do you give a man who has everything, Shelley?" Jack asked earnestly.

"I have the most beautiful girlfriend in the world who adores me, we have our health and we're rich beyond our wildest dreams. Seriously Shelley, what more could any reasonable person want? Well there is one thing but only Nikki can give me that. Oh, and don't be so sure that I wouldn't like to have that ménage."

"Hmmm, Ok a tie it is then," Shelley laughed. "Maybe I'll splurge and buy you two ties, Jack."

"As long as one's wrapped around your naked body Shelley and one's around Nikki's, that'll do just fine" Jack said. Before he knew it, Little Jack was beginning to strain at his pants.

"Look, Shelley, I've gotta go. I have several things to do before I meet with Nikki later so go out and buy me those ties and we'll catch up later, Ok?"

Hanging up the phone, Jack sat at his desk thinking how much alike Nikki and Shelley were. Their bodies were both voluptuous with generous breasts, slim waists, and long legs. Shelley was only an inch shorter than Nikki and if you were in a dark room with both of them naked you'd have a hard time telling them apart.

So Jack had his own little ménage of sorts right there in his office — in his vivid imagination. *No harm, no foul, Jack old boy and you'll be able to perform for Nikki tonight,* Jack smiled to himself.

❧

The knock on the back door tripped Nikki's heart into a staccato beat. Even though she had orchestrated this whole forthcoming encounter, it still gave her gooseflesh thinking about it.

She walked to the door through her lavishly appointed kitchen with the Italian marble countertop and large Italian floor tiles. She had every conceivable cooking accoutrement hanging from the ceiling over the almost obscenely large island bar.

She kept asking herself if this was the right thing to do. Would Jack really be amenable to her surprise? And even more intriguingly would she be able to go through with it? Is this what she wanted too? Would Shelley chicken out?

Shelley was a model who was always looking for acting jobs. She landed a few bit parts in commercials and did some community theater. But she was always looking for ways to augment her acting chops. She not so secretly wanted to be the next big discovery in Hollywood...that is, if the producers and directors deigned to discover a 40-something-year-old woman.

Shelley was drop dead gorgeous with a body that wouldn't quit, along with all of the other attributes necessary to make it in the acting world today. She just needed the powers that be to discover her.

Nikki opened the door and greeted her best friend, Shelley, with a warm hug and a continental kiss on each cheek.

Not wanting to waste any time, Nikki said, "Come on in Shelley. Are you ready for the big show?"

"Of course I am, Nik. You know how much I love Jack and how much I love you and you know I'd do anything for you guys. Even kinky stuff" Shelley laughed.

"What was that noise? Did you hear that Nik? Sounded like a door shutting or something. Is Jack home?"

"It's probably the air conditioning unit Shel. I've got the repairman coming tomorrow. Sometimes it shakes rattles and rolls whenever it kicks in. Boy you're really nervous about this aren't you? You need some wine my dear."

Nikki led Shelley down the hallway to her bedroom where they could look through her enormous closets and try to pick out just the right dress. She'd brought a bottle of Shiraz and two glasses with her so they could relax while picking out clothes and plotting Jack's surprise.

"Are you sure that you're up to it too, Nikki?" Shelley asked as she hugged her best friend and waited for her reply.

"Yep, we're gonna do it Shel. I've been thinking about this for a long time. Part of me is hesitant but when I give it serious thought I really think Jack is gonna love it...don't you?"

"Hell yeah, he'll love it Nikki. Now let's see if we can pull it off. This is so damn exciting. "Oh, by the way, I called Jack and asked him what he wanted for his birthday. You know what he told me?"

"Knowing Jack and his quirky sense of humor Shel, the possibilities are endless. What did he say he wanted?" Nikki said as she held up the first of what would be many dresses in front of her.

"Ties! He said he wanted freakin' ties!" Shelley laughed.

"Ok, so he wasn't the one who actually suggested ties but he wouldn't tell me what he wanted so I told him I'd buy him a tie and he agreed. And now I'm thinking about how I'm gonna use those ties. He'll be sorry he ever agreed to them" Shelley said as she and Nikki convulsed into peals of laughter.

"I'm getting nervous though as it gets closer. What if Jack gets upset with us? I tried to feel him out about a ménage a trois and he seemed up for it. Don't worry I didn't tell him anything, but I'm so nervous."

"Shelley, breathe, breathe. Do you really think Jack would be upset by this? You're not thinking clearly. Jack adores you, always has and even though you're just good friends you must know that he fantasizes about you. And what man would turn down his fantasy woman?"

Getting off the exquisite divan where she had been reclining, Shelley began pacing around Nikki's and Jack's magnificent bedroom suite. Their king sized bed was covered with a luxurious, sinfully thick quilt that one could get lost in.

Shelley said, "Nikki are you absolutely certain you want to go through with this? I don't want anything to change our friendship...yours and mine or mine and Jack's, or for that matter, yours and Jack's relationship."

Watching Shelley pacing the bedroom Nikki smiled and reached out and grabbed her friend's hand. She drew her over to her and stared intently into her eyes. "Shel, I love you. Jack loves you. And more importantly, I know that Jack loves me more than life itself. I'm not worried that this one time episode will escalate into anything else. Jack will just be ecstatic to get this out of his system, to make love to his fantasy woman while his adoring girlfriend makes love to him."

"I know you're right Nik, but still I worry," Shelley said as she pulled her hair up into a pony tail, securing it with the elastic loop that she had in her pocket. She was beginning to feel the excitement thinking about what was to come.

"Shelley," Nikki said in all seriousness," if this ruins our relationship, then Jack and I most likely won't be taking it to the next level. But I know Jack and he'll be embarrassed at first but don't you worry about him; it won't be any time – seconds maybe – before he's into the whole thing" Nikki laughed.

"You're a great friend Shelley... to both of us."

Shelley poured them each a glass of wine and then asked Nikki the question that had been on her mind for some time. "Nik, how come you and Jack have never actually taken it to the next level – getting married? You never say and Jack clams up whenever I bring up the subject."

"It's pretty simple, Shelley. He's never asked me!"

"So you can't ask him?"

"I've thought about it many times during all these years but I always chicken out. I mean, we have such a great thing going, we live together and really the only thing that separates us from married couples is a little piece of paper. At least that's what I always tell myself."

"You really would like to marry him though, wouldn't you Nikki? Why don't you just ask him? Ask him tonight. What a fantastic birthday gift that would be for Jack."

"I know Shel. We've danced around the subject from time to time as something that might happen *someday*. But Jack is so focused on his business and his charitable work that I don't think he really seriously considers it. Besides, I did tell him early on in our relationship that I was not the marrying kind. I let him know I would be perfectly content just living together. And that's how it's been."

"Well, if you're both happy that's all that counts, I guess. And you're right; it *is* just a piece of paper. Look at how many married couples have that piece of paper and end up in divorce court. Still, I think you should ask him. You two have what it takes to make a marriage last. You've already been together longer than a lot of marriages have lasted. Anyway, it's no business of mine. Just stay happy!"

"No worries on that part, Shel. We are indeed very happy."

Pouring them each another glass of the Shiraz from the Warratah's fine collection, Nikki began to lay out the plan of how and when she would make her appearance in the bed. They both giggled as they envisioned various scenarios and picturing Jack's reaction to all of them.

Taking the last sip of wine from her glass, Nikki said "Well, I guess this is it Shel. The magic hour is almost upon us. Shall we go?" Nikki then walked her good friend through her incredible home to the kitchen where they stood and chatted and giggled like two school girls.

Hugging each other farewell, Nikki then gave Shelley a loving kiss on the cheek and said "Ok, girl. Get ready to give the performance of your life. You're always looking for acting jobs so here's your chance to put on a performance worthy of any award!"

"Feet, don't fail me now," Shelley laughed. "I have the most important audition of my life coming up."

"Don't fret, Shel," Nikki said, giving her dear friend a reassuring pat on the shoulder.

"Now go get ready and above all, do not panic. We'll pull this off. And think about it." Nikki said with a sly smile on her face. "Do you seriously think he'll leap out of bed, offended, and throw us both out of the stateroom?"

Throwing her hands up in the air, in an exaggerated theatrical gesture, Shelley responded "Oh my god what was I thinking? Of course he won't be upset. How could he be? He'll be in bed with two women who love him and whom he loves and wants to have sex with. Still ..."

Noticing the sudden wistful look on her dear friend Shelley's face, Nikki asked, "What's wrong, Shel? Listen, if you don't want to go through with this, you ..."

Shelley held up her hand in protest and took a deep breath. "Nikki, of course I want to go through with it. It's just that ... just that I wish I had someone who loves me as much as Jack loves you. I wish it could be David who was waiting in the cabin for me."

Grabbing Shelley by the wrist, Nikki led her over to the kitchen table. "Here, sit down, hon. I'll be right back. We forgot something."

Seconds later Nikki returned to the kitchen with the fabulous dress she was lending Shelley, along with the half empty bottle of Shiraz. "We left this in the bedroom," she said, smiling at Shelley. Grabbing two wine glasses from the overhead rack, Nikki poured the remaining wine into hers and Shelley's glasses.

"Now, let's talk. What's this about David? I've always felt you two were perfect for each other but you never seemed to pay him any mind."

Taking a healthy swig of the wine, Shelley then nervously traced her fingers around the rim of the glass. Looking up at Nikki, Shelley smiled sheepishly and told her friend that she and David had had a delicious one night stand a couple of weeks ago. "It's true,

Nik," Shelley said, noticing the astonished look on her friend's face.

Her mouth hanging open, Nikki could only utter a surprised "What?"

"Two weeks ago David and I ran into each other at your marina. It was the first time we'd seen each other in about six months. The last time we were in each company's company, we had a little flirting thing going on but it never went anywhere. And don't even ask me why not because I don't know why not. Maybe I was apprehensive because he's eight years younger than I am. Or maybe he wasn't interested because I'm eight years older than him. Anyway it never went anywhere. We passed by each other one time. I was in a hurry to get home and feed Clancy and let him out and then make it to an audition on time. So it was just a quick hello. But still, I always felt there was something between us."

"Helllllloo, Shelley. Tell me how a 'quick hello' went to a roll in the hay ... or wherever you did it," Nikki exclaimed, barely able to contain her excitement.

"Tell me everything and don't leave anything out, not one single kiss or tongue fencing or caress or whatever!" Nikki giggled, feeling the light effects of the wind traveling through her body.

"I knew you two would make a great couple. And hey, why didn't you tell me this before? I've never known you to keep a secret."

"Well apparently David doesn't think we'd make such a good couple, Nikki, even though sometimes I do," Shelley lamented. Looking at the clock on the wall, she knew she didn't have time to dawdle but she also knew there was no way Nikki was letting her out of the house until she *fessed* up.

"Well, I was helping Uncle Bob polish the brass on his yacht. He has staff to do just that for him, as you know, but he uses my helping him as an excuse to talk about Aunt Sheena. Ever since she passed away, he's been so lost. So, anyway we were talking and polishing, enjoying our time together when Uncle Bob looked over my shoulder and yelled "Hey, my man."

I couldn't believe my ears ... or my eyes. When I turned around there was David standing on the dock looking absolutely stunningly handsome; and sexy as hell. I'm sure my mouth was agape and I couldn't think of a thing to say ..."

"Except, hello," Nikki laughed.

"Ha! I don't even think I said that, Nik. For some reason this guy just takes my breath away – literally. The next thing I know, David was asking Uncle Bob, 'Permission to come aboard, sir.' And that's what he did. He came on board, walked over to Uncle Bob, shook his hand, and said 'How are you, man? Sorry, I mean Captain.'"

"And the next words out of his mouth, before Uncle Bob got a chance to say anything, were, 'You've got the prettiest helper in the whole marina; lucky you.' And then he looked at me and winked! "

"Yeah, yeah, so now we've gone from hello to a wink. Get to the good part, girl," Nikki laughed, gesturing with her hand which almost knocked her wine glass to the floor.

"Well ... the three of us talked for what seemed like forever because I'm telling you all I could think of was getting him in the sack. Oh, I'm gonna burn in hell, I know it, but damn, I wanted him," Shelley giggled.

"And he wanted me too because he hung around. Even when Uncle Bob said that he had to leave, David smiled and said "You don't mind if I hang around and help Shelley with the polishing, do you, Bob?"

"I hope David didn't think he was pulling the wool over your Uncle Bob's eyes, Shel, because Uncle Bob is nobody's fool."

"Oh, hell no, Nik. I think Uncle Bob knew what was happening before I did. He just laughed and said 'Well I've never heard it called that before David but what do I know? I'm just an old geezer now I guess. "

Uncle Bob gave me a big hug and pointed to the sign next to the port hole. He actually looked a little happy when he left."

"What sign? I don't recall any sign on his boat – excuse me, I mean his yacht. And that sure is a Yacht with a capital Y."

"The sign that says 'If this yacht's a'rockin', don't come a'knockin.' I know, I know. I can't believe he keeps that tacky sign on there either. I guess it reminds him of all the fun times he and Aunt Sheena must have had."

Pointing an imaginary gun at Shelley, Nikki said with exasperation, "That's nice, it really is but if you don't get to the good parts quickly, I'm going to have to shoot you."

Squeezing Nik's finger, Shelley replied, "Well, save your bullets, Nik. Here's the good part – the Reader's Digest version. We talked, we drank, and we had hot and heavy sex. Here's the bad part - We talked, we drank, and we had hot and heavy sex and that was it! End of story. I didn't tell you about it because I was hoping to have a better story – one with a happy ending, but when that didn't happen I was too embarrassed to tell you."

Nikki gave her friend a loving hug and smiled. "Shelley, I happen to know for a fact that David really digs you. He's always had a thing for you but from what Jack's told me, he worries about the age difference. It doesn't matter to him but he thinks it bothers you. He also thinks he's not good enough for you."

Taking a sip of her wine, Shelley managed to smile and said "Well, he sure was good enough *to* me, Nik. Boy was he good. I could definitely go for more of that – a lot more! But he hasn't called and I'm too proud to call him."

"Well, perhaps you need to take your own advice, Shelley," Nikki smiled at her friend.

"Touche', Nik. You're absolutely right. I *will* call him. Thanks. But first ..."

Taking one last sip of the wine, Shelley put her glass down and got up from the bar stool. "I've gotta go Nikki. I have things to do to get ready for tonight. Don't worry about me. I'll be fine. Honestly. Especially if I call David and he wants to see me again. But I'm still unsure about calling. We'll see; maybe tomorrow."

Shelley picked up the dress she was borrowing from Nikki and carefully placed it over her arm. Nikki watched her friend walk out the door. She hoped that Shelley and David would hook up and be as happy as she and Jack are.

Nikki walked down the hall to her bedroom when she thought she heard the sound of the kitchen door closing. Wondering if Shelley had walked back into the house for something, Nikki called out "Shelley, is that you?"

When there was no answer, Nikki went back into the kitchen but found the door closed, and locked. "That's strange, I could swear I heard a noise coming from here ... and ... well, what do you know? It was you, you little devil," Nikki laughed as she spied the 'person' who was responsible for the noise in the kitchen nook.

She had spied Pierre, her spoiled gray and white *pound* cat, whom she suspected really did think he was a human, rolling on the floor with leaves of catnip clinging to his whiskers and fat belly. The wooden bowl that she kept the catnip package in was upended next to him.

"Bad boy, Pierre. Now, I'm going to have to find another place to keep your drugs," Nikki laughed as she picked up the 15 pound cat that she'd rescued from the local humane society nine years earlier.

He was one of those rare cats who were not cuddly or handsome. In fact, the workers at the shelter felt sorry for him, figuring he'd never be adopted because of his looks. He'd been brought into the shelter by a county worker who'd found him at the landfill scrounging for scraps of food.

Pierre was very malnourished and had evidence of previous altercations with other cats, judging by the missing pieces of his ears and chunks of missing fur. He was missing two upper teeth and one in the front on his lower jaw was broken. The shelter workers named him Rocky for his pugnacious attitude and heart and they gave him plenty of TLC.

It was a joyous day for all, the day that Nikki walked into the shelter in search of a cute cuddly little kitten. The fact that she walked out of the shelter with Rocky was testament to Nikki's kind nature and her inclination to champion the plight of the underdog ... or, in this case, the undercat.

Rocky, whom Nikki promptly renamed Pierre, believing he deserved a new and dignified start in life, thrived under her constant care and loving attention and multiple visits to the vet. Jack had always claimed that he was allergic to cats but miraculously lost his so-called allergy once Pierre won him over. He was definitely their baby and spoiled unashamedly by both Nikki and Jack.

Nikki placed the bowl back on the counter, cleaned up the remaining catnip and stuck the half-empty bag in the refrigerator. "You behave yourself Pierre or no more catnip for you, understand? I've gotta take my shower now, so try to stay out of trouble."

Relieved that it was just Pierre causing the noise and not an intruder, Nikki turned the shower on and then began undressing. She stepped into the shower and let the hot water run over her head and down her chest, soaping and massaging her breasts. She was going over the seduction plan in her head, growing more excited anticipating Jack's reaction to her birthday surprise. She was also contemplating Shelley's advice to her.

Shelley's phone rang, startling her. She was rehearsing her part in tonight's events when Nikki called. "Hey Shel, how are you, hon? You still on for tonight?"

"I guess ... yeah, Nik, I'll do it. I don't know ... I've been giving it a lot of thought and one part of me really wants to do it, and the other part, doesn't. It's exciting but is it wrong?"

"It's only wrong Shelley if you do it and don't want to. This is entirely your call. If you decide not to go through with it, you can just give Jack the ties, and I'll give him, well I'll give him something else that I know he'll enjoy," Nikki laughed.

"Either way, he'll be happy. You know how easy going Jack is and besides, he'll say it's the thought that counts."

"Nikki, I don't want to disappoint you. Tell you what, I'll go to the marina, and see what happens. If I chicken out, we'll just tell Jack what we were going to do and let the chips fall where they may." Ok, Nik? Please say you won't be upset if I can't do it. Then again, I may," Shelley giggled nervously.

"Whatever floats your boat, Shelley. Or whatever floats your yacht in this case. Wink, wink. It's all good and we'll make sure Jack has a great birthday. We'll all have fun. And don't you worry your pretty little head about it. Besides I've got his other big birthday gift for him, don't forget."

"Right you are. See you soon and thanks for being understanding, Nikki. Then again, you always are. No wonder we all love you."

"Thanks Shel. Love you too. Well, I have to do my makeup and hair and get dressed. I've changed my mind. I'm wearing the red sarong. Its' an oldie but Jack loves how it looks on me."

"Gee, you've changed your mind – again. What a surprise. I'd have been shocked if you didn't." Shelley laughed into the phone.

"Pot calling the kettle black, girlfriend. Okay we have to be at the marina in one hour so I'd better start moving. Don't forget, it's berth 10."

❧

Jack was almost dizzy with anticipation. What had his quirky, wonderful sweetheart concocted for his 50th birthday?

"I know Nikki and I know that she'll throw her entire being and imagination into this surprise" Jack said to Marcus, who had stopped by his office.

"Jack, just stop thinking about it. You're beginning to act a bit girly," Marcus laughed as he slapped his best friend on the back and gave him a few playful punches.

"If you over-think it you might end up disappointed and that would just kill Nikki."

Sitting in Jack's office, smoking a real Cuban cigar, Marcus began reflecting on how fortunate they both were, how well their lives had turned out and how incredibly lucky Jack was to have found such a gem as Nikki.

"Nikki and Shelley are two of the three best catches in Florida, maybe even the entire country Jack, and you reeled in one of the best. I almost envy you man" Marcus said with a twinkle in his eye, while blowing out a long swirl of smoke.

Jack sat up straight in his chair and exclaimed "Hold it right there Marc. What are you talking about? Two of the *three* best catches? Who's the third one? Been holding out on me, my friend?"

"Well," Marcus drawled, "you're rich beyond most people's dreams, and you're a successful and savvy businessman, but your skills of observation are sadly lacking, my friend."

Slapping his hand on one knee, Jack gave his friend a suspicious look. "What the devil are you talking about, Marc? I didn't amass my fortune and become a hugely successful builder of luxury yachts, by being stupid."

"Hold on there, Jack," Marcus laughed as he blew a smoke ring in Jack's face. "I didn't say you were stupid, bro. I just meant if we were yachts – that is, my girl and me – you'd have damn sure paid attention to what was unfolding right before your very eyes."

Marcus stood up and reached for the bottle of scotch. After pouring himself a generous serving, and one for Jack, he handed Jack the glass and said "I can't believe we've pulled the wool over your eyes for these past three weeks."

"Oh, hell, Marcus, if it's only been three weeks, you can't blame me for not noticing. It isn't like I see you every day and when I do see you, you're not talking to anybody but Jillian. Maybe I should have asked Jill who you're seeing. I'm sure she knows. Probably all the women in town do. That's a woman thing for you."

"Yeah, man. Jillian knows for sure," Marcus said, barely able to contain his glee.

"Ok, this is getting too girly, Marc. Tell me – who is this mystery woman who's been hiding right under my nose? I don't get it. I'd always hoped that you and Jillian would hit it off."

The laughter that arose from Marcus's throat stopped Jack in his tracks.

"Wait! You're kidding me. You? And Jillian? My sister? Get outta town! This is unfreakingbelievable."

"So I take it you approve, man?" Marcus said as Jack dashed over to him and gave his friend a huge bear hug.

Grinning from ear to ear Jack said, "I couldn't have picked a better guy for my sister, not that she let me, mind you. She found you on her own. I always said she was the smart one in the family. Well, congratulations, my friend. You know you're getting one hell of a woman. And if you two get married – you are going to get married, aren't you? – then you'll be getting one hell of a brother-in-law."

Marcus was happy that his best friend was happy for him. "We haven't set a date or anything yet, it's still early, but yeah, we both know this is it. It'll happen and of course you'll be my best man."

Marcus hesitated and then said, "Speaking of marriage Jack, when in the hell are you and Nikki going to take the plunge? I know she says she's happy just living with you, but do you really buy that? Don't you think most women want to get married?"

"Don't let *them* hear you say that Marc. That's not how the women of *today* think, or at least that's what it seems like. Hell, Marcus I've recently been giving the marriage thing serious thought; really serious thought. So much thought that I'm going to pop the question tonight, if you'll pardon the cliché. It's time. I'm 50 now and I think I'm ready to grow up. If Nik says no, then we'll just continue the way we have been and I'll still be the luckiest guy in the world. But ... I really hope she says yes! Man, I love this woman. I can't believe what an idiot I've been all this time."

"Hey man, we can get really girly now and start talking about a double wedding. Ha! Oh my god, don't you ever tell anyone I said that or I'll have to kill you," Marcus laughed.

"Don't worry about that Marc. This conversation never leaves this room ...girl," Jack said doubling over in laughter.

"Ok, ok, man" Marcus said, laughing himself.

"Point taken. Here, do you think Jillian will like this, Jack?" Marcus opened a small velvet-lined box and showed it to him.

"Damn, Marc, that's one hell of a diamond ring. Who wouldn't like that? Although knowing my sister she'll probably want you to exchange it for a smaller one and donate your money to charity."

Marcus put his drink down and relit his cigar that had gone out. Blowing the smoke out, he looked at Jack and said "that's one of the great things about your sister, Jack. She's just like you – always looking out for the under privileged. But I'm hoping I can convince her that once in awhile we have to enjoy our wealth."

"Speaking of wealth, Marc, I know this is a bit indelicate but where in the hell did you get the money to buy such a rock? Your yacht building business must be picking up and I'm really glad about that. There are plenty of customers around for both of us."

"Sometimes you need only one big job to make it all worthwhile. But you're right, I've been enjoying great success and then this one big contract came my way and I had to take it. We're really lucky Jack. I never lose sight of how fortunate we are."

"This is too much, man. Two great surprises in one day," Jack said while rubbing his palm along the back of his neck.

"And speaking of great surprises, Marcus, I've got some things to do before I meet Nikki at the marina. I want to stop by Rosella's pastry shop and pick up her favorite dessert, chocolate lamingtons. Did you know that Nikki helped Marlene, a fellow Aussie, open this shop? Don't know why Marlene would name a pastry shop after a parrot that only eats nuts and seeds, but some of those Aussies are a bunch of wags. But you've gotta love 'em. They're fun-loving people. Don't know what she's got in store for me, but knowing Nikki, you know it will be something different, to say the least."

"Oh yeah, it'll be different alright," Marcus agreed.

Both men walked to the door, smiling. "Well, I've got a date with an angel myself, Jack. So I'll catch you tomorrow. Happy Birthday buddy and all that."

As Marcus walked out the door, Jack hollered, "Well, tell your little angel she has some explaining to do to me, not telling me that she had hooked up with you."

Marcus grinned and kept on walking, raising his hand up over his head in a wave.

❧

Jack was whistling as he hung up the phone. He had left the office earlier soon after Marcus did. He'd encountered yet another surprise while taking care of business; one that was responsible for the whistling now.

He'd returned to his office, feeling gleeful and upbeat. He was looking forward to his birthday surprise more than Nikki could know. Jack was generous almost to a fault and loved to give even more than he loved to receive. Tonight he would do both.

As he was driving to the marina, the rain began to splash on his windshield. Jack and Nikki loved the rain, always saying that it was playing their song. So many wonderful memories of birthdays past played in his head like a slow motion slideshow. Memories of their ten years together, the happiest years of his life, interspersed with the sounds of their rain song, kept a smile on Jack's face and a thrill in his heart.

His thoughts drifted to Nikki's body, as they always did, and the wonderful way she used it to give him pleasure. He marveled at her skill in the bedroom or in her marina or in his office or anywhere they were alone. She loved sex and she loved him and she knew how to show it. Her tongue drove him crazy and her hands ... yeah, she knew what to do with her hands, and her tongue, and her body.

By the time he arrived at the marina the rain had stopped and the stars were winking down at him. It was one of those perfectly wonderful summer nights that turned everyone into a romantic.

Walking along the wharf, Jack took note of the berths until he came to number 10. His mind was so occupied with what would soon unfold that he didn't notice Nikki standing on the deck of the yacht next to berth 10, watching him.

"So far, so good," Nikki said silently to herself.

"He didn't notice me. This is off to a good start. Ok, Shelley, come on now. Jack just went on board and will be waiting. Come on, Shel," Nikki said, trying to urge her friend on telepathically.

The dock was quiet with only a few people coming to and from their boats. The male figure making his way onto berth 10 went unnoticed by Nikki; so absorbed was she in going over the upcoming scenario in her mind.

Within a few minutes Nikki caught sight of Shelley making her way along the dock. She checked her watch, made a mental note of the time and began the countdown. Soon Jack would realize just how much she loved him.

She loosened the belt around her stylish trench coat ensuring that it would slip off her easily and quickly, revealing her nakedness. She'd had another change of mind before she left their house and decided to forego the dress. Her body began to heat up in anticipation of such a daring act; a ménage a trois with the love of her life and her best friend.

After 15 minutes had gone by, Nikki disembarked from her friend's yacht and slowly made her way onto the yacht in berth 10. She didn't know what scene would greet her. Would she find Shelley and Jack in the throes of passion? Would she be jealous if she did? That thought was beginning to creep into her mind. If they were indeed having sex, would Nikki have the guts to join them and give Jack the thrill of his lifetime?

Or would she find them sitting in the saloon, embarrassed by the failed plan because Shelley couldn't go through with it? Would they be laughing? Would Jack be upset because he didn't get his ménage a trois? The uncertainty was driving her crazy.

"It's now or never, Nik. Here we go," Nikki said to herself. Creeping stealthily onto the deck, Nikki listened for sounds of ... of what? Of love making, of laughter? She didn't hear anything other than light music emanating from inside.

"Ok, Shel didn't back out, I guess. The music's a good sign. It's show time, Nikki." Quietly opening the door to the saloon, Nikki was greeted by a lighted room instead of darkness.

Staring back at Nikki's astonished face were the smiling faces of Jack, and Shelley. But even more astonishing was who was sitting next to Shelley with his arm around her: David.

"What? Wh ... What's going on? Jack, tell me ... what's going on here? Shelley?" Nikki said looking at her friend beseechingly.

"And David? Nice to see you but geez, what are you doing here? I'm sorry, I don't mean to be rude but I feel like I'm in the Twilight Zone," Nikki laughed self-consciously.

Jack walked over to Nikki and gave her a huge bear hug followed by a hot, passionate kiss that seemed to go on forever. "Well ... I have a confession to make Nik. Come here. Sit down. All will be revealed, if you'll just give me a few minutes to explain.

Jack began his explanation, pausing only to take a sip of his scotch and to give Nikki kisses. He explained how he had gone back to the house earlier, riding there on his bicycle because of the glorious Florida weather.

"So that's why I didn't see your Porsche in the driveway. I also didn't notice the bike parked anywhere. Then again I wasn't looking for anything. Go on ..."

With a sheepish look on his face, Jack continued explaining ... "I stopped by the house to pick up my allergy pills. I didn't have any left at my office. I'd had an attack while I was at the office right after Marcus left, and figured I'd just come home, pick them up, grab a bite to eat and then ride into town to do a few errands. You weren't home when I got to the house."

"But I never left the house all day Jack ... oh wait, I did go next door to lend Dolores my diamond and emerald bracelet that she wanted to wear to the charity ball this weekend. I couldn't have been gone more than five minutes though because I was waiting for Shelley to come over."

"Well that's when I came home then. I was in our bathroom when I heard you and Shelley come into the bedroom. I was getting ready to yell to you to let you know I was home so I wouldn't frighten you but you and Shelley were talking about your big plan and right away what you were saying got my attention. So I kept as quiet as a church mouse. I know I was eavesdropping or ear-wigging as you Aussies say," Jack laughed, "but I think you'd have done the same, right?"

"You've got that right! Lucky for you our bedroom suite is almost the size of some people's apartments, otherwise we may have discovered you."

"I know. I really lucked out on that one."

"So you stood there and listened to our devious plan? You heard ... *everything?*"

"Every giggle, every single word and I'll tell you what ... I was getting really worked up! It was all I could do to control myself and not burst into the bedroom and take you both right then and there," Jack laughed.

"Crikey!"

"Crikey is right. You almost caught me Nik. I breathed a big sigh of relief when both of you finally left the bedroom. I stood there in the bathroom pondering what I'd just heard. I was ready to sneak out when I heard you tell Shelley that you had forgotten something so I knew you were coming back to the bedroom. I quickly beat it out of there and ducked into the study, just missing colliding with you by seconds. I didn't realize I could be so stealthy, James Bond and all that. I stayed in the study until I heard Shelley leave and you go back into our bedroom. Then I sneaked out of the study, and crept into the kitchen nook where I was sidelined by Pierre. The little bugger ran right over my feet causing me to trip."

"That's too funny Jack. Sometimes I swear he does these things on purpose," Nikki laughed.

"I don't *think* he does, Nik. I'm sure of it," Jack said. "The little devil caused me to knock the bowl, where we keep the catnip, on the floor. I didn't even have time to scold him; I just beat feet out of the house, grabbed my bike and took off."

"Sure, as if you would scold Pierre," Nikki said laughingly.

"And he knows I wouldn't. He's spoiled rotten."

Taking a long drink from her glass, Nikki tried to gather her thoughts while swallowing. She was trying to recall every word that she had uttered when she suddenly remembered that she and Shelley had discussed the M word – marriage.

Oh please dear God, make him forget he heard that. Maybe he didn't. Sure, like that's possible. He said he heard every word!

"Well, sweetheart, if you heard our plans, what stopped you from going through with them? How did David get here?" Turning to look at Shelley who was sitting snug up against David, Nikki asked "And what about you, Shel? What changed your mind?"

Jack held up his hand and said "Whoa, Nik. Let me continue, babe."

Turning his attention to Shelley and David, Jack smiled broadly at both of them. "Shelley, I've known for quite awhile how

David feels about you and I also know that for all his bravado and machismo, he's really a shy guy. Then when I heard you say how you feel about him and that you two had a ... well, you know ..."

"A one night stand, Jack," David cut in.

"We can talk about it. We're all adults. But I was hoping it wasn't a one night stand. I wanted more but for some reason I got it in my head that Shelley wasn't that into me so I never called her. I'm sorry Shelley ... but I've already told you that tonight," David said, while kissing Shelley on the top of her head.

"Ok, I can dig that, David, but ..."

"So I called David, and asked him to meet me here at the marina. But first I explained everything to him on the phone," Jack said. "And I was actually going to turn Shelley down, that is if she had wanted to go through with it. I never thought I'd be happy for a woman to say no to me."

"And Nikki, when I got here, I knew I couldn't go through with it," Shelley interrupted.

"Sorry Jack, I love you but I guess that kind of thing just isn't in me. It sounded exciting to be sure, but with each step I took along the pier, I knew it wasn't going to happen."

Shelley looked at David and blushed." I kept thinking about David and what he would think. I was going to call him tomorrow and ask him out. And how would I explain me having a ménage a trois?"

Laughing aloud, Jack exclaimed "And you should have seen Shelley's face, Nikki, when she walked in here and saw both me and David sitting here. It was bloody priceless."

Squirming in her seat, Shelley managed to whisper "Not only priceless, but embarrassing as all hell. I hoped David would believe that I'd changed my mind."

"I believed you Shel," David said as he hugged her and pulled her closer to him. Jack's not bad looking and all that but I knew you thought I was hotter," he said as they all laughed.

"Definitely! Sorry Jack. We're still best friends, right?"

"You know it babe. You know why? Because I know I'm hotter than him!"

Nikki's voice interrupted the laughter. "You know what Jack?" I'm glad it didn't happen either. I was having my own doubts while standing on the deck of the Yankee Pride in berth 9. I didn't know what I'd find when I came on board. But I can guarantee you I didn't expect to see this scene."

Jack walked over to the refrigerator by the bar and brought up a magnum of Clos du Mesnil champagne.

"Jack," Nikki uttered, "that's extravagant. I know you can afford it love, but that's not like you to spend $750.00 on a bottle of bubbly. What's gotten into you?"

Jack deftly popped the cork and then poured the champagne into four glasses. "This calls for a toast."

"Hear, hear," everyone chimed in.

Raising his glass as everyone raised theirs in unison, Jack said "I know it's extravagant Nik, not by our standards of course because we can afford it, but it did make me feel a bit foolish spending that kind of money on a champagne that quite frankly I couldn't distinguish from a Dom Perignon, but you only turn 50 once, right?

"I don't know, Jack. I'll probably turn fifty at least four or five times."

They all laughed and Nikki said "And you are so worth it sweetheart."

"And so are you, love of my life."

Turning to Shelley Jack smiled and said "Shelley, you've been my lifelong friend and I love you – even though you wouldn't have sex with me." Everyone shared the laugh as Jack continued, "And David you're a damn good friend. I'm glad you and Shelley have found each other."

Then, wrapping his arm around Nikki's waist, clinking his glass against hers, he looked deep into her eyes and said "Nikki, I love you more than you will ever, ever know. I can't thank you enough for arranging the ménage. But as much as Shelley loves me and I love her too, I love you the most. You're my girl, my woman, my lover, my best friend. You're my world, my universe. You're my everything, Nikki. I don't want to make love to anyone but you, now and forever."

They all took a drink of their champagne and watched the love story unfolding before them.

Jack gave Nikki a kiss, a beautiful, loving, tender kiss, his tongue tasting of champagne which Nikki licked with her own tongue. Then he took a step back and put his champagne glass on the table. What he did next took Nikki's breath away – literally. They all watched, mesmerized, as Jack went down on one knee and took Nikki's hands in his.

"Nikki, babe, it's time. We've skirted around the marriage issue for years. We're not getting any younger. Especially me," Jack laughed nervously.

"This afternoon when I heard you say that I've never asked you to marry me, I realized what a fool I've been. It's all I've wanted for so long but didn't really realize it, I guess."

"Oh, Jack it's my ..."

"Wait, let me finish. Nikki, I love you more than life itself. Will you do me the honor of marrying me and letting me spend the rest of my life proving to you how much I love you? Will you, please? Nikki? Please? Say something, say yes."

"Well if you'll be quiet and give me a chance, Jack, I'll say not yes, but hell yes!" Nikki let loose in delight.

Jack stood up and swept Nikki into his arms, bending her backwards in the best old Hollywood movie star style. Looking down at her beaming face, Jack said "I love you, Nikki Robertson – soon to be Nikki Jameson. Oh hell, you will take my name, right? Or not. That's OK too. Whatever you want; just as long as you marry me."

"I'll do anything Jack, if you'll just let me stand up straight" Nikki laughed.

"And yes, I'll proudly take your name. Now let me up before I faint, Mr. Jameson."

"My pleasure, soon-to-be Mrs. Jameson" Jack said laughingly while lifting Nikki upright.

"And keep tomorrow open, ok?"

"Anything you say sweetheart ... but keep it open for what?"

"Silly girl. Didn't you notice something's missing?"

"Hmmm, white doves fluttering overhead, violins playing Pachelbel's Canon? What?"

"Well, most guys when they propose marriage reach into their pocket and produce a little black box with a sparkling diamond in it. Do you see any box, or diamond for that matter? No? So, tomorrow we're going to the jewelers for your engagement ring where you can select whatever diamond you want, whatever carat or cut. And while we're at it we can select our wedding rings because this is gonna be a short engagement, babe."

Cupping her face with her hands, Nikki felt the tears streaming down from her eyes to her lips, tasting the salty flavor. "I love you. I'm the luckiest girl in the world, sweetheart."

Shelley and David roundly applauded and shouted their congratulations and felicitations.

"May I kiss the bride-to-be, Jack?" David asked as he gave Nikki a kiss, not waiting for Jack's approval.

"My turn to kiss the groom-to-be" Shelley announced, while hugging Jack around the neck and planting a big kiss on his lips.

"Ok, time for a group hug and kiss," Nikki interjected, while gathering everybody to her, kissing them all and being kissed and hugged in return.

Jack's eyes looked at Nikki's trench coat and wondered what lay hidden underneath while thanking the gods that be that she was his. And he was hers. Forever. He was going to claim that body tonight with a renewed passion. He could already feel her legs wrapped around him and then resting on his shoulders as he entered her and prepared to make vigorous love to her.

His musing was interrupted by Nikki's voice. "Let's go out on deck, Jack. There's a little something I want to show you."

Taking Jack by the hand, Nikki ushered him to the cabin door. She glanced back over her shoulder and gave Shelley and David a knowing smile.

"You kids behave yourselves while we're gone Ok?" Then she walked out the door with Jack.

"Where are we going, babe?" Jack asked, as they made their way past berth 11, coming to a halt at berth 12.

"Just walk right here to berth 12, Mr. Jameson, look to your left and Bob's your uncle. Well ... What do you think?" Nikki asked Jack as she pointed to the dinghy suspended on the side of the boat.

"You've got to be kidding me, Nikki. This dinghy is ... no, it can't be."

"Yes, it is Jack. It's the little boat you built when you were fifteen; the original Mother Ocean. Your dad's had it in storage all these years. Even though it had deteriorated a bit your parents couldn't bring themselves to throw it away. It was what led you to where you are today. This is their surprise for you too."

Jack hugged Nikki so tight she could feel the air being expelled from her lungs in a loud whoosh.

"Nikki, I can't believe this. You have no idea how much this means to me."

Catching her breath, Nikki said, "I'm not finished yet Jack. Aren't you curious why it's on this yacht? Walk with me."

Jack squeezed Nikki's hand as they took several steps along the pier and then turned left at the starboard side of the yacht.

"Whoa, Nikki! Babe!" Jack shouted. "Now it's my turn to ask what's going on. So ... what's going on? The Mother Ocean Too?" Jack's jaw was dropping and his eyes were misting over.

"It's a long story Jack. Let's just say I wanted to get you something you'd never get for yourself and I also wanted to help out a friend, our friend."

"Marcus! So this is the lucky contract that he got that's enabling him to marry my sister. You made this possible for him Nikki. You! You're ... you're ..."

"I'm what, Jack? The luckiest girl in the world who's rich beyond her wildest dreams? A girl who is marrying an uber rich man whom she loves more than anything? And a girl who likes to help out her friends? What's money Jack if you can't use it to make others happy? This gift makes Marcus happy, Jillian happy, me happy and most importantly, it makes you happy."

Jack then did something he'd only done a few times in his life – once when his best buddy, his Lab/Dalmatian mix died of old age, and when his mother was seriously ill – he cried. But these were tears of joy now. Tears of utter happiness.

Jack placed the index fingers of each hand under his eyes and rubbed the moisture away. He grabbed Nikki around the waist and guided her back to the portside of the yacht. He said, "Well, we've already had the champagne. I think it's time to christen the Mother Ocean Too in a different way now, don't you, my beloved?"

"Oh yes, yes I do. Wait until you see her inside, Jack. Marcus did almost as good a job as you would. She's just beautiful and ..." Nikki hesitated, smiling.

"And what, Nik?" Jack asked with a curious smile on his face.

"And the master stateroom has the biggest, most luxurious damn bed I've ever seen. It vibrates, can be moved up, down, sideways and ..." Nikki laughed.

"I love you Nikki Robertson not-soon-enough-to-be-Mrs. Jameson," Jack whispered in Nikki's ear. "And as you Aussies would say, 'I'm as happy as Larry,' whoever the devil Larry is but I think I'm even happier than him."

Arms intertwined around each other's waists, they kissed as they stood outside the cabin door, feeling the gentle drops of rain that had begun falling again.

Jack's hands drifted down to Nikki's well-rounded bum, squeezing it while pulling her tightly to him. "I want to see what's under that trench coat, as if I didn't know; nothing!" he smiled.

They swayed gently to the music playing in their heads. "It's playing our song Nik. What could be more perfect? I'm crazy in love with you."

"I know Jack. I love you with all my heart. Now let's go inside, christen this baby and set the date. Happy Birthday, my love!"

Chocolate Lamingtons

A deliciously favorite Australian dessert. Small squares of plain cake dipped in melted chocolate and sugar and coated in desiccated coconut.

Sponge Cake

Ingredients -

3 eggs

1/2 cup castor sugar (super fine granulated sugar)

3/4 cup self-rising flour

1/4 cup cornstarch

15g (1/2oz) butter

3 tablespoons hot water

Chocolate Icing

3 cups desiccated coconut

500g (1lb) icing sugar

1/3 cup cocoa

(extra cocoa can be added, according to taste)

15g (1/2oz) butter

1/2 cup milk

Directions

Beat eggs until thick and creamy. Gradually add sugar. Continue beating until sugar is completely dissolved.

Fold in sifted self-rising flour and cornstarch, then combined water and butter.

Pour mixture into prepared lamington tins (7in x 11in).

Bake in moderate oven approximately 30 minutes.

Let cake stand in pan for 5 min before turning out onto wire rack.

Sift icing sugar and cocoa into heatproof bowl.

Stir in butter and milk.

Stir over a pan of hot water until icing is smooth and glossy.

Trim brown top and sides from cake.

Cut into 16 even pieces.

Holding each piece on a fork, dip each cake into icing.

Hold over bowl a few minutes to drain off excess chocolate.

Toss in coconut or sprinkle to coat.

Place on oven tray to set.

(Cake is easier to handle if made the day before.

Sponge cake or butter cake may be used.

May be filled with jam and cream.)

(www.aussie-info.com and from my Robertson family recipe collection)

"And even if the sun refused to shine
Even if romance ran out of rhyme

You would still have my heart until the end of time

You're all I need, my love, my Valentine "

V is for Valentine

· ·

Valentine's Day was looming. Alanna found it strange that she should use that particular word "looming" to describe the upcoming sweetheart's day. It was a day that she always eagerly anticipated; a day in which she'd be showered with long-stemmed red roses – her favorite – and the requisite heart-shaped box of chocolates, inside which would be tucked an exquisite piece of jewelry and a love note from Bryce.

Bryce was thoughtful and generous like that but it seemed the other 364 days of the year he was preoccupied. He worked by day and attended Southern Oregon University at night; his goal of being a science teacher always foremost on his mind.

This year would be different. This year Alanna would be spending Valentine's Day in Hawaii, instead of her home state of Oregon. She loved Oregon, especially the little town of Ashland where she'd moved to a dozen years ago. She'd spent her childhood years in Portland and loved it but when her grandmother had died and left her house and property in Ashland to Alanna, she'd fallen in love with the little town at first sight.

Alanna and Bryce loved attending the Oregon Shakespeare Festival and the Ashland Independent Film Festival. She also loved living in a town that was home to The Bathroom Readers' Institute and Bathroom Readers' Press and the ever popular Uncle John's Bathroom Reader books. She dreamed that one day it would be known as the home of her books.

She was the successful author of a series of popular little 'How To' books ranging in subject matter from 'How to Find and Keep Love' to 'How to Tell Him it's Over and Remain Friends' to "How to Win Him Back' to 'How to Have Your Cake and Eat it Too – a Woman's Guide to Dating Like a Man'. She had twenty-one books in the How To series with many more bouncing around in her head and one more due for publication in April.

As an author she could live anywhere and make a good living so she had taken advantage of that, living a nomadic existence for several years. She wrote two of her books while staying in a villa in Tuscany, another book written while on a tour of Scandinavia; she even wrote one of her books during a three week visit to Iceland – 'How to Thaw His Heart and Make Him Melt'. Surprisingly that was one of the more popular books in her series and one that, truth be known, she'd written as a lark. You never knew what would sell in this business she'd often remind herself.

She found herself wondering how she was going to break the news to Bryce, that she would be spending the next six weeks in Hawaii, keeping her there until a week after Valentine's Day. Bryce loved Alanna, of that she had no doubt. He was the most caring, considerate lover she'd ever had. He knew all of her pleasure spots and tended to them with an eagerness she'd never experienced with anyone else.

But Bryce was not adventurous like Alanna was. Bryce was steady, a rock, reliable; always there for her, never pressuring her into anything. He's too steady, too reliable. Where is the enthusiasm she wondered; the fire, the passion for life. There was nothing wrong with his passion when it came to making love or his passion for science and being a science teacher but that's where it stopped.

He would never think to just drop everything and take off for parts unknown, to explore the world; experience all the flavors of exotic places and new people, waking up in a new and strange city; all the things that excited Alanna.

She tried not to be unfair to Bryce, after all he was studying hard to get his degree but she wished he had a little more exuberance; to take a vacation during school break. Just once would show her that he had some spark to him. But that was not Bryce. He was as slow and steady as an Oregon rain.

She regretted that her visit would keep her in Hawaii past Valentine's day but her sister-in-law, Sunny, Alanna's brother's wife, would be recuperating from major surgery and would need her help in caring for her two young sons and her not so small menagerie of pets. Widowed for three years she was still having a hard time accepting her lot in life. Alanna was having a hard time accepting her brother's sudden death from an accidental drug overdose. But they had the boys to live for and to care for, not to mention the non-human responsibilities, and that was helping a great deal.

Alanna wondered how she'd be able to meet her publisher's deadline for her next book, 'How to Change Your Man Without Him Knowing It'. This had been the hardest of all her books to write so far. How could she tell others how to change their man when she couldn't change her own?

The phone rang; it was her publisher. "How's my favorite 'How To' author? Banging out that latest book?" Victor asked her with trepidation. He was always nervous when Alanna gave him her latest book proposal but he also knew that she always came through. This one though he thought would be really difficult; he knew about the differences between her and Bryce. He wondered how a girl filled with so much wanderlust could settle down with a staid schoolteacher-to-be.

"I'm as fine as frog hair, Victor. How are you? Wringing your hands and pacing the floor worried about my latest book? Don't bother answering, I already know the answer. You think I've gone off the deep end and gotten myself into serious trouble."

"Well I don't know how serious but yeah, I do think this is gonna be a hard one for you. However, as usual I have the utmost confidence in your ability to tell others to do what you cannot do yourself," Victor laughed.

"Right as usual Victor. I've started this book over and over, typing and revising until I think I'm going to collapse and puke. Maybe I should - puke, that is – maybe it'll get all the negativity out of me allowing me to start fresh."

"You know best Alanna. Puke to your little heart's content if you think that'll help. I just wanted to check in and see how it's going."

"Speaking of going, Vic, I'm leaving on January 5th for Hawaii. I'll be there for about six weeks, visiting my sister-in-law; she's having major surgery and needs me there to take care of her. And Vic, don't worry. I'll be working on the book in between feeding the kids, driving them to and from school, emptying litter boxes, walking dogs, and not to mention taking care of my sister-in-law. I hope to squeeze in a little touristy stuff too. Oh and somewhere in there I'll write several thousand words a day. I promise."

Alanna said goodbye to Vic and found herself thinking of the irony of how busy she was going to be, just like Bryce. No time for anything spontaneous. Just like Bryce.

❧

The ringing of the doorbell brought Alanna's thoughts back to reality. She had been busy working on the book and it was giving her fits and starts. Had she bitten off more than she can chew she pondered. Could she really write a believable book about changing your man without him knowing it? First of all she pondered the ability to change a man and even the wisdom of it. Secondly how could it be accomplished without him knowing it?

She was formulating several ideas that might work just at the moment the doorbell rang. She saved her document, closed her laptop and walked to the door to admit Bryce into the living room.

"Hey Alanna, sweetie," Bryce said softly as he took her in his arms and kissed her. He leaned back, looked into her beautiful blue-violet eyes with the golden flecks in them. They were her most outstanding feature; a feature that mesmerized all who saw those beautiful orbs and Bryce was no different. He could gaze into her eyes forever.

"Hi, love. Mmm, kiss me again. I need something to make me feel good after struggling with my book all day."

They kissed lovingly and by mutual silent agreement Bryce led them toward the bedroom door. Alanna had been working at her desk wearing only a skimpy teddy which Bryce found delightful; easier to remove and affording quicker access to her beautiful breasts – and the rest of her inviting body.

She was 5'5", and 125 pounds of feminine pulchritude; meshing perfectly with his 5'11" perfectly muscled and toned body. His naturally wavy blonde hair that was worn to chin level complemented by his goatee gave him a rugged and leonine appearance.

He lay down on his back on the bed and Alanna slowly crawled on top of him, her long black hair hanging down, brushing over his face. She kissed his pouty and masculine lips, lips so hot they could melt glaciers. If there was any real cause for global climate change Alanna was certain it was Bryce's lips.

They made love vigorously and breathlessly with steam practically emanating from all their pores. Bryce's hands slid up and down Alanna's back, stroking her from the nape of her neck, grabbing her hair and twisting it through his fingers and then sliding his hands down to her buttocks where he'd squeeze and lift. Alanna would run her tongue around Bryce's mouth darting it in and out in concert with Bryce's movements until they would finally collapse in satisfied exhaustion.

They were hot for each other and had been since they'd first met at night school. Alanna had been auditing a writing class and Bryce was taking his first organic chemistry class.

They'd met in the hallway where Alanna had her nose in a text book and had inadvertently bumped into Bryce. She'd apologized for walking while reading which Bryce found both amusing and endearing.

They laughed about the incident and stood in the hallway talking until the break was over and each had to go back to class.

When class was over, Alanna was delighted to find a pair of beautiful blue eyes coupled with that shaggy mane waiting for her in the hallway opposite her classroom. He invited her to have coffee with him in the college cafeteria; the first of many coffee dates which ultimately led to the beginning of a wonderful relationship.

"Was that good for you too," Bryce laughed. "You have a hell of a smile on your face."

"I was remembering how we'd first met that night at school. How I bumped into you and what a great life we've had together since then. And yes, to answer your question, it was good for me too. As if you don't know – it's always good for me."

"Mmm, you always say the right thing, but then again you're a writer so why wouldn't you? And speaking of writing, my little Hemingway, are you ever going to tell me what your latest 'How To' book is about? You've been keeping me in the dark about this one and you've really got my curiosity on high alert."

"Well, although I appreciate the Hemingway compliment, Bryce, I'd feel much more complimented if you compared me to Anna Quindlen, thank you very much. That said, I'm not ready to tell you about my latest book because I'm not sure I can write it. It's challenging my writing skills. No, that's not right. It isn't challenging my writing skills. It's challenging my imagination. Oh my god Bryce, my last book might actually end up being my last book!"

"No, no that's not true. You've got a lot of 'How To' books left within you sweetheart. Maybe you should just give up on whatever this one's about and move on to another one. Maybe 'How To Stop Bugging Your Boyfriend To Be Spontaneous'. No? Come on that's funny. Admit it."

"Actually that's very funny sweetheart and you're right. I could write volumes about that. But I can't write that book just yet. I have something to tell you, and also to ask you. But can we have some dinner while we talk? You always make me so hungry."

"You bet, me too. Let's go out, maybe to Roma's Ristorante'. I am so in the mood for Italian now, after just having had the best in English-Scottish fare," Bryce joked as he flicked a stray lock of hair from Alanna's forehead.

"If you don't mind Bryce, I think we should just order in. Would it be okay if we just had some pizza and beer? I'd really like to talk here at home where it's private."

"Uh oh, this doesn't sound very promising, but whatever you want is fine with me. Shoot."

Alanna got up off the bed and stood over Bryce, grabbing his hands and pulling him up. She led him into the bathroom where they took a quick shower together, then dried off and dressed. They walked together, arms around each other's waists, into the living room where they settled down on the couch.

Alanna opened her cell and called their local pizza place and ordered a large pizza with all the toppings and a side order of pasta with Alfredo sauce.

While they waited for their food to be delivered, Alanna opened two beers for them, Stella Artois for both, and told Bryce about her upcoming trip to Hawaii; that she would have to be there for at least six weeks. This would be the first time they'd be apart since they'd begun dating in earnest. They had become inseparable.

It was true that when they were together they weren't always really together; Alanna would be on the couch with her laptop working on her latest book and Bryce would be on the other end of the couch studying chemistry or physics or whatever class he was presently enrolled in. They would take frequent little breaks to grab a kiss or a bite to eat; sometimes their breaks would consist of hot and heavy sex. But they were together and that's all that mattered.

"Okay," Bryce said as he took a deep breath. "I understand. I really do. Doesn't mean that I like it but we've been through worse things. We'll get through this too. It's a good thing we have Skype so I can still look at your beautiful face each day. It won't be the same as holding you in my arms of course but we'll make do."

"Thank you hon; you're one hell of a guy and I'm so glad you're mine."

"Okay, that takes care of the telling me something but you said there was a question too. I hope you aren't going to ask me to go to Hawaii with you Alanna, because as much as I'd love to you know I can't. Even though I'll be on winter break for some of the time while you're in Hawaii, I still couldn't go. I have an incredible amount of studying to do and I have to maintain my 4.0 average if I want to get into grad school. Oh please tell me you weren't going to ask me to do that sweetheart."

Of course not Bryce why would I ask you to do something spontaneous for just once in your life? Just once. Just one lousy weekend, would it kill you?

The doorbell rang. Pizza! A temporary reprieve; time to give Alanna a few minutes to compose herself. She didn't want Bryce to see how upset she was. He was a wonderful, kind man who always did whatever was in his power to make her happy. He hated to refuse her anything and she knew it. And she felt like crap for the petty thoughts that had just gone through her mind.

"No, of course I'm not going to ask you to join me Bryce, not even for just a couple of days. I understand how important school is to you and how critical it is for you to maintain your 4.0."

Bryce's face broke into a broad smile of relief. Alanna was glad she didn't break down and ask him to join her, if only for a weekend. He had the money; she knew that wouldn't be a problem.

Bryce took a big bite of his pizza slice, chewed it and swallowed, the whole time looking at Alanna with a questioning look on his face. "So what's the question? Or is this 'Twenty Questions' and I have to guess?"

Wiping some Alfredo sauce from her lips with her napkin, Alanna took the few moments to think of a good question she could ask him. 'Oh, it's nothing' wouldn't cut it. Bryce wouldn't let her get away with that. He knew her and he knew if she said she had something to ask him then she definitely had something to ask him.

"I was wondering if you'd like to pose for the cover of my latest book. I know you said before you weren't interested in being a 'pin-up' as you called it, but I thought perhaps you might consider it. It wouldn't be a picture of you per se but a cartoon drawing of you. I just thought I'd ask; that's all."

That's seriously scary Alanna, how quickly you can lie. Whew!

The smile on Bryce's face allayed her fears that he was aware she was lying. It also made her feel bad; she'd never lied to Bryce before. To be sure it was merely a little white lie but still it gave her pause.

"Well, let me surprise you babe. Since you'll be leaving me for such a long time – and yes I think six weeks is a long time to be away from you – I've changed my mind; I'd love to pose for your book cover, just as long as it isn't a 'How To Cheat On Your Man and Get Away With It' book."

"Don't be silly Bryce, I could never, and would never write a book like that. So we'll discuss this further when I return from Hawaii. I'll miss you so much but my sister-in-law really needs me. I have to go. She's always been more like a sister than an in-law. My brother loved her dearly and so do I."

Blake took a swig of his beer and picked up another piece of pizza. Before biting into it he said "I know, my love and I know you have to go just like you know I have to stay here. I know you'd like me to be more spontaneous, well actually just spontaneous; to be more spontaneous would imply that I'm already spontaneous to a degree and we both know I'm not."

"It's okay Bryce. I'm a free bird and you're a methodical person who likes all his ducks in a row, in a very straight line actually, nothing out of place, a place for everything and everything in its place. But I love that about you too. I just wish that once in awhile you'd step out of your comfort zone and live it up a little; rob a bank or something."

Bryce nearly choked on his pizza while laughing. "Sometimes I wonder if you might indeed like to see me do something like that."

Some beer escaped from Alana's mouth and drizzled down her chin as she laughed along with him.

They enjoyed their shared laughs; each of them appreciating how precious, and short life is. Other people might have laughed at their separation anxiety, upset by having to be away from each other for a mere six weeks.

To Bryce and Alanna though, each of them having suffered the sudden loss of a loved one, they considered each day a gift; a gift that could be snatched from them in a heartbeat. Six weeks of separation to others might seem a trivial matter but to Bryce and Alanna it could be a lifetime apart.

They knew the heartbreak of losing someone so precious to them; she losing her older brother and Bryce losing a younger sister, ironically both of them to the disease of addiction. Alanna's brother, Scott, had been hooked on crack cocaine and heroin and Bryce's younger sister, Bryanna was a slave to prescription pills. Alanna had toyed with writing a 'How To' on addiction – 'How to Say Yes to Life and No to Drugs' but that was one book she positively knew she couldn't write.

Nobody could write that book Alanna knew; there was no cut and dried method of curing addiction. She would just have to have faith that science would unravel this particular mystery of the brain and develop a cure.

☙❧

Bryce drove Alanna to the airport allowing plenty of time for them to sit and talk before her plane departed. She was anxious but excited; sad but happy. She and Bryce talked about everything, exchanging I Love Yous over and over and kissing discreetly.

They intensely disliked this part of the separation; the minutes leading up to when Alanna would give Bryce a last hug and kiss before walking up to the checkpoint, and removing her shoes while silently cursing Richard Reid, the so-called Shoe Bomber, while wondering how many germs she might be gathering on her feet from the grubby floor.

Yuck!

Alanna arrived at Honolulu International Airport on the island of Oahu. She loved Hawaii; one of her favorite places in the world. She loved visiting the International Market Place and standing in awe of the beautiful banyan tree in its center; a tree that would be leveled if future developers have their way. She liked the little independent shops and didn't want to see a string of well-known high end stores taking over and eliminating the charm that so typified this area.

For now, she had to get to her sister-in-law's house in the beautiful Mililani area. Fortunately her brother had left her well off so she could continue living in such a beautiful place. He'd purchased their home outright not wanting her to be left with a mortgage should – no, not should – *when* something happened to him. He knew his addiction was spiraling out of control and he wouldn't live long. She had to give him that – he provided for hers and their children's future.

Alanna was greeted by vociferous barks and the sounds of bois-terous boys yelling "Aunt Alanna, Aunt Alanna!" The three cats wisely sought shelter on top of the bookshelves or under the sofas. She always felt at home when she visited her family. Even with Scott missing, the home was still filled with love.

"I'm sorry I couldn't pick you up at the airport Alanna," Sunny said, her voice barely above a whisper. She always spoke low when she was nervous and Alanna knew she had good reason to be ner-vous now. Her surgery was scheduled for the day after tomorrow and she was dreading it.

"Your flight couldn't have arrived at a worse time; I'm sorry but I couldn't cancel Dylan's orthodontic appointment, not after we'd waited so long for it to be scheduled. I didn't want to postpone it; that would only have added to your burden next week."

"Not to worry, Sunny. I made it all the way from the mainland to the airport without any problems; and it was a lovely ride here. Don't you worry your pretty little head about anything. Under-stand me? All you have to concern yourself with is keeping a pos-itive attitude. The surgery will be over and done with before you know it."

Sunny didn't like going to doctors let alone having invasive sur-gery and this was going to be quite invasive; a unilateral nephrec-tomy with the recovery time expected to be eight weeks. After Alanna's departure, Sunny's sister, Annie, would arrive to take over all chores. She'd be back from her trip to New Zealand by then; Sunny would be well on the way to recovery, and she and Annie could spend quality time together.

❧

The surgery was uneventful, even better than they had hoped for. Alanna enjoyed being with her nephews, playing with them and helping them with their homework. She wondered how she'd ever get any part of her book written because there seemed to be nowhere in the house that wasn't filled with noise; the dogs tearing around the house chased by Dylan and Liam, or the boys playing loud video games or the phone ringing off the hook for them.

It was quite a busy home and Alanna loved every minute of it. She especially enjoyed the companionship of the three cats, Little Pippi, Squeaky and Sugar. They were always vying for her attention, each one trying to be king of the hill on her lap. When they tired of jumping on her laptop and getting shifted away, they'd climb on her shoulder or sit on the arm of the sofa.

They shared her bed with her each night purring contentedly. They loved their Aunt Alanna too, but to anyone who knows cats it was obvious they mainly loved her warmth. They weren't fooling Alanna one bit but she didn't mind. She loved them and appreciated them for what they are; cats!

Most of all Alanna looked forward to Bryce's nightly Skype calls. Steady, reliable, always dependable Bryce. He was more reliable than any clock. She looked forward to seeing his gorgeous face every night but oh how she wished he were here with her in person; but not Bryce; no he couldn't do that. That would be spontaneous!

The weeks went by surprisingly quickly; Sunny was home and healing and Alanna was actually getting a decent amount of writing done. She'd learned how to write with a background of chaos going on all around her.

She'd scrapped the 'How to Change Your Man Without Him Knowing It' and gave a sigh of relief when she realized she wasn't going to be bothered with it anymore. Her heart just wasn't in that one and besides who'd want a man so wimpy that he could be changed, she asked herself.

On to the next book; 'How to Accept Your Mate for Who He Is and Still Love him'. Not the easiest book I've attempted she smiled to herself, but infinitely easier than trying to write one on how to change a man.

Skype time had arrived on Valentine's Day and Alanna was eagerly looking forward to talking to her sweetie. She had to admit a deep disappointment though when the mail had arrived and there was nothing from Bryce; no love letter, no special delivery of flowers, nothing.

"Happy Valentine's Day, sweetheart," Alanna said as she stared at the screen, looking into Bryce's eyes and wishing they could be together.

"Alanna, I'm sorry I didn't send you anything, or have flowers delivered but you'll be home in a few days and I'd rather be with you when I give you your gift, and the chocolates and flowers of course. Good old dependable Bryce, never spontaneous, I know, I know. But wouldn't you rather have reliability than spontaneity?"

"You mean I can't have both?" Alanna laughed.

They talked for even longer than usual, excited they'd be seeing each other within a few days when Alanna would arrive home. Alanna was happy that her sister-in-law was doing so well but sad that she'd have to leave them all. She was really going to miss them and hoped she could return soon.

Well, good old Bryce, he certainly wasn't so predictable today. Today of all days, Valentine's Day he decides to be different.

They hung up and Alanna dove back into the book, having a hard time coming up with more reasons to accept the mate for who he is and still love him. She wrote until she was bleary-eyed and then decided to call it a night. She was too tired to fight with the cats so she let them have their way and she positioned herself on the bed as best as she could. It was no time before Little Pippi was curled up on her chest with the other two snuggled up against her, one against her hip and one against her ankle.

꙳

The next day Sunny and Alanna were enjoying a quiet brunch, discussing the events of the last 5 weeks, the children, the pets, Sunny's amazing recovery which Sunny attributed to the Florence Nightingale attributes of Alanna and Alanna's imminent departure.

"Alanna, you're such a free spirit, so unpredictable. I never know what to expect of you from one minute to the next. I just don't see what the attraction is to Bryce whom you say is so, well, so unlike you."

"Great sex! Let me rephrase that – phenomenal sex" Alanna said; her eyes crinkling as she laughed. "And he truly is a wonderful, kind man. I'd have to travel the world over to find a better man. But yes I wish for once he could do something exciting, something different. I'd love to marry him – not that he's asked mind you – but I keep wondering if life with him would be one big snooze fest with wonderful sex in between. Is that enough?"

Alanna's cell rang, interrupting their conversation. It was Bryce. "Hey sweetheart, how's this for spontaneity? It isn't even nighttime and it's not Skype. And yet here I am talking to you. Damn! Hold on a minute, babe I've got another call. It's Dr. Smithfield, my professor and I have to take it. I promise I won't keep you waiting."

Sunny excused herself; getting up to let the dogs in from the back yard and leaving Alanna to have a private conversation.

"I'll get it," Alanna called to Sunny as she walked into the living room to answer the doorbell which had just rung; holding the cell phone to her ear so she wouldn't miss when Bryce came back on the phone.

Bryce's timing was impeccable. He came back on the phone and said "It's me, Mr. Spontaneity," as Alanna opened the door and stood there with her mouth agape, not daring to believe her eyes.

"Bryce! Oh my god, is it really you?" Alanna threw her arms around him and smothered his face with kisses, throwing her head back to look at him and then throwing herself into him again. They kissed with their usual passion if not more so; with Bryce's arms held behind his back.

"Here, sweetheart," Bryce said as he brought his right arm around from behind his back presenting Alanna with a small bouquet of red roses followed promptly by a heart-shaped box of chocolates presented with his left hand.

"Bryce I don't know what to say. I truly don't. I'm not much of a wordsmith am I? I'm speechless. What's going on? Flowers, chocolates – here – in Hawaii?"

"Of course; I'm Mr. Spontaneity. Didn't you know that?"

They stood at the door kissing again. Alanna was aware of Sunny's presence behind her. "Well you have to be the one and only Bryce; am I right?" Sunny exclaimed while sizing him up and liking what she saw. "But you ..."

Bryce laughed heartily. "Right – but I don't do things like this. I'm sure Alanna has been filling your ears about my predictability. Well, I guess I showed both of you didn't I?"

"Alanna, bring this gorgeous man inside. Come in Bryce. My sister-in-law isn't usually this rude, but I'm sure you know that."

They moved inside, Bryce shutting the door behind them. "I'll be out of your hair in just a bit guys but right now I think this calls for some Mimosas," Sunny said as she walked into the kitchen to mix up a batch.

While Sunny was making the Mimosas, Bryce and Alanna canoodled on the sofa; "How long is long enough to be polite and talk to Sunny before we can take off to your bedroom?" Bryce asked.

"I want you Alanna, right here, right now. It's been a hell of a long five weeks without you, without feeling your bare breasts against my chest, without kissing them, without feeling your sugar walls. Hell, it's been way too long."

Sunny entered the living room, pitcher and three glasses in hand and paused. The heat in the room was enough to set off the fire alarm, judging by the smoldering looks in Alanna's and Bryce's eyes and the closeness of their bodies to each other's. She was surprised steam wasn't rising from their heads.

"You know what guys? I think these drinks can wait. Why don't the two of you go upstairs and unwind? Bryce, I know you'll want to unpack and maybe even take a nap. I know it's only about a 5 hour plane trip from the mainland to here but still, it's uncomfortable sitting in those small seats. We can celebrate together later."

"You're a wise woman Sunny," Bryce said while casting a sly wink in her direction.

Alanna and Bryce walked up to Alanna's room and closed the door. They didn't stand on ceremony and hurriedly peeled each other's clothes off, fondling each other and kissing; Bryce brushing his tongue over Alanna's moist lips while she drew his tongue into her mouth.

Their lovemaking was hot and furious, five weeks of passion eager to seek release. Neither was disappointed that it didn't last long. They knew they'd be back at it again later tonight; this time slower and more romantic but still with plenty of passion.

"I think you could use a nice, hot bath Bryce. Shall we take one?"

They lay in the oversize tub, with Bryce leaning back against it. His arms were wrapped around Alanna as she lay against him, her back resting on his chest while he soaped her breasts and belly, occasionally letting his fingers dip down beneath the soap bubbles. They luxuriated in their togetherness and the warmth of the water.

They didn't do much talking. All they wanted was to relax in the tub together, kissing and touching and just enjoying being together. The only interruption to this romantic interlude was when Alanna asked Bryce about his sudden decision to surprise her.

"Why didn't you arrive yesterday Bryce, on Valentine's Day? Don't get me wrong, I'm not complaining; not at all. I just don't understand."

"Because, my little minx, if I'd arrived yesterday on Valentine's Day that would be so plebian, so predictable, so unspontaneous. So I decided to arrive today; when you wouldn't expect me. I've gotta tell you there might just be something to this spontaneity. I'm enjoying it a lot," Bryce said as he tickled his fingers over Alanna's chest, evoking a sigh of appreciation from her.

"From now on babe, we'll celebrate Valentine's Day on February 15th. It'll be our own special celebration. That okay with you?"

Alanna turned her head and leaned back, kissing Bryce on the lips as he leaned down to meet hers. "It's a date Bryce." They stood up in the tub, showered the soap off of them and then got out of the tub and dried off.

Bryce and Alanna fell asleep on the bed, Bryce on his back and Alanna lying next to him, her arm lying across his chest and her face nuzzled up against his neck with one leg straddled over his.

They awoke an hour later. "Mmm, are you thinking what I'm thinking, sweetheart?" Bryce murmured in Alanna's ear.

Alanna gave him little love nips on his neck while running her hand from his chest down to his groin, squeezing and rubbing, driving Bryce to distraction.

"Yeah babe, I'm thinking red hot sex followed by some really good food." Alanna moved her leg across Bryce's body, pressing her knee into the mattress and pushing herself up on him. She was straddling his whole body now, a hand on either side of his head supporting her while she lowered herself on to him and began working her magic; her hair flying wildly as she flung her head back and then brought it down again kissing him and teasing her tongue into his mouth. It wasn't long before they were both sated and quite happy.

"You two enjoy your bath and nap?" Sunny asked with a smile and a wink for Bryce, as he and Alanna descended the stairs into the living room.

"Uh oh, here comes trouble. Boys, stop running and for goodness sakes keep the dogs under control before they knock us all over."

"Too late, Sunny," Bryce yelped as the dogs charged him, yapping and barking, all wagging tails and drooling mouths and big paws flying around in a blur.

"I think they like me."

"Well, don't think too highly of yourself Bryce; I hate to tell you but they greet everyone that way. They've never met a person they didn't like," Alanna told him.

"I like them too," Bryce said, rubbing their heads and backs and nuzzling them. "But you've gotta let me go now guys. I have some important business to tend to."

Bryce excused himself and took his cell phone out of the pocket of his jeans while walking into the kitchen. He found Sunny's phone book on the counter next to the land line and looked up the number for Charley Wong's; an upscale restaurant one of the flight attendants had told him about.

He held his breath as he dialed the number knowing it might be difficult to make a reservation on such short notice at such an upscale restaurant. He was gambling that there would be no problem though since this was the day *after* one of the most popular dining out days of the year.

His gamble paid off and he'd secured a reservation for 8 p.m. He couldn't wait to sample the Hawaiian fare that he'd heard so much about.

He joined Alanna and Sunny in the living room where he poured himself and Alanna some of the left over Mimosas; Sunny was not partaking of any alcohol being cautious not to impede her recovery with toxins no matter how delicious those toxins were.

"Okay now it's time for me to go upstairs and get dressed. How *should* I dress, Bryce; fancy, casual, in between, what?"

"Well I've heard that you can never go wrong with the LBD. How's that sound?" Bryce laughed as he showed off his newfound knowledge of women's apparel. He was leaping out of his comfort zone, learning about the things that mattered to Alanna, dropping everything and flying to Hawaii without a second thought.

Good old predictable Bryce, huh? Well he's gone, left him back on the mainland. This is the new and improved Bryce.

"So, is this okay?" Alanna asked as she stood on the open staircase, a half hour later, looking down at Bryce and Sunny who were sitting on the sofa getting to know each other.

"Wow!" Bryce and Sunny exclaimed at almost the same time. That's one great LBD, Alanna; the little black dress in case you're wondering what the initials stand for," Bryce laughed.

"Alright, where is the real Bryce and what have you done with him?" Alanna joked.

"I'm right here, sweetheart, totally mesmerized by this vision before my eyes. I'm not sure if you're more beautiful naked or dressed to the nines. But I know how I like you best," Bryce said with more than a twinkle in his eyes.

"You're breathtaking; but then you're always breathtaking. I'll be the envy of every man – and woman – in the restaurant."

Alanna walked down the staircase, sashayed over to Bryce, kissed him on the lips and then swatted him on the butt as he stood up. "Now get yourself upstairs and dressed. I'm famished. And besides I want to show myself off in my LBD," Alanna giggled.

Bryce's entrance was no less stunning than Alanna's; a vision of leonine perfection cloaked in a form-fitting black Armani suit that showcased his lean but muscled body.

He called for a taxi to take them the short distance to the restaurant; both of them a vision of beauty worthy of any red carpet event.

❦

Bryce was surprised to find the restaurant situated on the third floor of an office building. Had he been misled, he wondered. His fears were allayed when they stepped off the elevator and were greeted by the wait staff eager to usher them to their table.

They were seated and handed the menus with the server asking them their drink preference. "Do you by any chance have Schramsberg's J. Schram 1999?" Bryce asked.

"Ah, I see you know your American champagnes sir. Excellent selection, and yes we do have it. I'll return in just a minute."

Alanna's eyes were almost popping at her suddenly unspontaneous lover. "Bryce, how do you know about this champagne? The most hoity toity champagne that I know of is Dom Perignon or Perrier Jouet and the only reason I know about the Perrier Jouet is because it's the bottle with the white flowers on it that is always featured in TV shows or movies," Alanna laughed.

"Well I suppose you just need to be more spontaneous and unpredictable my little ingénue." Bryce let her stew over that one for a minute before confessing that the same flight attendant who'd told him about the restaurant had also told him about the champagne.

"I can only imagine how much it costs but don't tell me. Okay? I don't want to ruin the evening by getting indigestion."

"I won't tell you then. I'll let you think I spent a fortune on it. I didn't but even if I did, you're worth every penny of it ... But it wasn't cheap," Bryce said sotto voce laughing as he said it.

The server brought them the champagne and popped the cork and filled their flutes. Alanna noticed some of the other patrons eyeing the bottle. She smiled, feeling very special.

The server asked for their orders. "I'll have the ginger crusted onaga," Bryce declared, "and ... Alanna?"

"I'll have the seafood bowl, please."

They didn't drink the champagne immediately. Alanna had some questions first.

"So Bryce," Alanna started, after the server had left their table, "tell me how this all came about, why you decided to just up and fly here? What about school? We haven't had time to talk since you arrived, not that I'm complaining sweetheart; you've kept me very busy but I'm ready to listen to it all right now. Please tell me what's going on."

Alanna listened to Bryce's explanation, how much he loves her, and missed her and decided he was going to try it her way for once. "Alanna you were right. It felt so good to make those airline reservations; the excitement I felt knowing I would be seeing you again; and not only seeing you but surprising you. You've no idea how exciting this has been for me."

"Bryce, knowing that you would do this for me just leaves me speechless. But there *is* one thing I have to say: I love you more than you'll ever know and I know now that I would never want to change you. You're kind, you're considerate, you're thoughtful, you're obliging, you're mannerly, you're polite, you're gorgeous and you're incredible in bed."

"Really; you think I'm all those things? That's a pretty long list of superlatives, babe."

"You're all that and even one thing more Bryce. I never thought I'd say this but you're, oh my, you're spontaneous! It's amazing. It never crossed my mind that the name 'Bryce' and the word 'spontaneous' would be uttered in the same sentence. I'll remember this forever."

Bryce cleared his throat. "Something else I'd like you to remember forever, sweetheart, but I want you to know I was happy you didn't mention there was no jewelry in the box of chocolates this year."

Alanna smiled at Bryce and said "Sweetheart, I was so excited to see you nothing else mattered. You could have put a 'Crackerjack' toy in there and I wouldn't have cared. You're all that matters to me."

"And you're all that matters to me Alanna, my love. Here," Bryce said as he put his hand in his suit pocket and withdrew a sparkling one carat Princess cut diamond, and placed it on the ring finger of her left hand. "Do you think you could spend the rest of your life with a dependable and sometimes slightly spontaneous science teacher?"

"I, I ... again I'm speechless. I'm gobsmacked. Bryce, I love you! I am so much in love with you."

"Well?"

"Well, what?"

"I really *have* frazzled you haven't I? Will you marry me Alanna?"

"Oh, oh, I'm sorry. Of course I will Bryce. Yes, yes, yes, a thousand times yes. Kiss me, my wonderful, thoughtful, handsome Bryce."

"That's it? What happened to all those other adjectives," Bryce asked as he kissed Alanna's hand and grinned at her. Then he pulled her to him as he leaned across the table and kissed her, his bride to be, the love of his life.

Bryce picked up his flute and raised it in the air as Alanna picked hers up. He toasted her. "You're the love of my life Alanna. Here's to spontaneity and here's to reliability and here's to us and the memories we're making now that will last us a lifetime."

"You said it all sweetheart. I love you."

They enjoyed their delicious meal that the server had brought earlier. They could both see why this restaurant had been so highly recommended.

They were still smiling at each other when the server arrived back at their table offering them dessert. "We have a wonderful new dessert," Kim, their waiter said. "It's Hawaiian Chocolate Haupia Pie that I'm sure you'll both love. May I bring you some or would you like one of our wonderful coconut desserts?"

Bryce looked at Alanna and they both shook their heads in agreement. "That sounds wonderful Kim, we'll both try it.   This is a night for celebration."

"Very well" Kim said as he smiled and made his way for the kitchen returning quickly with their mouth-watering dessert.

Bryce poured more champagne and then raised his glass to Alanna's again. "Happy Valentine's Day sweetheart," Bryce said; "our very own special Valentine's Day. I love you!"

"Happy Valentine's Day to you too, my love; I love you and I love my diamond!" Alanna exclaimed.

"It doesn't sparkle anywhere near as much as your beautiful eyes, babe. Hey, what do you say we celebrate Valentine's Day every year in Hawaii?"

"Mmm, sounds wonderful to me, absolutely wonderful. But we don't want to be too predictable do we Bryce? Maybe we should go to Rio one year or Sydney or Pago Pago," Alanna said, arching her eyebrows waiting for Bryce's response.

"Sure, wherever you want, my love; just as long as we're together from now on."

"Kidding you sweetheart. February 15th will always be special to me and spending it here in Hawaii will be even more special. And you were open to spending the day elsewhere; *that* is special to me. But I still love you no matter where you want to spend our special day."

"Maybe you can even write another little book about this. Hmm, I'm thinking 'How to Go from Reliable to Spontaneous in Five Easy Steps and Propose to Your Girlfriend and' ... Too long, huh?" Bryce laughed as Alanna rolled her eyes at him.

"How about we forget about books and everything else for tonight sweetheart? I'm ready to go back to the house and crawl into bed, "But seriously, this has been the most wonderful Valentine's Day of my life even if it *is* the 15th and not the 14th. And I have a wee surprise for you, love," Alanna smiled slyly. "If you're a good boy – or a bad boy - I'll show you later."

Grinning, Bryce, ever the old-fashioned gentleman, stood up and stepped to Alanna's chair, grasped her hand, and helped her up. After paying for their exquisite meal, Bryce led Alanna to the elevator just as it opened disgorging a group of people and allowing them to enter.

The doors closed. "I hope there aren't any security cameras in here," Alanna whispered breathily into Bryce's ear, as he grabbed her body, pulled it to him and hungrily lifted her silky dress, delighted to find his hands caressing a luscious, rounded bare bottom. He unzipped his fly, freeing himself and then grabbed her buttocks with both hands. He lifted her off the floor and lowered her body onto him.

"Nice surprise babe, very, very nice. Now who do you think's gonna arrive at the destination first – the elevator ... or us?" As excited as he was he was putting his money on the elevator coming in second. Bryce smiled, enjoying his witticism ... and his precious Alanna.

❧

Macadamia Nut Crusted Dark Chocolate Haupia Pie

Serves 8

Ingredients

Crust:

3/4 cup flour

1/8 cup granulated sugar

1/8 cup packed brown sugar

3/4 stick cold butter (6 TBS)

1/2 cup uncooked Quaker Oats

1/4 cup chopped Macadamia Nuts

Filling:

6 ounces good quality dark chocolate

1 13.5 oz can coconut milk (or a little over 1.5 cups)

1 cup 2% milk

1 cup granulated sugar

1/2 cup cornstarch

1 cup water

Whipped cream:

1 cup heavy whipping cream

1/8 cup granulated sugar

1/2 tsp vanilla extract

Instructions

Preheat oven to 350 degrees. Butter a 9 inch pie pan. Mix flour, granulated sugar and brown sugar in medium bowl; cut in butter with a fork until mixture resembles coarse crumbs. Stir in oats and nuts. Press the mixture into bottom and sides of prepared pie pan. Bake for 15-20 minutes or until golden brown.

While crust is baking, make haupia by whisking coconut milk, milk and sugar together in a saucepan. While bringing coconut mixture to a boil, whisk cornstarch and water together in a separate bowl. Reduce coconut mixture to a simmer and pour in cornstarch mixture. Continue whisking until mixture is thick.

Remove crust from oven when done and put in fridge to cool slightly.

In a medium microwave safe bowl, microwave for 1- 1 1/2 minutes and stir with a fork to melt. Pour half of haupia into the chocolate and mix well. Pour chocolate haupia into pie crust. Pour remaining white haupia in a layer on top of chocolate haupia. Place pie in refrigerator to cool at least 1 hour.

Whip heavy cream, sugar and vanilla until stiff peaks form. Pipe or spread onto pie and top with shaved chocolate. Cool another hour in fridge. (dianasauerdishes.com)

"Love is my religion, - I could die for it."

~JOHN KEATS

"Well I love a rainy night
It's such a beautiful sight

I love to feel the rain On my face

To taste the rain on my lips
In the moonlight shadow"

"Stormy Weather"

. . . .

Larissa was panting, trying to catch her breath, her whole body tingling from head to toe. Her hair was matted from perspiration which was sliding down her neck and onto her chest. Her palms were sweaty and her throat was dry. Her heart was racing. Every part of her body was on fire from Charles's handling of her body; how he maneuvered her, how he brought her to the edge over and over until he finally brought her over the top.

Damn! That was great sex!

She was lying on her back with Charles lying on his front beside her, his left arm draped over her with his hand resting down between her thighs. In no time Charles's hand would begin moving, rubbing Larissa between her legs, moving his hands up to her belly and then down to her groin again and then he'd pull her on top of him, ready for another energetic romp. Once was never enough for him.

After round two, as she always thought of it, he'd be snoring. Within seconds of their second go round she could always count on Charles to be fast asleep snoring.

Would a little cuddling afterward be too much to ask, she wondered. A kiss or two? Anything to show that she was a person, not an object to be used. But what could she expect from him? He was her boy toy, a mere 21-years-old with more energy than any 10 men. He lived for sex, but that was about it. He was a 21-year-old sex machine but she supposed most guys his age were the same way. She wanted more though, she wanted a relationship and she knew it wasn't going to happen with Charles.

She would miss him. She would miss his model looks, his gorgeous smile with the most perfect straight white teeth, his unusual hazel eyes, his muscular physique, and his kisses. But mostly she would miss the outrageous sex as he lay under her with his strong muscled legs wrapped around her, as he stroked her tenderly and then more urgently and deeply as he kissed her feverishly.

Charles was an athlete in bed. He was a man who could take her to the heights of pleasure even though he wasn't trying. He was far too interested in his own pleasure but that just proved how great he was at this sex thing; he could give pleasure while thinking only of himself.

That was the part she wouldn't miss; his narcissism. He wouldn't think to ask her 'was it good for you'? The thought just wouldn't occur to him. Of course to be fair to him it was quite obvious that she enjoyed sex with him. Why ask a question to which you already know the answer? But that wasn't the point. It would be nice to know that he cared enough to even ask.

Their once weekly tryst was just that – a tryst – nothing more. Larissa had just discovered that Charles was seeing other women when he wasn't with her. Emotionally it wasn't a big deal for her but she was wary of his conduct when he was with other women. Did he wear a condom? Would she contract an STD from him? So far, so good, but one could never be too careful.

As phenomenal as the sex was she decided that the risk far outweighed the pleasure; well perhaps it didn't *far* outweigh it but she was growing more concerned. It didn't help matters when Charles had brought up the subject of condoms.

"Larissa baby, we've been seeing each other long enough that I think it's time we got rid of the condoms. We don't need them and sex would be so much better without me having to always put a jacket on it, babe."

Those words kept echoing in her head. If he's saying this to me, he's probably saying it to his other sexual partners. Only an idiot would think otherwise, she told herself. She wouldn't even ask him because she doubted he'd tell her the truth.

There would be no more worries now. Of course there would be no more out of this world sex. And there'd be no more being treated like an object.

Charles's reaction to her breaking off their once a week assignation had surprised her. He seemed genuinely hurt. She was only a once a week fling though. She felt certain he had six others, well maybe only five; after all the guy had to rest some time.

But even if Charles had acted hurt, Larissa knew that nothing would have changed. Charles would still care only for himself and his needs and he would still see other women. And her life would still be in jeopardy for all she knew. He needed to grow up and she knew that one day when he did, he'd probably make some woman very happy.

⚜

Six months had passed since Larissa had made the decision to end her relationship with Charles. She'd had herself tested and was relieved to find that she was free of disease. She wondered if perhaps she'd acted too hastily in calling off her relationship with him but in her heart of hearts she knew it was the right thing to do.

It was a beautiful, typical Florida day with clear skies and temperatures in the high 80s. But it was early in the day and afternoon thunderstorms could still rear their heads. Larissa was on the float lazing around the pool; a cold iced tea in her hand and her cell phone protected under a towel on the deck within reaching distance. The phone rang. It was her BFF, Keisha and Keisha was most definitely her Best Friend Forever. They were bonded stronger than sisters.

"Hey girlfriend what's up? Wait, before you answer that. I'll tell you what's up; the annual downtown Melbourne Art Festival which I'm sure you've chosen to forget about. But Shemar and I are dragging you there anyway."

"Keesh, hold it right there. You know …"

"Yeah, yeah I know. You're not up to dating or putting yourself out there only to be disappointed again. And you've lost interest in your art because you don't feel worthy anymore, all because of *him*. It's the same old song Larissa but I'm tired of listening to it. Shemar and I are both tired of it and we're not going to take it anymore. You're coming with us and you're going to enjoy yourself. I have declared it. Queen Keisha has spoken."

"You know Keesh, if you keep it up I'm going to tell our friends that your first name really *is* Queen. You were Queen before Latifah. And I know how much you dislike your first name. I don't understand why you dislike it so much though since you act like a damn queen sometimes. I swear, you're something else. So how's Shemar?"

"Uh uh Larissa. Forget it. You are not changing the subject. I'm used to your tactics. We're going to the art festival and we are going to have fun. And by the way, Shemar is just fine thank you and one day you'll find your own Shemar; because you sure can't have mine."

"I'd steal him from you if I could Keisha but BFFs don't do that to each other so I'll go to the art festival with you just to get you off my back."

"Good girl, Larissa. That's the attitude; positive. You're young, you're beautiful, you're healthy, intelligent and you're a great person. And you know how to work it, girl. You were way too good for what's his name."

"Well, he didn't think so Keisha. One woman wasn't enough for him. He was just too young. I do miss the sex though. And his name is Charles as if you didn't know."

"But Larissa, he only wanted you for sex. You deserve a man who will want you for the wonderful and beautiful person you are. He's out there somewhere I promise you; maybe not at the art festival but he's there somewhere. And you'll never find him if you stay cooped up in your house. You need to find your enthusiasm again, rediscover your art, and get in touch with *you* again."

"Okay. I know you're right and thank you but it's so demoralizing knowing I have a lot to offer a good man and yet I can't find him. I know I don't need a man to be happy but it would be nice to be appreciated by someone other than you and Shemar, and my cats and ... well gee, who would have guessed – the weather has suddenly turned. Gotta get out of the pool. The skies are threatening to spill all over me. So I'll see you tomorrow. And Keisha ..."

thanks for always looking out for me, always trying to help me, always being a true BFF."

Larissa quickly emerged from the pool as the storm clouds gathered and the sound of thunder pierced her heart. She reminisced about hers and Charles's lovemaking on her enclosed back deck as the rains fell, listening to the roar of the thunder and watching the lightning flashing in the distance.

Come on Larissa, stop making it into a love affair. Once we'd had sex and Charles had his nap, he'd be gone and I wouldn't see him for another week. Don't ever forget that.

❧

The next day arrived and Larissa promised herself she was going to be upbeat and positive. She would enjoy the art show because she loved art. She was an artist herself. She knew she was attractive, standing at 5'7" long blonde hair, eyes greener than anyone's ought to be, and 120 pounds with a great rack, as Charles used to say, and nice long legs.

She was sure if there was something lacking in her personality someone would have told her by now but the truth is she was very well liked. What she wanted was to be well loved.

The doorbell rang, Larissa opened it and was greeted by "Oh, baby, you're lookin' fine." Shemar! Trust him to always say something to lift my spirits, Larissa thought.

Keisha hugged her and said "You really do look fine girlfriend. Shemar has great taste in women."

"Thank you. I love you both. Now let's get this show on the road. Believe it or not I'm actually looking forward to this. I'm in the mood to see what all the other artists have to offer. Maybe I'll get some inspiration. You both know I haven't been on my game since ... well since I bid adieu to that selfish, self-centered what's his name rat bast..."

"Wow! You go girl. You *are* ready to move on and we're here to help you on your way. To the art show we go."

Later, Larissa found herself admiring some really fine pieces, everything from acrylics to pottery and just about every medium in between. She was comparing her art to the work of others and was feeling pretty upbeat about her artistic talents.

She had been admiring a painting done by a local artist and was strongly considering buying it, when her thoughts were interrupted by the sound of a familiar voice.

"Excuse me, you look very interested in this painting and it caught my eye too," the stranger next to her said. "Do you think it's a quality painting?" I don't know anything about art, but I know what I like and I like this piece. Do you think it's worth the asking price ... if you don't mind my asking?"

Larissa took an even closer look at the painting which resulted in her standing closer to this stranger. She turned from the painting, and looked up into the face of a very handsome man who was smiling at her.

Keisha grabbed Shemar's arm and began leading him away from the booth. "What are you doing Keisha? We said we were going to stay with Larissa and help her to start socializing again. We shouldn't leave her on her own."

"Shemar, how do you spell 'dense'? Come on, spell it."

"This is silly. Okay, I know you want me to say S h e m a r ..."

"Damn right. Now look at her, she's talking to another person and that person is a male and a damn fine looking one at that. And he's smiling at her. Let's get the hell out of here ... now! We can watch her from the American Indian jewelry booth. And while we're there you can buy me something ... just because you're happy to have me."

Shemar threw his head back and laughed and threw his arms around his beloved wife. Indeed he was truly happy to have her. He'd buy her anything her heart desired but he wasn't going to tell *her* that. He was madly in love but he wasn't a fool, he laughed to himself. They headed over to the other booth and kept a watchful but careful eye on their dear friend.

Mesmerized by the handsome stranger's voice and his face – where had she seen that face -Larissa was momentarily at a loss for words. She hadn't even noticed that Keisha and Shemar had strolled away from her. She finally managed to speak and said that it was indeed a very good painting done by a well known local artist with an excellent reputation.

"But you can't really go by my taste. I'm quite partial to paintings with dark, gothic scenes and I love this one. I love thunderstorms and this painting evokes memories of breathtaking storm-filled days."

"I love thunderstorms too," the handsome stranger said in that mesmerizing voice with the handsome face that was driving Larissa mad. She thought she recognized him from somewhere but couldn't quite place where.

"Here I am living in Florida which is known for its sunny skies but give me a good heart-stopping thunderstorm and it actually brightens my day. I suppose that doesn't make sense to you, ahh ..."

"Larissa. Hi, I'm Larissa Johnstone. I'm glad to meet you." She offered her hand to the stranger beside her and he grasped it with a strong yet gentle and warm hand.

"I'm Ted, and I'm really glad to meet you too. Are you an artist Larissa?"

Larissa smiled what she hoped was a beguiling smile and said "Yes, I am. I work in several mediums but I prefer watercolors. Are you an artist, Ted?"

Ted looked at Larissa and this time his whole face lit up. He was taking in every feature of her beautiful face and he was captivated. "Some might say I'm an artist," Ted laughed as if the very thought of him being called an artist amused him.

It was dawning on Larissa that she was really enjoying talking to Ted but she was still distracted by that voice and face. Where had she heard it? Where had she seen him? "What is it that you do, Ted? Do you sculpt or ..."

"My voice would be my medium and my profession is that of meteorologist. I'm on our local weather station, Channel 13."

"*That's* where I know you from!" Larissa exclaimed. "You're Ted Turner; the other Ted Turner, of course, not the wealthy founder of CNN and ex-husband of Jane Fonda."

Ted laughed as he stood there admiring this exquisite creature standing before him. "No, I'm not *that* Ted Turner. Wish I had his money though instead of just sharing his name and good looks. I'm kidding you Larissa. I'm much better looking than he."

"And ever so modest," Larissa said as she smiled.

Ted laughed again, "I can't believe I'm saying these things. You're just bringing out the kid in me I think. I always did like to laugh and joke around. I haven't done that in awhile. Anyway ..."

"I'm sorry Ted. I've been going over in my mind where I recognize you and your voice from and I couldn't quite place it. I'm embarrassed to say I usually have my head in my laptop while I've got the TV on. But I have seen you and of course I've heard your voice. I don't know why I couldn't connect the dots right away."

"Hmm, I guess I'm pretty forgettable. That's a real ego deflater for sure but that's okay; I don't have a big ego. It's a good thing too."

"Then let me make amends for that. Your voice has helped me through many a thunderstorm; so soothing and reassuring. I've loved your voice for so long now. I'm thrilled to hear it in person."

"Tell you what Larissa. I'm going to purchase this painting. I have it on the best authority that it's a quality painting," Ted said as he leaned his head closer to hers and smiled into her eyes.

"Maybe you could come over to my house and help me decide where to hang it. I have two places in mind but I'm not sure which one would show the painting off to best advantage. One of the places is on the wall above my bed," Ted said as he gave Larissa a sly smile.

"Oh, I catch your drift Ted but I'm not ready for ... for sex. I don't know you and I don't even know if you're married although I notice you're not wearing a wedding ring. Also there's no telltale white mark where a ring would have been so I'm guessing you're not married. But still, I know nothing about you and I'm not the kind of girl to hop into bed with the first handsome man I meet."

"Well, thank you for the compliment! Okay, single, never married, engaged once but she was only using me for sex. Yes I know it's usually the other way round but she wasn't interested in anything about me. I'll bet she couldn't even tell what color my eyes are if asked. Own my own home, have two dogs and two cats, no kids, no diseases, no debts. I'm 37, 6 feet two inches, 190 pounds, a Pisces, not that I believe in that mumbo jumbo, graduated from the University of Oklahoma where I studied meteorology, worked at several small TV stations in Tulsa, where I grew up, and then landed a great job as a meteorologist at WKMG in Orlando. For more information, call my mother. She'd love to tell a woman all about me. She's my biggest fan."

"Well I think that covers it all Ted except for two things."

"Hmm, okay, I lived in Israel for a year; that was with the woman who used me for sex, and I was also in the Navy for four years. There; I think that about covers it. Oh I did have chicken pox when I was 13."

"That's a lot of information, Ted but the two things I want to know are the names of your dogs and cats and do you love them and treat them well?"

"Technically," Ted burst out laughing, "that's three things. But okay, the two dogs are Smudgie and Heidi. Smudgie is a white mutt with a black mark across her nose that looks like a smudge of something on it. I found her on the street, very bedraggled and rail thin. Heidi is a German Shepherd that I rescued from the pound. She's an older dog and her days were numbered. The two cats are, well don't laugh, Frick and Frack. They're also rescues. And yes I love them all and not only treat them well but I spoil them rotten."

"That's so sweet and very interesting Ted; but don't the cats get confused with such similar sounding names?"

"Oh my god Larissa, you don't have any cats do you?" Ted laughed barely able to contain his incredulity.

"I could call one Beethoven and the other Dudley Do-Right and they still wouldn't come when called or pay me any mind if they didn't feel like it. They're cats. Sorry, I didn't mean to laugh but I just thought it was funny, them being confused and ..."

"That is pretty funny isn't it? I can appreciate that, Ted," Larissa laughed too.

"Actually I do have two cats myself. No dogs, but my two buddies, Abbott and Costello. They're what keep me going each day. Somebody dropped them off in front of my door when they were only about a week old. It was touch and go for awhile but the veterinarian and I managed to keep them alive and healthy. They're 10 years old now, had them since I was 25."

"So, Larissa, I think we've covered a lot of ground but there's so much I want to learn about you. Where you're from, where you work, all your likes and dislikes and anything and everything. Well, now I know how old you are. But right now I want to know what kind of food you like because I love to cook."

"We're perfect for each other then," Larissa said. "You love to cook and I love to eat." Ted laughed along with her.

"You'd never know you like to eat judging by that gorgeous body; if I'm not being too impertinent. But when you're built like that you have to know that men notice."

"Thank you Ted; it's nice to be appreciated and to know that someone's interested in me, but there's more to me than my body."

Ted grabbed Larissa's hands, at the same time leaning his body into hers, pulling her to him, and allowing his arousal to caress her. He brought his lips close to hers, hovering over them, eagerly anticipating kissing them, his arousal growing stronger and harder until he finally could wait no longer. He pressed his lips against hers, holding her head in his hands. He could have kissed her longer and harder if only they weren't surrounded by people.

"Ted, we're not exactly alone here. If we were ... well, if we were ...wait a minute, my friends seem to have deserted me." Looking around, Larissa spotted Keisha and Shemar in the booth opposite where she and Ted were standing. They both gave her sheep-ish smiles which were returned by Larissa who also gave them a thumbs up before returning her attention to Ted.

"Your friends seem to understand you'll be leaving with me. They must be very good friends. I hope to meet them, but not tonight," Ted whispered, his breath hot in Larissa's ear.

"Let's talk to the artist and I'll pay for the painting and then would you accompany me to my place? First we'll have to stop by the store to pick up a few things for dinner and then we'll have a nice candlelight dinner accompanied by my special frozen chocolate covered cappuccino crunch cake. It'll be a long dinner and we'll have time to get to know each other and then ... well then after dessert we can *really* get to know each other. Whatever happens or doesn't happen is your call although I hope you're feeling what I'm feeling. But I'm a gentleman Larissa."

Ted took her into his arms, kissed her and said "Just ask my mother, she'll tell you."

⚘

Frozen Chocolate-Covered Cappuccino Crunch Cake

- 1 (10 3/4 oz.) frozen pound cake, thawed

- 3/4 cup heavy whipping cream

- 1 3/4 cups (11.5-oz. pkg.) NESTLE® TOLL HOUSE® Milk Chocolate Morsels

- 4 cups (1 quart) coffee ice cream, softened

- 1 cup frozen whipped topping, thawed

- 1 3/4 cups coarsely crushed malted milk balls

- Frozen whipped topping, thawed (optional)

- Coarsely crushed malted milk balls, (optional)

- Slice pound cake into 1/8- to 1/4-inch slices. Place half of the slices on bottom of 9-inch spring form pan; press down firmly. Set remaining slices aside.

- Bring cream just to a boil in medium saucepan. Remove from heat. Add milk chocolate morsels; let stand 5 minutes. Whisk until well combined and smooth. Pour half of the chocolate mixture over pound cake in pan, spreading evenly to within 1/4-inch of edge of pan.

- Cover; freeze for 1 1/2 hours or until chocolate is set.

- Combine softened ice cream and whipped topping in large bowl. Fold in 1 3/4 cups crushed malted milk balls. Spread over chocolate layer in pan. Cover;

- Freeze until ice cream is firm, about 2 hours.

- Top ice cream with remaining pound cake slices; press down firmly. Spread remaining chocolate mixture over pound cake. Cover; freeze at least 6 hours

- To serve, remove sides of pan. Garnish with additional whipped dessert topping and sprinkle with crushed malted milk balls, if desired. To cut cake easily, run a knife under hot water and dry with a paper towel before making slices.

www.allwomenstalk.com

"*Love conquers all things; let us surrender to love*"

Virgil

Acknowledgements

I want to thank everyone who encouraged me to write this book, to friends who allowed me to use either their first name or last name, and some friends who shared titbits of their stories, permitting me to embellish them for the book.

My special thanks as always to my good friend and book designer, Amy Zofko. This is my fourth book for which Amy has designed the cover and each one has surpassed the previous one. Her talents are limitless.

My thanks to my critique partner and friend, Gloria Schramm, for her helpful suggestions and encouragement.

Saving the best for last, as always my husband has been my single greatest source of encouragement and inspiration, contributing ideas for the book and offering critical suggestions. His loving ways inspired many of the heroes in the stories.

No acknowledgement could be complete without mentioning the other two loves of my life; my sons, Dale and Scott. They've made my life worthwhile and joyful.

"You are always new; the last of your kisses was ever the sweetest."

John Keats

Sheryl Letzgus McGinnis was born in Australia and has lived most of her life in the United States, growing up in New Jersey and now residing in Florida with her husband and remaining son. She is a member of the Parent Advisory Board of The Partnership for a Drug-Free America (The Partnership at Drug-Free.org).

Sheryl and her family are passionate about animal welfare and are owned by three spoiled rotten cats.

Sheryl is the author of three books on drugs and addiction and numerous articles both online and in print publications. She's also the author of articles in print magazines both here in the United States and England on various subjects ranging from tea-cups to parenting. She's been interviewed on TV and radio shows both in the USA and Canada.

"Romance Chocolates" is her first book in the romance genre.

Made in the USA
Lexington, KY
19 December 2010